"HERE THERE BE NO DRAGONS," SAYS ANNE McCAFFREY

Instead there are:

* Enchantments
* Things Magical and Strange
* Devils and Demons
* Professors of Potent Powers
* A Pompous Bishop
* Witchcraft and Wizardry
* The King in Yellow
* Bodychangers
* An Exorcist
* Magicians and their Magicks

—and other such strange phenomena, all brought together in a witch's brew by Anne McCaffrey to delight her myriad fans!

Also by Anne McCaffrey
Published by Ballantine Books:

Alchemy
AND
Academe

*A Collection of Original Stories
Concerning Themselves with
Transmutations, Mental and Elemental,
Alchemical and Academic*

SELECTED BY
Anne McCaffrey

A Del Rey Book

BALLANTINE BOOKS • NEW YORK

"Weed of Time" by Norman Spinrad printed by permission of the author and his agents, Scott Meredith Literary Agency, Inc., 845 Third Avenue, New York, New York 10022.

"Night and the Loves of Joe Dicostanzo" by Samuel R. Delany is an original work and appears here for the first time by the permission of the author and Henry Morrision, Inc., his agents.

"Ringing the Changes" by Robert Silverberg printed by permission of the author and his agents, Scott Meredith Literary Agency, Inc., 845 Third Avenue, New York, New York 10022.

Acknowledgment is made to the following for permission to reprint their material:

ALFRED A. KNOPF, INC.
"The Dance of the Solids," copyright © 1968 by John Updike. Reprinted from *Midpoint and Other Poems*, John Updike, by permission of Alfred A. Knopf, Inc.

A Del Rey Book
Published by Ballantine Books

Library of Congress Catalog Card Number: 73-129892

ISBN 0-345-28643-X

This edition published by arrangement with Doubleday & Company, Inc.

Printed in Canada

First Ballantine Books Edition: January 1980
Fifth Printing: June 1984

Cover art by Rowena Morrill

DEDICATED TO THE MEMORY OF
Nancy Graves Bache, playwright
Rosel George Brown, author
Nancy Hood Brown, poet

"They told me, Heraclitus, they told me you were dead,
They brought me bitter news to hear and bitter tears
          to shed.
I wept as I remembered, how often you and I
Had tired the sun with talking and sent him down
          the sky.
And now that thou art lying, my dear old Carian
          guest,
A handful of grey ashes, long, long ago at rest,
Still are thy pleasant voices, thy Nightingales,
          awake,
For Death, he taketh all away, but them he cannot
          take."

WILLIAM JOHNSON CORY
Paraphrase from Callimachus

CONTENTS

FOREWORD

People often ask me, with expressions of puzzled, wondering awe, "How do you think up such ideas?"

My replies vary between evasion and a forthright answer, depending on which story prompted the inquiry. For this Anthology, however, in which I have have no auctorial part, I can cite the exact genesis.

In May (1968) on a bright and brilliant morning, I had traveled cross-state to spend some hours with my good friend and colleague, Sonya Dorman. We put our time to good use, by milfording* each other's latest stories. Sonya had handed me hers, saying with a self-deprecating sigh that she feared it was sword and sorcery.

"It is not!" I declared, deeply appreciating the *typisch* Slavonic ending. "It's alchemy and academe."

"Say, that would be a good title for an anthology," Sonya said.

We spent the next hour projecting a ponderous tome with stories on this theme. (Prime on our list was Charles Harness' "The Alchemist," which was to both our minds the epitome of this category.)

By the time we had settled on the best possible editor for such an anthology and the publisher most likely to snap at the chance for such a notable book, it was time for me to go home and attend to mundane and maternal matters.

Our selected editor bounced the job smartly back with a "Why don't *you* do it, Anne?" The publisher astonished me by enthusiasm for the project, although it

* To milford—to subject a story to the workshop scrutiny learned at the Milford (Pennsylvania) Science Fiction Workshop.

was felt that stories written to the theme would make an even better collection. That's why "The Alchemist" is absent from these pages.

However, the auspices continued fine. The Anthology seemed possessed of a certain magic. Authors developed severe cases of Inspiration and feverishly demanded the exact parameters of the theme. Heavens! Weren't they obvious?

No. They were not.

What aspect of Alchemy? What did I mean by Academe?

The good *Encyclopaedia Britannica* disclosed an accurate definition of "alchemy":

> In the narrow sense of the word, alchemy is the pretended art of making gold and silver, or transmuting base metals into noble uses.
>
> Alchemy in its wider and truer significance stands for the chemistry of the Middle Ages. The idea of transmutation in the country of its origin (Greece) had a philosophical basis and was linked up with the Greek theories of matter then current. . . .
>
> The fundamental theory of transmutation of metals is to be found in the Greek alchemists. Regarding all substances as being composed of primitive matter—primae materia— . . .

Chicanery, philosophy, atomic structure. Surely there were parameters . . . or directions in which Inspiration could speed, particularly for writers versed in the science fiction and fantasy field.

"Primae materia" could be said to be "atoms." Only now plasma physicists and quantum chemists have had to extend their parameters light-years into new areas of pure research. They examine not Democritus' Air, Fire, Water, Earth but complicated shells, suborbital levels, particles, mesons, boasting energies barely understood at the theoretic level. Deep serious study is progressing at universities all over the world, for science must take itself seriously.

Aye, and that's one of my personal complaints of science fiction: it takes itself much too seriously. So I told my contributors that I would appreciate Humor as well as Humors in this Anthology.

I explored further afield to define the theme. Imagine my double delight at discovering, in *Scientific American* (of all places), verses by the American poet John Updike, which begin:

> All things are Atoms: Earth and Water, Air
>> And Fire, all, *Democritus* foretold.
>> Swiss *Paracelsus*, in's alchemic lair,
>> Saw Sulfur, Salt, and Mercury unfold
>> Amid Millennial hopes of faking Gold.
>> *Lavoisier* dethroned Phlogiston; then
>> Molecular Analysis made bold
>> Forays into the gases: Hydrogen
> Stood naked in the dazzled sight of Learned Men.

Calloo, Callay! What a joy, to find an example of the poet's alchemy so apt to the theme: alpha and omega.

And, behold the magic of the Anthology waxes stronger, drawing to it as does a lodestone needle, another pointed description of alchemy by Roger Zelazny, surely one of the purest word-alchemists in science fiction.

"No matter what your scientific background, emotionally you're an alchemist. You live in a world of liquids, solids, gases, and heat-transfer effects that accompany their changes of state. Those are the things you perceive, the things you feel. Whatever you know about their true natures is grafted on top of that. So, when it comes to the day to day sensations of living, from mixing a cup of coffee to flying a kite, you treat with the four ideal elements of the old philosophers: earth, air, fire and water."*

"Emotionally, you're an alchemist"—now there's a definition, a whole new sector for observation.

Russell Baker is also illuminating on the philosophical content of "alchemy." Man has been dabbling on other aspects of "Magick." Mr. Baker, in an editorial in the *New York Times,* June 16, 1968, discusses a general resurgence of this ancient art and a keen interest in the occult. Mr. Baker suggests that advertising is the "sophisticated son of Abracadabra," with TV commercials promising to turn a housewife into a queen if she'll but change her brand of margarine. More ominous, he suggests

that the alchemists of the present day—the people who believe in the short-cut to riches—are members of the drug cults. With pot or LSD, or something else exotic from a chemical retort, they believe this leaden old world can be turned into instant gold. They talk about it in terms of "expanded consciousness," or "turning on" as if minds were light bulbs. . . . It is entrancing to think that chemistry can turn the magic trick in an instant, especially if you doubt your strength or ability to love life for itself, and it is just about as realistic as expecting to turn lead into gold without a nuclear reactor.

That rather points to where alchemy's "at." So, let me define "academe." (Yes, yes, of course it was the alliteration that teased and pleased but the significance goes deeper.)

Webster's Seventh New Collegiate Dictionary defines "academe" thusly:

* Roger Zelazny, *Isle of the Dead* (New York: Ace Books, Inc., 1969).

ac-a-deme *n* [irreg. fr. L *academia*] **1 a:** a place of instruction **b:** academic environment **2:** ACADEMIC; *esp:* PEDANT

A place of instruction is not *de rigueur* a chalky school hall; it could be within the chambers of the heart, or the twisted paths of the mind, or both, wherever instruction—of whatever sort—takes place: a sleepy English garden, a slum-tenement fire escape, a bar, an open field, a Camp Fire Girl meeting, a botany laboratory, a plasma lab.

Considering recent university problems, extrapolate the college of the future. Certainly an academic environment suggested by Sonya Dorman's "A Mess of Porridge" might be a delightful solution for contemporary institutions struggling with the sour anarchism of SDS. As John Updike remarks in Stanza 9 of "Dance of the Solids,"

Textbooks and Heaven only are Ideal; . . .

And that is as good a place as any to stop *explaining* the parameters within which these good authors wrote.

By happy alchemy of mind
. . . turn to pleasure all you find.*
Anne McCaffrey
1970

*Martin Green, "The Spleen."

The Dance of the Solids*

JOHN UPDIKE

—

Editor's Note: These verses were composed after the writer had read the issue of SCIENTIFIC AMERICAN (September, 1967) devoted to materials. They appear in his book *Midpoint and Other Poems,* and are reproduced with the generous permission of Alfred A. Knopf, Inc.

Argument: In stanzas associated with allegory the actual atomic structure of solids unfolds. Metals, Ceramics and Polymers. The conduction of heat, electricity and light through solids. Solidity emerges as being intricate, giddy, playful.

All things are Atoms: Earth and Water, Air
  And Fire, all, *Democritus* foretold.
  Swiss *Paracelsus*, in's alchemic lair,
  Saw Sulfur, Salt, and Mercury unfold
  Amid Millennial hopes of faking Gold.
  Lavoisier dethroned Phlogiston; then
  Molecular Analysis made bold
  Forays into the gases: Hydrogen
Stood naked in the dazzled sight of Learned Men.

* *Scientific American,* January, 1969.

1

The Solid State, however, kept its grains
   Of Microstructure coarsely veiled until
   X-ray diffraction pierced the Crystal Planes
   That roofed the giddy Dance, the taut Quadrille
   Where Silicon and Carbon Atoms will
   Link Valencies, four-figured, hand in hand
   With common Ions and Rare Earths to fill
   The lattices of Matter, Glass or Sand,
With tiny Excitations, quantitatively grand.

The *Metals,* lustrous Monarchs of the Cave,
   Are ductile and conductive and opaque
   Because each Atom generously gave
   Its own Electrons to a mutual Stake,
   A Pool that acts as Bond. The Ions take
   The stacking shape of Spheres, and slip and flow
   When pressed or dented; thusly *Metals* make
   A better Paper Clip than a Window,
Are vulnerable to Shear, and, heated, brightly glow.

Ceramic, muddy Queen of human Arts,
   First served as simple Stone. Feldspar supplied
   Crude Clay; and Rubies, Porcelain, and Quartz
   Came each to light. Aluminum Oxide
   Is typical—a Metal is allied
   With Oxygen ionically; no free
   Electrons form a lubricating tide,
   Hence, Empresslike, *Ceramics* tend to be
Resistant, porous, brittle, and refractory.

Prince *Glass, Ceramic*'s son, though crystal-clear,
   Is no wise crystalline. The fond Voyeur
   And Narcissist alike devoutly peer
   Into Disorder, the Disorderer
   Being Covalent Bondings that prefer
   Prolonged Viscosity and spread loose nets
   Photons slip through. The average *Polymer*
   Enjoys a Glassy state, but cools, forgets
To slump, and clouds in closely patterned Minuets.

The *Polymers,* those giant Molecules,
   Like Starch and Polyoxymethylene,
   Flesh out, as protein serfs and plastic fools,
   The Kingdom with Life's Stuff. Our time has seen
   The synthesis of Polyisoprene
   And many cross-linked Helixes unknown
   To *Robert Hooke;* but each primordial Bean
   Knew Cellulose by heart: *Nature* alone
Of Collagen and Apatite compounded Bone.

What happens in these Lattices when *Heat*
   Transports Vibrations through a solid mass?
   $T = 3Nk$ is much too neat;
   A rigid Crystal's not a fluid Gas.
   Debye in 1912 proposed Elas-
   Tic Waves called *phonons* which obey *Max Planck*'s
   Great Quantum Law. Although amorphous Glass,
   Umklapp Switchbacks, and Isotopes play pranks
Upon his Formulae, *Debye* deserves warm Thanks.

   Eletroconductivity depends
   On Free Electrons: in Germanium
   A touch of Arsenic liberates; in blends
   Like Nickel Oxide, *Ohms* thwart Current. From
   Pure Copper threads to wads of Chewing Gum
   Resistance varies hugely. Cold and light
   As well as "doping" modify the sum
   Of *Fermi* Levels, Ion scatter, site
Proximity, and other factors recondite.

Textbooks and Heaven only are Ideal;
   Solidity is an imperfect state.
   Within the cracked and dislocated Real
   Nonstoichiometric crystals dominate.
   Stray Atoms sully and precipitate;
   Strange holes, *excitons,* wander loose; because
   Of Dangling Bonds, a chemical Substrate
   Corrodes and catalyzes—surface Flaws
Help Epitaxial Growth to fix adsorptive claws.

White Sunlight, *Newton* saw, is not so pure;
 A Spectrum bared the Rainbow to his view.
 Each Element absorbs its signature:
 Go add a negative Electron to
 Potassium Chloride; it turns deep blue,
 As Chromium incarnadines Sapphire.
 Wavelengths, absorbed, are reëmitted through
 Fluorescence, Phosphorescence, and the higher
Intensities that deadly *Laser Beams* require.

Magnetic Atoms, such as Iron, keep
 Unpaired Electrons in their middle shell,
 Each one a spinning Magnet that would leap
 The *Bloch* Walls whereat antiparallel
 Domains converge. Diffuse Material
 Becomes *Magnetic* when another Field
 Aligns domains like Seaweed in a swell.
 How nicely microscopic forces yield,
In Units growing Visible, the World we wield!

"Textbooks and Heaven only are Ideal,"
Line 1, Stanza 9,
"Dance of the Solids"
John Updike

A Mess of Porridge

SONYA DORMAN

—

She came in by the door which was barred with words and a thumbprint, though she did not speak or raise her hand. Brynt, with his customary icy competence, was trying to repair the planetary computer; Macio had fallen asleep over an unfinished poem; old Argoyle was sitting on the window seat at the top of the tower inscribing a ledger by hand. The apprentice, Hoo, was dusting the crystal banks; he was the first to see her.

"Great Hoyle," was what Hoo said, when the six-year-old girl came in through the door without a thumbprint or a word. Her yellow hair was long and shaggy, there were holes in her leggings, her boots were untied and her nose was runny. Argoyle looked down and saw her, and nearly fell off his window seat, he was so shocked.

Macio woke up and grumbled, "What is it?"

Brynt put down his tools and came over to examine the unwelcome guest. They were all, except Hoo, on winter holiday and annoyed at being interrupted. Argoyle climbed laboriously down from the tower where he had been relaxing from his daily schedule with an interminable project of writing *The Galactic Guide to Terran Cooking*. He had just finished the recipe for Noodles with Fleshballs and was irritated at being unable to go on to the next. He was also interested and curious, and could feel the old ague in his bones from sitting in one position for too long. Nobody stayed in good health forever, not even the three Masters.

They talked among themselves. "Child." "Girl." "How did she get in?" "How can we get her out?"

She ate two pieces of their soft bread, drank a cup of cold tea, and fell asleep on the floor, curled up in Argoyle's old cloak from which the stars were fading. She lay right up against the heat panel. Her added body warmth caused the vanes of the radiometer to spin rapidly in their niche one the wall above, where they caught down-radiations from both suns, and up-radiations from the heat inside, and reacted to maintain a comfortable climate indoors. This did not prevent the big room from being full of drafts.

The tower and its lower floors had been hodge-podged together by student engineers and things didn't always operate as they should. The tower itself was sealed off with plastiglass, and Argoyle's electric heater comforted him up there, although it had proven anathema to the owls because of its fiery glare at all hours. Brynt and Macio quarreled continually about what temperature should be kept during sleep hours. Macio said he got a headache from sleeping in a hot room, which adversely affected his poems, sonatas, and philosophies, while Brynt said he got such swollen sinuses from sleeping in the cold that he could scarcely lecture, let alone equate.

Hoo, being clever and young, slept anywhere he could and ate twice as much as the older men. After all, he was the only one who went Out.

A check of the radar screen showed no vessel within

planetfall. Macio asked, "Do you think something crashed, and she survived?"

Brynt said, "I'm sure not, she couldn't have lived on rainwater and air pie for two months, and it was two months ago we had that minor disturbance on the screens."

Argoyle thought she might have managed on berries and rainwater, but did not say so. Macio took the cards from his sleeve, shuffled them, cut them, counted six for her years, and laid the seventh on the table. It was the Empress, with her crown of stars and the symbol of Venus on her shield.

"Get her out of here," Brynt said immediately, scowling.

"But she's only six," Macio objected.

Argoyle looked down at the sleeping child and shook his head. "Brynt's right, she must go. We have all those students in stasis in the back room. Give her eight or nine years and she'll raise hell with them. The last thing we need at the University is an Empress."

Hoo ate a piece of bread with jelly spread an inch thick on it. "Perhaps you'll need one," he suggested. "Most of the students have to go elsewhere once they've obtained their degrees. Don't you think they might profit by the experience?"

All three of his elders and betters turned simultaneously to look at him and he felt his flesh begin to shrivel on his bones. "I just thought—" he mumbled.

"Don't think!" Brynt said. "You're here only to learn."

"Yes, sir," Hoo said, finishing the bread and wondering, for the hundredth time, how he was supposed to study and learn without thinking. It was a trick he hoped to learn after some more academic years. You eat porridge for fifty years, Hoo thought, and after your fangs have fallen out you don't want anything else but porridge. He would have rebelled if he could; he'd been sent to the University in lieu of an older brother who'd run away to space. Hoo would have preferred that himself, and was afraid porridge wouldn't nourish him.

"This is very upsetting," Macio said and sat down to think about it.

Argoyle fingered his white beard, and said, "I can't see any problem. We'll send her off on the next ship that stops by."

"But she came in without warning," Brynt said. "Hoo, you must check the door circuits, something's wrong."

"Fuss, fuss," Hoo murmured to himself, for Brynt always worried about things not working, even after Hoo had repaired them. Hoo took the screwdriver from his leg pocket and approached the circuit box at the side of the door, pointing the plasti-shield handle and saying the proper words to disengage the voltage. The hinged door of the box was decorated with a cross, a scimitar, a mezuzah, an octagonal crystal, and two maroon circles. The circles went dark as the voltage died. Hoo opened the box, took the insides out, examined each wire, cog, bolt, and India-ink tracing, put it back together, and closed the box. He said the words backward, and was satisfied to see the maroon circles glow with returning life.

"Nothing but an engineer," Brynt remarked, and turned away. He was going to go down to the Facilities Room but Macio was already at the door, and since it was not urgent, tomorrow would do for Brynt just as well. Brynt still enjoyed it now and then, but selected a tape at random, while Macio was young enough to choose his tapes with care and spent some time deciding between an acrobat and a belly dancer.

Old Argoyle hadn't been down to the Facilities Room for years. He climbed back through the plastiglass door to the tower, mentally congratulating the original planners for including the Room. Half an hour of it, with no responsibility or any residue of emotion when it was over, and the younger men were ready to go back to work.

He had by now forgotten his own Empress, whom he had loved: her long, dark hair, her belly as big as the western ocean, their hundred years together. He liked the dusty and windy tower, the peace to work or take a nap, or to employ owls. Dr. Argoyle plugged in the heater. It buzzed and lit up, and he rubbed his hands before it. Hoo was right in a way, the old Master thought. There was nothing like real experience, in the long run. All the simulated engagements were of small value, compared to a real one. Then all the more reason for that sleeping baby breeder to be shipped out as fast as possible.

Argoyle picked up his stylus and ledger and began to write his introduction to the recipe for CRUSHED DUCK:

> Originating with the Chinese, this delicious main course has, over the centuries, been adapted to the kitchens of the furthest Outposts, and is served in the finest restaurants, except those of China where ducks no longer grow. The absence of ducks from their native habitat is assumed to be the result of the manipulations of the feather merchants, who went east when the western birds had been picked clean.

"Oh, dear," Argoyle sighed when he saw Brynt climbing up to interrupt once again. Brynt came in and clapped his hands gently together in front of the heater, not to warm them so much as to show a respectful appreciation of the bright red glow.

"How do you suppose she got in?" he began, as Argoyle was sure he would. "Those door circuits are not defective."

"How do you suppose an Empress ever gets in? Who could ever keep her out?" Argoyle replied in his rhetorical way.

Brynt hitched himself up on the window seat beside his colleague. "Are you telling me that even at this age, or stage, we can do nothing?"

"I think it's best if we feed her only until the next

ship comes, and then send her to a proper school somewhere. That is, of course, assuming she has lost her
family."

Brynt was thoughtful for a while. Then he asked,
"What sort of schools do they send girls to?"

"Today the nonuniversities are all coeducational, I'm
told."

Brynt was mortified. "But then how do they prevent—" He could not go on.

"Oh, they don't," Argoyle said with amusement.
"They don't try to." The second sun was beginning to
go down and shadows like fingers were moving up the
side of the tower. In a little while the windows would go
dark. "We've lived here such a long, long time, Brynt. I
think, if we were to go Out to the other planets, we'd be
considered quaint old things."

"We are respected men," Brynt said coldly. "The
best families send their sons to us for education."

Silence again. As darkness began to fill the tower
room the heater glowed more brightly, and then the
light panels began to glow, too, shining on Argoyle's
thin white hair, and on Brynt's dark, lined face.

At length Brynt asked, "What if we put her into
stasis?"

"What purpose would it serve? She has a right to her
own life, somewhere else."

"She is very small," Brynt said.

"She is very female."

Brynt stood up. "What if a ship does not come before
the next semester?"

Argoyle made a resigned gesture. "Well, as we keep
pointing out to each other, she's only six. A ship will
come this year, sooner or later."

When Brynt went downstairs he found the child still
asleep, curled up in the old cloak of the Master, and
Macio sitting at the table wrestling with a dimensional
poem. He was having difficulty with the first stanza,
while the second was complete and part of the third existed at the base near the floor. Several blank spots

shifted back and forth through the lines, where he had not found the right words. As the blank spots shifted, the sense and rhythm shifted, and occasionally Macio would sit back and scan the structure.

Where at ease   sleepy   lies
                     at ease   the morning
     at morning   ease   the woman
     the woman lies   O   sleepy

"Are you busy?" Brynt asked him.

"For Kepler's sake, you astronomer," Macio shouted, "of course I'm busy, can't you see I'm making a poem?"

"Where's Hoo?"

"In the Facilities Room," Macio said, removing a noun. "As far as I can make out he does nothing but eat and use Facilities."

"He has some potential as an engineer, you know."

Macio sighed. "I spent most of my youth writing symphonies."

"If you hadn't you wouldn't be here."

Macio deconstructed the poem and put the pieces back in the amber box. "Well, what is it? I assume you want to talk about something?"

Brynt snorted. "How did she get in through the door?" he said.

"If we knew she was outside, any one of us might have let her in," Macio reminded him. "Not consciously, of course," he added in his most pious voice.

Hoo shut the door of the Facilities Room and came upstairs, his hair still rumpled from the helmet. "I'm starving," he said. "Is there any of the oat bread left?"

The two Masters looked at each other, and away. Hoo found the remains of the loaf and was spreading jelly on the heel of it when Brynt touched his shoulder and said, "I think you'd better sleep in the tower room tonight."

Hoo looked at him, chewed, looked at the sleeping

child. He swallowed the mouthful and said, "She's as safe with me as with you."

Brynt closed his hand into a fist and tapped Hoo once over the heart. The bread fell from the boy's hand, landing jelly side down on the floor, and the blood drained from his face. "You smidgeon," Brynt roared. "You morsel, you will go into stasis for fifty years if you ever speak to me like that again."

A mouse came softly out of a chink by the doorcircuit box. Her eyes glittered as she ran across the floor, snatched the fallen bread, raised her snout for an upward glance at invisible owls, and ran back, over the prism which served as a sill, her feet sparkling red, orange, blue. Back into her crevice she went, leaving no crumbs.

"Yes, sir," Hoo said, as the color slowly returned to his face. He moved toward the tower stairway, thinking bitterly about how the three men lived inside themselves, in their own small fires. It was a pity they never understood what was Out there—fire of suns, auroras, civilizations crumbling into dust and new life riding somewhere else on the light of years.

In the morning, when all met in the big room, the child was awake, smiling. She said, "Good day, Uncles."

"We are not related," Argoyle said.

"Everybody's relative. Is there any bread to eat?"

Hoo looked guilty, and gave himself away with a glance at the food panel.

"Do you mean to say tea isn't ready yet?" Brynt demanded.

Hoo began thumbing the buttons in awful haste; out tumbled soft toast, bread puddings, saucers of soaked biscuit, bowls of applesauce. Argoyle strode over to Hoo and pulled him away from the panel. "Sit down," he said in a voice of great authority. "This is a mess."

In a few moments it had been cleaned up, and a pot of hot tea and bowls of porridge had been produced. They found, after experiments, that a mug of milk could be brought forth for the child. When she had finished eating she came to their table and looked around on it. Not finding what she wanted, she took Brynt's sleeve and very delicately wiped her lips with it.

He snatched his arm away. "What are you doing?" he yelled.

"Excuse me," she said, astonished but not alarmed. "Don't you like me?"

"What's your name?" Macio asked hurriedly.

"Peggy. Don't you like jelly on your toast? I do."

Hoo spread some jelly on a piece of bread, and she thanked him for it. "It's better than berries. And I ate eggs, but I couldn't cook them so they were gooey."

"Just as I thought," Argoyle murmured. "Months on berries and water, and she's survived."

"That doesn't prove anything," Brynt remarked.

Macio said, "It does too. Courage, ingenuity, endurance. It proves a lot."

Hoo started his chores by going to the back room to check the feeder tubes. Students were not permitted off-planet until they received their degrees, or flunked out and were sent to traders' schools. During holidays they were put into stasis, though not the same kind employed for space travel. Student stasis was far more luxurious; they wore the helmets associated with the Facilities Room. It was simply a slowing down: a dream a week, a bowl of soup a month. It was restful and pleasant, they came back refreshed to their studies. No radical ideas or experience of violence intruded into their years of intellectual discipline, and they were able to emerge fully prepared as teachers, philosophers, or researchers.

Unlike the group in stasis who had five or six years more ahead of them, Hoo was only a year short of his degree. He would stay on with the Masters, to study more, to assist with lectures. There were times when he was resigned to this idea; other times, such as now, he felt bitter and cheated.

Macio, reading his face, said kindly, "Why don't you

go down to the Facilities Room if you've finished your chores?"

"I just came up from there an hour ago," Hoo said.

"Before breakfast?" Brynt asked.

"I can't think of a better time," Hoo said, sliding away from him. "I'd better check the weather vanes this morning, before the winds come." He was out the door with his backpack of tools before Brynt could reproach him.

"Oh, to be young," Argoyle said cheerfully.

"What can I do today, Uncles?" Peggy asked.

"We are not your Uncles," they told her.

"Then you must be Cousins. We are all related. My father showed me the tree on which we all grew, with our little great-father hanging from the lowest branch."

Argoyle clapped himself on the forehead in horror, Macio wrinkled his face in disgust. "Wherever are you from?" he asked. "What planet?"

"Sheboygan," Peggy said.

They echoed the word. "Sheboygan, Sheboygan, never heard of it. What do they publish there?"

Brynt scanned the charts, list after list, and could not find it. "You must be lying," he said to her.

"I don't lie. If I lie my mother washes out my mouth with whiskey."

"Contrabanders." "Stasis-breakers!" "Non-universi-tists." "Anti-profs."

"Oh yes, Aunties," Peggy said. "They all come for dinner on Greatsday."

"Claptrap," Brynt snarled, and walked off. He had half a dozen lectures to prepare before the semester began, and it would begin soon enough.

"Do you read?" Macio asked the child.

"A little. I was being teached. I can spell tarradiddle."

"I was being taught," Macio corrected her.

"Oh was you? What did you learn?" Peggy asked.

"How to spell claptrap," Macio replied, and they smiled at each other.

Argoyle gently took Macio by the arm to turn him around, and suggested, "Why don't you go and scribe the circuits for your first lecture on harmony?" Macio took the hint and went off to his study corner. Argoyle set up the viewer for Peggy, ran in several of the simplest tapes he could find, including Darwin and Busby. "What does your father do?" he asked her.

"He's a weathermaker. Could I see some molecules, please?"

"I'll find you some. What do you know about them?"

"If something is thick, like a floor, there are lots of molecules, and they dance so slow you can't see them. But if something is thin, like air, they dance so fast you can't see them. So I never saw any. But my mother said that is the dance of the universe."

"And what does your mother do?"

Peggy looked into the viewer and regarded the molecular structure of hydrogen blankly and fearlessly. "She doesn't do anything, Uncle. She is an Empress."

"So I feared," Argoyle said. "I am going upstairs and do not wish to be disturbed. We are all at work here. Is that clear?"

"Yes. May I push this thing if I want to see something else?"

"You may," Argoyle said, and leaned over to whisper, "the blue button on the right of the food panel will produce bread pudding."

He closed the plastiglass hatchway behind him and climbed on up to his room. He intended to get down to work immediately, but found his ledger and stylus where he'd left them the night before. It was tempting. He'd worked a long time on the guide to Terran cooking and fully expected to publish within a year, just as he'd expected to publish last year. He settled himself in the window seat, and wrote out his introduction to the recipe for CROW PIE:

The history of this delicacy is shrouded in secrecy, perhaps because it has been traditional on Terra to consume this by oneself, in solitude. There is a legend that says the Pie was served to the Kings of England, but we have no evidence to support that. Our scholars believe that although eating Crow is a genuine Terran gourmet feat, it is the least likely to become popular on other worlds. However, since even today a Terran may be heard to say he is going to eat some, or serve it to another, we feel it should be presented in this collection. It is said to be served with great pleasure.

At this point, feeling both drowsy and restless, Argoyle slid off the seat to glance downstairs. Peggy was eating bread pudding. A small owl was looking at her from his perch on the edge of an empty porridge bowl. Peggy offered a piece of bread pudding, which the owl took, and instantly spat out. Peggy giggled. "My poor bird," Argoyle said, and went back to his window seat. He had a stiff course in histories to prepare, and began to think about it, and soon was asleep.

Hoo finished his Outside chores for the morning, and stood in his cleated boots on the roof of the south wing. The air was cold, very clear, a salmon color from the rising of the first sun. A crescent of low mountains, dark as iron, lay behind the University building. He breathed deeply and even enjoyed the slight dizziness he felt. It was a relief after the solid stance he must hold indoors. "Out there," he said to himself, "and I'm stuck here."

As the first sun rose, so did the morning winds, and within a few moments the high gusts buffeted him so that he had difficulty crossing the smooth roof surface to get back to safety. When he returned to the big room he found that Macio had opened the poem box and was sitting at the table with Peggy. Hoo looked at the formed words with surprise and fascination, wondering if Macio had gone into the collapse he was always threatening.

Day squirts through   the holes
    between the tenth   and the eleventh
you know   be careful of interstices

Poor old thing, Hoo thought. As he watched, Peggy reached into the box, took out the complete words "how to" and inserted them in the last line.

Brynt was checking the crystal packs in the computer, frowning slightly as he ran through them. "Absolutely no record," he said aloud, "none at all, and there would have to be some record if a ship came down. How did she get here?"

Hoo thought that if a ship had come down softly on the other side of the planet, or even in the valley which lay beyond the low mountains, there might not be a record of it. The computer wasn't in even fair shape, since it was the basis for Brynt's most difficult lecture-demonstrations, and the crystals were smeared with thumbprints, two of the buttons stuck like old piano keys and rarely rose to necessary occasions. There were other malfunctions which Brynt simply bypassed.

Many times Hoo fairly sweated with impatience to get his hands on the thing and make proper adjustments, though he suspected there were worn parts for which they had no replacements.

What can I make you
  see   saw   grundule
  of the summer   rains

Peggy posted these words in a nice pattern, and Macio watched her with a sleepy but avuncular fondness. "Oh, I like this," Peggy said. "It's more fun."

"What's grundule?" Hoo asked curiously.

"I don't know. I just like the sound of it, don't you?"

"Don't stifle her," Macio warned.

Brynt interrupted them, saying, "We're to go up to the tower. I'm sure the child can manage for a few minutes."

They went through the hatchway and up the stairs to the tower to join Argoyle. He had just written, in his old ledger, the introduction to a famous dessert.

He said, "Ah, yes," when they arrived. "We must have a deliberation. Before the students come out of stasis, only too soon, that'll be, Peggy must be taken care of—I mean, of course, we must see that she's returned to her family, if they are still extant. Or at least returned somewhere else."

"Actually, she's only six," Macio said. "I don't see any rush to make the decision."

Brynt sat down with his fists on his knees, and there was a portentous silence. Hoo stood, feet planted apart, back to the wall. Talk, talk, he was thinking, and nothing but farina for supper.

Brynt spoke. "If, possibly, a ship did crash, would there be any chance of making repairs to it? We must consider this carefully."

"Even if it could be repaired, and put into operation, how could a small child handle it?" Macio asked.

"I'm sure these little modern ships are fully automated," Argoyle said. "Given a reasonable amount of food, and some amusements, she ought to manage, if a course could be plotted for her."

Another silence. Slowly, all three Masters turned to look at Hoo. He said, "I think—"

"Don't be so infernally independent," Brynt cautioned him. "Just do what you're told and everything will be fine." He added, "As a matter of fact, you weren't invited here, and you may be excused. We will let you know our decision."

Hoo bolted down the stairs, nearly losing his footing in his rage and frustration. As he came into the big room Peggy looked up at him severely. "They're talking about me, aren't they, Hoo?"

"Yes, they are."

"Are you a Master?"

"Not yet. But I'm studying to be one."

"Why?" Peggy asked.

Hoo gritted his teeth. Why indeed, he thought, and gritted them again to make sure they hadn't gone soft, or fallen out. If she lived on berries and raw eggs, I could too, he thought. He glanced at the wind gauge. The worst of the morning blow had passed, although it was still rough out there. Berries were no worse than porridge, Hoo thought. Better; they required chewing.

He picked up his backpack of tools and began to strap it on. Peggy watched him. When he got to the door, she asked quietly, "What will they do with me?"

"Nothing," Hoo said, and smiled gently at her. "Not a thing, so you don't have to worry. The worst they can do is bore you to tears."

"Not me," Peggy said. "Good-bye." He stepped over the prismatic glint of the doorsill and disappeared. She put the poem box carefully on the floor, and stood up. At Brynt's computer, she imitated him by punching out a question for it: What is for supper?

FARINA, it replied reassuringly. FARINA

POTATO SOUP OR CUCUMBER STEW

"Rats," Peggy murmured. She must learn how to operate the machinery behind the food panel: Spaghetti and meatballs, fried chicken, and hot fudge syrup on apple pie with walnuts. She pushed the blue button but instead of bread pudding it served her a dish of applesauce. It took her a long time to eat it because she didn't like it, and after a still longer time the men came down the steep stairs from the tower.

"Where's Hoo?" Brynt asked crossly.

"I suppose he's in the Facilities Room," Macio said. "Though it's really my turn."

"Perhaps he went out for another vane check," Argoyle suggested, glancing at the gauges as if they could tell. He asked Peggy, "Do you happen to know where Hoo went?"

"No, sir," Peggy said. "I don't know where he went."

"But you must have seen him when he came down, he didn't just disappear," Brynt said.

"I think he did," Peggy replied.

Argoyle sighed. "Well, there's no use worrying now. We all have lectures to prepare and had better get on with them." He toiled upward again to his tower, and settled himself. Where do you suppose that young man has gone to? he asked himself, nodding a little. His lecture notes were over by the door, which meant he'd have to get up to get them, but his ledger and stylus were right to hand. He'd just finish off the page before getting down to serious work. He opened the ledger and wrote:

HUNGARIAN PRUNE PASTRY

The Hungarians were fond of horses and sour milk, and made great use of the prune. In fact, Hungarians were the discoverers of sour milk. At one time these people rode their horses for long distances, carrying supplies in leather saddlebags. On an occasion they tried to transport fresh milk in the saddlebags during hot weather, and after a long gallop over the plains, they stopped to eat a meal, and were astonished to find they had kurds. This

Argoyle began to snore. In the big room downstairs, the needles of the wind gauges grew still; the vanes of the radiometer spun contentedly; Macio revised for the fifth time his Scherzo for Samisen in B quarter; Brynt copied his notes from last year's lecture on Quant's *Universal Properties of Fire*. Peggy found that by pushing the red button simultaneously with the blue button, and giving the bottom of the food panel a sharp kick right afterward, she could produce a fairly good stew with meat in it.

She had just finished a big bowl of the stew when there was a slight rocking motion of the building, and the radar burped angrily before it settled into its tracking beep, beep, beep.

"Whatever was that?" Macio asked, startled. "It was very disturbing."

Brynt looked at the radar screen where a little luminous blip was rapidly fading Outward. "I suppose, possibly, there was a ship, after all."

The activity had wakened Argoyle and in spite of his resolve not to do the stairs again today, he came down, his cloak trailing from one arm. "Something occur?" he asked. "Have we recorded something?"

Macio said, "I believe so."

Argoyle suddenly sniffed the air, swung around, and looked at Peggy. "What did you eat?" he asked. "What did you get from the food panel?"

"Beef stew."

"You mustn't think of such things," Brynt warned her.

"I didn't do it by thinking," Peggy said. "I wish we had some peppermints."

With raised eyebrows, Brynt turned to his colleagues and asked, "What shall we do?"

Argoyle said, "We don't need to decide now, she's only six. We have plenty of time to talk about it."

Gratefully, Macio said, "That's good. We can talk about it tomorrow."

Academe: a place of instruction; an academic
environment

The Institute

CAROL EMSHWILLER

What are all these old ladies? Why these are . . . why
recent graduates, I would suspect, of the Old Ladies Institute of Higher Learning. See how thin and ascetic
they all are. How proud!

I've been wondering about the possibilities of doing
an article on the O.L.I. of H.L. For instance: It was
about that time that the Old Ladies Institute of Higher
Learning was founded, though not, mind you, by the
old ladies themselves, for they needed help before they
could take over on their own. By now, of course, the
O.L.I. of H.L. is completely run by the old ladies,
partly on Bauhaus principles, though not forgetting
Gaudí, partly à la Chicago U. "Angry" old ladies, one
could say, conscious of themselves as a force for change
in a changing society.

But run, old ladies, this is your last and only chance
to do so many things, dance at the Judson, for instance
(age is no factor there), your last chance to read Koch
and look at Rauschenberg or get into New Campus
Writing, swim the freestyle relay, jump the high jump
(literally and figuratively). Oh, my dear grandmother,

if you were here I'd bring you up as my own dear child,
feed you steak and liver and wheat germ oil, start you
off on push-ups and squats, buy you a book by Freud
(to *begin* with). "The child is father of the grandmother?"

Yes, the child *is* father of the grandmother, therefore,
well, why not start with Camp Fire Girls?

I have twelve girls, a coven of Camp Fire Girls (including me, that is) every Friday at 3:30, and it does
seem in some way significant that every afternoon on
that day I boil a tongue (cow's tongue) seasoned with
rosemary, savory and cloves (significances all of them).
Maybe the OLs do have the magic to, if they wanted to,
make a high jump record ("There was an old woman"
as the old rhyme goes, "tossed up in a basket seventeen
times as high as the moon . . ."), but I think swimming would suit the OLs better.

We might draw up a schedule of the O.L.I. of H.L.
thus:

7:00	Rising bell
7:30	Breakfast
8:00	First class, The Existentialist Woman's Role and Simone de Beauvoir
9:00	Developments in psychology since 1945 except Tuesdays and Thursdays, the Homosexual in Literature from Gide to the Present
10:00	Nudity in Art Through the Ages
11:00	Swimming
12:00	Lunch
1:00	Poetry since 1960 except Tuesdays and Thursdays, Biology with dissecting of frogs, etc., also emergency first aid for grandmothers such as how to perform a quick tracheotomy in case someone swallows a balloon
2:00	The Kama Sutra and related literature
3:00	Sports and exercises (tennis, archery, . . .)

4:00   Swimming
6:00   Cocktails
6:30   Dinner
8:00   Avant Guard movies (Vanderbeek and Brak-
       age, Jack Smith) with occasional poetry
       readings to music

(My grandmother was a shy woman, which doesn't
mean she was lacking in strength. On the contrary, I
suspect she had hidden wells of power that were left
forever untapped and now it is too late.)

But, as I said, I have these twelve girls with which to
lay the foundations of the Old Ladies I. of H.L. "I desire to seek the trail" (all Camp Fire Girl Trail Seekers
say this) "that shall become a delight to my feet. . . ."
Oh, nine-year-olds, I desire that you should seek the
trail that would delight me when you and I reach grand-
motherhood. Wohelo stands for work, health and love.
There's certainly nothing wrong in that. Struggle,
strength and sex? Agonies? Despair and courage? Self-
sacrifice? Wohelo, then.

In those days, those difficult beginning days of the
Institute, the OLs worked (tirelessly) rebuilding (with
their own hands) the old resort hotel that had been cho-
sen as the site of the School for Higher Learning.

> Patching the swimming pool with cement.
> Pulling the weeds out of the tennis courts.
> Shoring up the outbuildings.
> Blocking in the projection booth.

Three years later, let us say, Grandmother, a shy
woman even at the age of seventy-six, entered, like a
little orphan, through the high iron gates. One black bag
contained all of her personal belongings: 1 pr. reading
glasses, 3 aprons, 4 dresses, 2 foundations, 1 string of
jet beads, aspirin, APC pills, 6 pink rayon bloomers
without lace, 1 pr. support stockings, and so on.

But had not Grandmother once been a Camp Fire

Girl? "Wohelo," Grandmother said to herself, trudging off to meet the unknown, walking down the long entranceway that all the other grandmothers came down in private cars or taxis or airport limousines (Grandmother was a scholarship student), noting the unkempt lawns (the OLs haven't much time left over for gardening) and (later on) the monklike rooms, white-walled, noticing (this even later) the lack of tablecloths and that (and this was later still) they forgot about Thanksgiving altogether (though they did remember Christmas with Santa Claus and all). It wasn't, in many ways, exactly to Grandmother's taste. She liked flowers on her curtains.

However, Grandmother entered bravely, meeting the hatchet-faced president of the O.L.I. of H.L. (who was wearing a hand-loomed gray and tan shift with handmade silver jewelry. This even though the OLs didn't bother with such craft-sort-of-things themselves). (The president, by the way, also taught the course on Literature Related to the Kama Sutra.) But Grandmother did enter bravely and, once there, Grandmother persevered. ("Old Woman, Old Woman, Old Woman, said I," as the old rhyme goes, "Oh whither, oh whither, oh whither so high?")

Sex, she learned in Sex 101, is symmetrical, vertical, central and (usually) ventral. (Grandmother had not realized this before.) Grandmother not only drew a picture, as follows:

but wrote her first sonnet on the symmetricality of love, which began:

> When I have fears that sex may cease to be,
>   And dry, oh desert dry I lie like nuns . . .

and so forth.

Grandmother had a lot to learn, but she made good progress. Her first semester she had three Bs and one C, but after that she always had a sprinkling of As.

It was in her senior year that she discovered that her medium was really movies. She talked two other old ladies into posing for her films. Grandma had close-ups of their wonderful old skin, like around the eyes and under the arms, etc. (Grandma had learned by then to see *everything* though she only got a C in the freshman course, Finding New Things to See. Not such an easy course either.) And sometimes she had them pose together on a cot, but . . . well, that's how Grandmother landed in jail and never quite got to graduate. She died before she served out her time.

But don't think she didn't know what she was doing. These days things are a lot easier for old ladies everywhere, partly because of her, and now most all O.L.I. of H.L. graduates get into *Who's Who* (of course they

can't stay there long. Some promising students even die
before they get to their junior year, let alone last out an
issue of *Who's Who*). But those days it was Marguerite
Belquintine, Hatty Witbaum, Emilia Juisinbalvo, and
(my grandmother) Jenny Carswell . . . names we all
know now. They had to fight and suffer for the rest of
us. They were the first to forge the way for old ladies
everywhere.

So here I am with my Camp Fire Girls. Some way we
have to get started on this now (and my grandmother's
dead). They sing:

Wo - he -lo for aye, wo - he -lo for aye, wo -

And finding other creatures less than perfect,
create my own, with Alchemy, breathe life into
. . . Pygmalion?

Condillac's Statue

or WRENS IN HIS HEAD

R.A. LAFFERTY

—

Condillac made a man-sized statue. You did not know
that he could make a statue? All philosophers can do all
things whatsoever, if only they put their hands to it. He
made the statue from a thrust of granite that already
stood there. This granite seemed sometimes brown,
sometimes green, sometimes deep blue, but always frog-
colored, and never lifeless. Three big men did the rough
work, a smith, a wood chopper, and a stonecutter; and
Condillac himself did the fine work. He intended the
statue to be of noble appearance. It would have been
noble if cut out of travertine marble; but things cut out
of granite can only be comic or outré or grotesque.

His friend the brainy doctor Jouhandeau—but that
crabby old occultist was a friend of nobody—added a
thing to the statue according to the plan they had.

The statue stood on the edge of Condillac's estate of
Flux, near Beaugency, in the small park there just off
the mule road that ran north to Châteaudun, and just
off the river Loire itself. It was a fine small park with a

28

gushing spring that fed a bucket-cistern and a large horse-trough. And people came there.

Wagonmen and coachmen and mulemen stopped at this park. It had heavy grass all the way from Flux to the river. Horsemen and honest travelers, vagabonds and revolutionaries stopped there; boatmen from the Loire came there to enjoy a few hours. There were big shade trees and fine water in the summer, and plenty of underwood and stone hearths for the winter. There were old sheep sheds toward the river where one could sleep in the sour hay.

Children came there from town and country. Basket-women came out from Beaugency to sell bread and cheese and apples and wine to the travelers. And everybody who came there would like the statue.

It was a burlesque thing, a boy-man mass with a lump-ish loutish body and a very big head on it. It had a grin almost too wide for that head. Its face was slack and vacant most of the time, but in a certain shadow-hour it became a face of curious profundity. It was a clodhopper, a *balourd*.

The statue stood there a month, "till it should be accustomed to the site," as Condillac and Jouhandeau said. After that, the two of them came in deep evening and opened the head of the statue. (Even the kids who climbed on it had not known that the head would open.) Jouhandeau made the first connection in that head. Then they sat on one of the great stone benches of the park and talked about it till the late moon arose.

"Are you sure it is still alive?" Condillac asked the crabby doctor.

"I myself do not believe in life," Jouhandeau said, "but it is still alive, as *you* understand life."

"And you are sure that it was wiped clean?"

"Oh, absolutely, indiscussably. It gets its first sensory impressions now."

"If you can do such a thing, Jouhandeau, then you can do a thousand other things. It shakes me even to think of them."

"I can do them, and I will not. I do this only to oblige you, to aid you in your studies. But you will be proved wrong; and you will not admit that you are wrong; so it will all be for nothing."

"But others will someday do what you can do now, Jouhandeau."

"Perhaps in two hundred years. I am not much more than two hundred years before my time. After all, Cugnot's automobile is regarded as mere curiosity by everyone. It will be more than a hundred years before such things are made commercially. And here is one greater than Cugnot: myself."

After a while, night men came out of the boscage of the river meadows to look for prey; and Condillac and Jouhandeau slipped back through the trees to the estate house before the rising moon should discover them to the night thieves.

And now the statue was getting its first sensory impressions.

"Old Rock can smell now," the kids told the people.

"How would a statue smell with a stone nose?" the people asked. "Does he snuffle or move or anything? How do you know that he can smell?"

"We don't know how he can smell with a stone nose," the kids said, "and he doesn't snuffle or move or anything. But he can smell now, and we don't know how he can."

Old Rock could smell now all right. And there was one other thing he seemed to do sometimes, but it was hard to catch him at it.

Lathered horses, foam-whitened harness, green goop in the horse trough, those were smells of the little park and the big country. Wet flint stones, grackle birds and the mites on them; river grass and marl grass and loam grass; oaks and chestnuts, wagon-wheel grease, men in leather; stone in shade, and stone in sun; hot mules, and they do *not* smell the same as hot horses; mice in the grass roots, muskiness of snakes; sharpness of fox hair, air of badger holes; brown dust of the Orléans road, red dust of the road to Châteaudun; crows that have fed today, and those who have not; time-polished coach wood; turtles eating low grapes, and the grapes being bruised and eaten; sheep and goats; cows in milk, new stilted colts; long loaves, corks of wine bottles, cicadas in pigweeds; hands of smiths and feet of charcoal burners; whetted iron on travelers; pungent blouses of river men; oatcakes and sour cream; wooden shoes, goose eggs, new-spread dung, potato bugs; thatchers at work; clover, vetch, hairy legs of bumblebees. There are no two of these things that have the same smell.

The kids said that the statue could smell even with a stone nose. He stood and smelled for a month, and the smells informed his stone.

Then Condillac and Jouhandeau came at night, opened the head of the statue, and made the second connection. Afterwards, they sat on one of the stone benches and talked about it till the late moon rose.

"I will prove that there are no innate concepts," Condillac said. "I will confute all foolish philosophers forever. I will prove that there is nothing in the mind but what goes in by the senses. You have obtained prime mature brain matter, snatched out of its dwellings at the moment before its deaths, blended in its several sources, and swept clean by your own techniques. It is an empty house here, and we introduce its dwellers one by one. Why do you say I will be proved wrong, Jouhandeau?"

"I do not believe that there are any innate concepts either. I do not believe that there are any concepts of any sort, anywhere, ever. But what you call concepts will crawl into that mind, not only by the senses through the stone apertures, but by means beyond you."

They argued till the night-bats and the night-sickness flew up from the river to look for prey; then they slipped back through the trees to the estate house.

"Old Rock can hear now," the kids told the people.

"Oh, cut the clownerie, kids," the people said. "How could a statue hear with stone ears?"

But he *could* hear. And there was the other thing that he still seemed to do, and now the kids caught him at it sometimes.

Ah, a whole catalog of different sounds and noises. Old Rock stood and listened for a month to the manifold noises that were all different. By the sounds and the noises he informed his stone. He began to understand the sounds.

That month gone by, Condillac and Jouhandeau came at night, made the third connection inside the head of the statue, and sat and talked about it till the late moon rose.

"Old Rock can see now," the kids said.

"Ah, there is something funny about that statue," the people agreed. "It no longer has stone eyes, but live eyes that move. But what is so wonderful about seeing? A pig or a chicken can do the same thing."

But there was that other thing that Old Rock-Head did, that he had been doing for some time. The statue laughed, openly and loudly now. He chuckled, rooted in the chuckling earth.

"Well, how can he laugh?" Condillac asked. "We haven't made such a connection. Indeed, we haven't provided him with such a connection; we couldn't have. We couldn't have influenced him in this unknowingly?"

"Impossible," said Jouhandeau. "Neither of us has ever laughed."

Well, Statue stood and saw with his eyes for a month. Perhaps it was not wonderful (wonderful is an innate concept, and therefore cannot be), but it was a new dimension. The bumpkin eyes twinkled and stared by turns, and the stone grin became even wider.

Condillac and Jouhandeau came by night to their monthly appointment, opened the head of the statue, made a fourth connection, and sat talking about it till the late moon rose.

"The Rock-Head can talk now," the kids told the people.

"Oh, we know that," the people said. "He talks to us too, but what is so wonderful about talking if it is no more than his talk? Big as he is, he talks like a half-grown kid. The fellow must be retarded."

Yes, he was, a little; but he began to catch up.

But the first person that Statue had talked to was his maker, Condillac himself.

"Statue, you are a *tabula rasa*," Condillac said to him.

"I don't know what that is," said Rock-Head. "Talk honest French, or I cannot understand you. Such is the only talk I have heard in the month I have stood here with loosened ears."

"Your brain was a tablet shaved smooth," said Condillac, "and we have let sensations into it one sense at a time, from the most simple to the most complex. This is to show that you may be functional without innate ideas. I will have to give you a name, Statue."

"Rock-Head is my name," said Statue. "The kids named me. They are friendly most of the time, but sometimes they are rock-throwing rogues."

"But you can have no idea of friendly or unfriendly," Condillac said. "These are only empty words that people use. You can have no idea of good or bad, of beauty or ugliness, of form or deformity, of pleasure or pain. Yours was mature brain matter, though swept clean, and none of the childish entrances could have been made, as with others. We have not yet hooked up your sense of touch, and we may not; it would mean running tendons all through you. Contamination may enter by the sense of touch. But now you can have no idea of justice or injustice, of elegance or inelegance, of wealth or of poverty. In fact, all these opposites are meaning-

less, as I will prove through you. They are only the babbling of blind philosophers."

"But I do have these ideas, Condillac," Rock-Head
insisted. "I have them strongly. I learned right smells
and wrong smells; right tones and wrong tones; right
shapes and forms and colors, and wrong. Oh, may I always choose the right things, Condillac!"

"Statue, you sound like an idiot preacher-man. There
are no right things or wrong things, there are no innate
ideas. There are no things in-place or out-of-place. I
prove this through you."

"Condillac, you are the Abbé of Mureaux, and you
draw pay for such," Rock-Head said. "You would be
in-place there. You are out-of-place on your estate
Flux."

"What is the matter with you, Statue?" Condillac demanded. "You are flighty and wan-witted."

"Wrens in my head, they say of me. It's a country
expression, Condillac. Besides, I have them literally,
quite a pleasant family of them inside my stone head.
Learn from the wren wisdom!"

Condillac angrily beat on the lower part of the statue
with his leaded cane, breaking off toes. "I will not be
lectured by a rock!" he crackled. "You have not these
ideas originally, and mature brain matter will reject
such. Therefore, you have them not! Reason is the
thing, Statue, rationality. We promulgate it. It spreads.
It prevails. The tomorrow world will be the world of
total reason."

"No, it will be the Revolution," said Rock-Head. "A
world condemned to such short fare as bleak reason will
howl and cry out for blood."

A long-tongued woman came to Rock-Head. "My
confessor told me that, whenever I feel impelled to repeat gossip, I should go whisper it to a statue, and then
forget it," she said. So she whispered it to Rock-Head
for an hour and a half.

In the cool of the evening, Rock-Head repeated it,

loudly and stonily, to the quite a few people who were enjoying the evening there, and he found himself the center of interest. But he was uneasy about it; he didn't understand why the confessor had instructed the woman to tell him such things.

One evening the revolutionaries gathered and talked at the foot of Statue.

"It should have happened in our fathers' time," one of them said. "Let it now be in our own time. We may not rightly push this thing off on our sons. The poor become poorer and the corrupt become more corrupt. How many does it take to upheave a world? There are five of us here. Up! Up! Five for the Revolution!"

"Six," cried Rock-Head. "I am for the Revolution too. Up, up, arise!"

"Statue, Statue," one of them asked, "how long have you been able to hear?"

"I'm in my third month of it, fellow."

"Then you have heard us before. You know what we stand for. We will have to destroy you."

"It is only a statue, Fustel," said another of them. "It would be superstition to destroy it. And we are enlightened."

"But what if he blurts out our slogans which he has heard, Hippolyte?"

"A good thing. Let the statue cry slogans, and the people will be amazed."

"Up with the Revolution!" Rock-Head cried again. "But I am not sure that you fellows provide a sufficient base for it. I visualize creatures with a narrower and more singular bent. I will string along with you, but meanwhile I will see what I can do about having real revolutionaries made."

"Have you noticed the new carp in the horse trough, Rock-Head?" the occult doctor Jouhandeau asked as he came by to visit one day.

"Yes, the kid seems to be in some kind of trouble. I'd

comfort him if I could get down to him. But how do you know he's a new carp? People don't notice such things."

"I put him there, Rock-Head," said Jouhandeau. "And I put a human child's brain into him, shaved smooth, of course, and trimmed to fit. He can smell and hear and see, but he could do as much when he had a child's brain."

"Jouhandeau, that kid's scared to death."

"Couldn't be, Rock-Head. Where could he have the idea of scared? Are you contradicting the wise Condillac?"

"Jouhandeau, I am friend to revolutionaries, but all the revolutionaries sound deficient to me. Make me revolutionaries who will do the thing!"

"Anything to oblige a stone-headed friend. I have already done some thinking along this line. I will not even have to transfer brains, or flop like vultures over the dying to rob them of these things. I can take sturdy farmers and townsmen and intellectuals as they stand, destroy certain small nodules in their heads, and we will have them ready to go. I treat them for the escarbilles, a disease of which I have never heard, and they even less. But I stop them in the roadways and tell them that they are afflicted and that I can cure them in a moment. And I do cure them in a moment, of something, but not of the escarbilles."

"Will they have a narrower and more singular bent?"

"They will, Rock-Head, so narrow and singular that you could hardly believe it."

A young fellow was smooching his girl and loving her up in the park.

"I want to do that too," Rock-Head called out loudly.

"All right, come down and do it," said the girl. "It's fun."

"But I can't come down," Rock-Head complained.

"Then you can't do it," the girl said, and they laughed at him.

"I wish that guy would get his truffle-grubbing hands off my girl," Rock-Head grumbled. "But how do I know it would be fun? Is not fun an innate idea? And there are none such."

A thief rode up one cloudy afternoon, opened Rock-Head's head, stuffed a large bag of gold inside, closed the head again, and rode off furiously once more. How did the thief know that Rock-Head's head would open? Why, the gentlemen of the trade can sense a good hiding place every time.

The thief was caught by pursuing horsemen. He was beaten, crying his innocence all the time; but he was not hanged. You cannot hang a thief without boodle.

But the bag full of gold weighed heavily on Rock-Head's brain. Moreover, it crowded the wrens in his head. He had great affection for the wrens, though they did sometimes pick his brains. This gold did have effect.

"This gold, at least, is not an innate idea," Rock-Head mused. "In its particular, it is a thing intruded directly into my head. It is a heavy thing, and I cannot ignore it. There is a new idea and a new attitude in me. I am a man of means now, and my thinking can never be quite what it was before."

Rock-Head began thinking in a new way.

"Jouhandeau," he said when that doctor came to visit him again, "tell Condillac that I want to talk to him. There is something wrong with that man, I believe."

"Condillac is dead now, Rock-Head," Jouhandeau told him. "That is the most recent thing wrong with him."

"How did he accept it? I've been afraid there would be some trouble there."

"He didn't accept it. He believes that life and death are both innate concepts, and that there are no innate concepts. Naturally, he will not believe that he is dead."

"How are you coming along with the revolutionaries, Jouhandeau?"

"Quite well. There are a hundred of them now, and I

will leave them to themselves. They will propagate their own kind, and in two hundred years they will take over the world. I will not hurry it. I am two hundred years before my time in so many ways already."

There was blood on the bread. There was blood on the land, and on every thing. It would bubble and speckle. Then it would flow.

Rock-Head had become an orator. He had the fire, he had the sparkle, he had the quick deep thunder of a true rouser. He had the freshness of morning rain and the resonance of the groaning earth.

So naturally he became something of a leader among the old-fashioned revolutionaries of the neighborhood, and they came for him one night.

"Time for talking is over with, Rock-Head," they told him. "Now is the time for action." They ripped his brains out of the rock case, they ripped out all the sensory appendages that went with them. They loaded these in two hampers on a mule.

"Lead us, Rock-Head," they said. "We begin to burn the world down tonight. We start with the estate house Flux and the town of Beaugency. We burn and we slay."

"What will become of my wrens when I am not in my head with them?" Rock-Head asked.

"We care nothing for wrens, we care nothing for people," they cried. "We only care that the burning may begin."

"What will become of my sack of gold when I am not in my own head to guard it?" Rock-Head worried.

"We care nothing for gold," they said, "we care less for bread. The burning is the thing." And they had come to the estate house of Flux. They began to butcher the gentlepeople and servants fluttering around and to set fire to the place.

"Wait, wait," Rock-Head called. "Have some respect for property. Wait."

"How can we have respect for property?" they asked as they killed and burned. "A revolutionary cares nothing for property."

"This one does," said Rock-Head. "We must have a revolution with full respect for property. I am a man of property now. I own a bag of gold. Up the revolution! Up respect for property!"

"This cannot be," the revolutionaries held council. "A person who owns one bag of gold cannot be a true revolutionary; though, oddly enough, a person who owns one thousand bags may sometimes be."

They began to kill Rock-Head there, in brain and sensories.

"Tell Jouhandeau to call off his thing," Rock-Head gasped out of his dying cerebrum; but these old-fashioned revolutionaries didn't understand him. They knew nothing of the creatures of Jouhandeau which would so soon obsolete them.

They killed Rock-Head in all his parts. They sold his remains for cat meat to a basketwoman there, and they went on with their burning.

Oh, the statue is still there, and there are still wrens in the head. There have now been more than one hundred generations of wrens there. These are the rich wrens and they have a good thing. They pay tribute to the shrikes in small gold coins, so they will not kill them. And the wrens are left alone.

The old-fashioned revolutionaries failed, but the new revolutionaries made by Jouhandeau could not fail. Failure is an innate concept, and there are no innate concepts. A hundred of them, with the few young boys they had pupped in the meanwhile, would overturn that land nineteen years later, that land with blood on the bread.

And later, a thousand of them would—, and ten thousand of them would—, and ten million of them would—, for they propagated their own kind. They were people so narrow and so singular that you would hardly believe it.

Doctor Jouhandeau was two hundred years before his time in so many ways, but he estimated the time of it nicely.

Sophisticated Sons of Abracadabra are
these . . .

The Sorcerers

L. SPRAGUE DE CAMP

—

They say the men of magic all are dead.
No more does the diviner in his swoon
Perceive the future in his mystic smokes;
No more the reckless sorcerer invokes
A demon fell to serve him. Xaltotun,
Imhotep, Merlin, and the rest, it's said
       Are gone from modern life.

But yesteryear, one who, the tale relates,
Was called MacGregor Mathers, Kabbalist,
Had built his Order of the Golden Dawn,
Donned robes, and struggled with the Devil's spawn—
The wizard Crowley, skulking Satanist—
And, exiled, played at four-men chess with Yeats,
       A ghost, and Mathers' wife.

Then, too, in London sat, with cigarette
In hand, unkempt and testy, azure-eyed,
The uncrowned empress of the occult world—
Huge Helena Blavatsky. Round her swirled

A horde of chelas who, though daily plied
With dicta from Mahatmas in Tibet,
      Were locked in frenzied strife.

And what bewhiskered alchemist of yore
Made gold from lead with such astute address
As Mrs. Eddy, Hubbard, and their kind
Turn doctrines full of gibberish refined
To fortunes from the dupes that they impress?
With such, as in the mystic times before,
      The world will long be rife.

Bend time itself to the critical need. Could there be a chemical which is the "alkahest of time," which is as dangerous—in subtler ways —to man as that which the ancients sought to turn base metal into gold?

The Weed of Time

NORMAN SPINRAD

—

I, me, the spark of mind that is my consciousness, dwells in a locus that is neither place nor time. The objective duration of my life-span is one hundred and ten years, but from my own locus of consciousness, I am immortal—my awareness of my own awareness can never cease to be. I am an infant am a child am a youth am an old, old man dying on clean white sheets. I am all these me's, have always been all these me's will always be all these me's in the place where my mind dwells in an eternal moment divorced from time. . . .

A century and a tenth is my eternity. My life is like a biography in a book: immutable, invariant, fixed in length, limitless in duration. On April 3, 2040, I am born. On December 2, 2150, I die. The events in between take place in a single instant. Say that I range up and down them at will, experiencing each of them again and again and again eternally. Even this is not really true; I experience all moments in my century and a

43

tenth simultaneously, once and forever. . . . How can I tell my story? How can I make you understand? The language we have in common is based on concepts of time which we do not share.

For me, time as you think of it does not exist. I do not move from moment to moment sequentially like a blind man groping his way down a tunnel. I am at all points in the tunnel simultaneously, and my eyes are open wide. Time is to me, in a sense, what space is to you, a field over which I move in more directions than one.

How can I tell you? How can I make you understand? We are all of us men born of women but in a way you have less in common with me than you do with an ape or an amoeba. Yet I *must* tell you, somehow. It is too late for me, will be too late, has been too late. I am trapped in this eternal hell and I can never escape, not even into death. My life is immutable, invariant, for I have eaten of Temp, the Weed of Time. But you must not! You must listen! You must understand! Shun the Weed of Time! I must try to tell you in my own way. It is pointless to try to start at the beginning. There is no beginning. There is no end. Only significant time-loci. Let me describe these loci. Perhaps I can make you understand. . . .

September 8, 2050. I am ten years old. I am in the office of Dr. Phipps, who is the Director of the mental hospital in which I have been for the past eight years. On June 12, 2053, they will finally understand that I am not insane. It is all they will understand, but it will be enough for them to release me. But on September 8, 2050, I am in a mental hospital.

September 8, 2050, is the day the first expedition returns from Tau Ceti. The arrival is to be televised, and that is why I am in Dr. Phipps' office watching television with the Director. The Tau Ceti expedition is the reason I am in the hospital. I have been babbling about it for the previous ten years. I have been demanding that the ship be quarantined, that the plant samples it will bring back be destroyed, not allowed to grow in the soil of Earth. For most of my life this has been regarded as an obvious symptom of schizophrenia—after all, before July 12, 2048, the ship has not left for Tau Ceti, and until today it has not returned.

But on September 8, 2050, they wonder. This is the day I have been babbling about since I emerged from my mother's womb and now it is happening. So now I am alone with Dr. Phipps as the image of the ship on the television set lands on the image of a wide concrete apron. . . .

"Make them understand!" I shout, knowing that it is futile. "Stop them, Dr. Phipps, stop them!"

Dr. Phipps stares at me uneasily. His small blue eyes show a mixture of pity, confusion and fright. He is all too familiar with my case. Sharing his desk top with the portable television set is a heavy oak-tag folder filled with my case history, filled with hundreds of therapy session records. In each of these records, this day is mentioned: September 8, 2050. I have repeated the same story over and over and over again. The ship will leave for Tau Ceti on July 12, 2048. It will return on September 8, 2050. The expedition will report that Tau Ceti has twelve planets. . . . The fifth alone is Earth-like and bears plant and animal life. . . . The expedition will bring back samples and seeds of a small Cetan plant with broad green leaves and small purple flowers. . . . The plant will be named *tempis ceti*. . . . It will become known as Temp. . . . Before the properties of the plant are fully understood, seeds will somehow become scattered and Temp will flourish in the soil of Earth . . . Somewhere, somehow, people will begin to eat the leaves of the Temp plant. They will become changed. They will babble of the future, and they will be considered mad—until the future events of which they speak begin to come to pass. . . .

Then the plant will be outlawed as a dangerous narcotic. Eating Temp will become a crime. . . . But as with all forbidden fruit, Temp will continue to be eaten. . . . And finally, Temp addicts will become the most sought-after criminals in the world. The governments of the Earth will attempt to milk the secrets of the future from their tortured minds. . . .

All this is my case history, with which Dr. Phipps is familiar. For eight years, this has been considered only a remarkably consistent psychotic delusion.

But now it is September 8, 2050. As I have predicted, the ship has returned from Tau Ceti. Dr. Phipps stares at me woodenly as the gangplank is erected and the crew begins to debark. I can see his jaw tense as the reporters gather around the Captain, a tall, lean man carrying a small sack.

The Captain shakes his head in confusion as the reporters besiege him. "Let me make a short statement first," he says crisply. "Save wear and tear on all of us."

The Captain's thin, hard, pale face fills the television screen. "The expedition is a success," he says. "The Tau Ceti system was found to have twelve planets, and the fifth is Earthlike and bears plant and simple animal life. Very peculiar animal life. . . ."

"What do you mean, peculiar?" a reporter shouts.

The Captain frowns and shrugs his wide shoulders. "Well, for one thing, they all seem to be herbivores and they seem to live off one species of plant which dominates the planetary flora. No predators. And it's not hard to see why. I don't quite know how to explain this, but all the critters seem to know what the other animals will do before they do it. And what we were going to do, too. We had one hell of a time taking specimens. We think it has something to do with the plant. Does something strange to their time sense."

"What makes you say that?" a reporter asks.

"Well, we fed some of the stuff to our lab animals. Same thing seemed to happen. It became virtually impossible to lay a hand on 'em. They seemed to be living a moment in the future, or something. That's why Dr. Lominov has called the plant *tempis ceti*."

"What's this *tempis* look like?" a reporter says.

"Well, it's sort of . . ." the Captain begins. "Wait a minute," he says, "I've got a sample right here."

He reaches into the small sack and pulls something out. The camera zooms in on the Captain's hand.

He is holding a small plant. The plant has broad green leaves and small purple blossoms.

Dr. Phipps' hands begin to tremble uncontrollably. He stares at me. He stares and stares and stares. . . .

May 12, 2062. I am in a small room. Think of it as a hospital room, think of it as a laboratory, think of it as a cell; it is all three. I have been here for three months.

I am seated on a comfortable lounge chair. Across a table from me sits a man from an unnamed government intelligence bureau. On the table is a tape recorder. It is running. The man seated opposite is frowning in exasperation.

"The subject is December, 2081," he says. "You will tell me all you know of the events of December, 2081."

I stare at him silently, sullenly. I am tired of all the men from intelligence sections, economic councils, scientific bureaus, with their endless, futile demands.

"Look," the man snaps, "we know better than to appeal to your nonexistent sense of patriotism. We are all too well aware that you don't give a damn about what the knowledge you have can mean to your country. But just remember this: you're a convicted criminal. Your sentence is indeterminate. Cooperate, and you'll be released in two years. Clam up, and we'll hold you here till you rot or until you get it through your head that the only way for you to get out is to talk. The subject is the month of December in the year 2081. Now, *give!*"

I sigh. I know that it is no use trying to tell any of them that knowledge of the future is useless, that the future cannot be changed because it was not changed because it will not be changed. They will not accept the

fact that choice is an illusion caused by the fact that
future time-loci are hidden from those who advance sequentially along the timestream one moment after the
other in blissful ignorance. They refuse to understand
that moments of future time are no different from moments of past or present time: fixed, immutable, invariant. They live in the illusion of sequential time.

So I begin to speak of the month of December in the
year 2081. I know they will not be satisfied until I have
told them all I know of the years between this time-
locus and December 2, 2150. I know they will not be
satisfied because they are not satisfied, have not been
satisfied, will not be satisfied. . . .

So I tell them of that terrible December nine years in
their future. . . .

December 2, 2150. I am old, old, a hundred and ten
years old. My age-ruined body lies on the clean white
sheets of a hospital bed, lungs, heart, blood vessels, or-
gans, all failing. Only my mind is forever untouched,
the mind of an infant-child-youth-man-ancient. I am, in
a sense, dying. Beyond this day, December 2, 2150, my
body no longer exists as a living organism. Time to me
forward of this date is as blank to me as time beyond
April 3, 2040, is in the other temporal direction.

In a sense, I am dying. But in another sense, I am
immortal. The spark of my consciousness will not go
out. My mind will not come to an end, for it has neither
end nor beginning. I exist in one moment that lasts forever and spans one hundred and ten years.

Think of my life as a chapter in a book, the book of
eternity, a book with no first page and no last. The
chapter that is my life-span is one hundred and ten
pages long. It has a starting point and an ending point,
but the chapter exists as long as the book exists, the
infinite book of eternity. . . .

Or, think of my life as a ruler one hundred and ten
inches long. The ruler "begins" at one end and "ends"

at one hundred and ten, but "begins" and "ends" refer to length, not duration.

I am dying. I experience dying always, but I never experience death. Death is the absence of experience. It can never come for me.

December 2, 2150, is but a significant time-locus for me, a dark wall, an end point beyond which I cannot see. The other wall has the time-locus April 3, 2040. . . .

April 3, 2040. Nothingness abruptly ends, non-nothingness abruptly begins. I am born.

What is it like for me to be born? How can I tell you? How can I make you understand? My life, my whole life-span of one hundred and ten years comes into being at once, in an instant. At the "moment" of my birth I am at the moment of my death and all moments in between. I emerge from my mother's womb and I see my life as one sees a painting, a painting of some complicated landscape: all at once, whole, a complete gestalt. I see my strange, strange infancy, the incomprehension as I emerge from the womb speaking perfect English, marred only by my undeveloped vocal apparatus, as I emerge from my mother's womb demanding that the ship from Tau Ceti in the time-locus September 8, 2050, be quarantined, knowing that my demand will be futile because it was futile, will be futile, is futile, knowing that at the moment of my birth I am have been will be all that I ever was/am/will be and that I cannot change a moment of it.

I emerge from my mother's womb and I am dying in clean white sheets and I am in the office of Dr. Phipps watching the ship land and I am in the government cell for two years babbling of the future and I am in a clearing in some woods where a plant with broad green leaves and small purple flowers grows and I am picking the plant and eating it as I know I will do have done am doing. . . .

I emerge from my mother's womb and I see the gestalt-painting of my life-span, a pattern of immutable events painted on the stationary and eternal canvas of time. . . .

But I do not merely *see* the "painting," I *am* the "painting" and I am the painter and I am also outside the painting viewing the whole and I am none of these.

And I see the immutable time-locus that determines all the rest—March 4, 2060. Change that and the painting dissolves and I live in time like any other man, moment after blessed moment, freed from this all-knowing hell. But change itself is illusion.

March 4, 2060, in a wood not too far from where I was born. But knowledge of the horror that day brings, has brought, will bring can change nothing. I will do as I am doing will do did because I did it will do it am doing it. . . .

April 3, 2040, and I emerge from my mother's womb, an infant-child-youth-man-ancient, in a government cell in a mental hospital dying in clean white sheets. . . .

March 4, 2060. I am twenty. I am in a clearing in the woods. Before me grows a small plant with broad green leaves and purple blossoms—Temp, the Weed of Time, which has haunted, haunts, will haunt my never-ending life. I know what I am doing will do have done because I will do have done am doing it.

How can I explain? How can I make you understand that this moment is unavoidable, invariant, that though I have known, do know, will know its dreadful consequences, I can do nothing to alter it?

The language is inadequate. What I have told you is an unavoidable half-truth. All actions I perform in my one-hundred-and-ten-year life-span occur simultaneously. But even that statement only hints around the truth, for "simultaneously" means "at the same time" and "time" as you understand the word has no relevance to my life. But let me approximate:

Let me say that all actions I have ever performed, will perform, do perform, occur simultaneously. Thus no knowledge inherent in any particular time-locus can affect any action performed at any other locus in time. Let me construct another useful lie. Let me say that for me action and perception are totally independent of each other. At the moment of my birth, I did everything I ever would do in my life, instantly, blindly, in one total gestalt. Only in the next "moment" do I perceive the results of all those myriad actions, the horror that March 4, 2060, will make has made is making of my life.

Or . . . they say that at the moment of death, one's entire life flashes instantaneously before one's eyes. At the moment of my birth, my whole life flashed before me, not merely before my eyes, but in reality. I cannot change any of it because change is something that exists only as a function of the relationship between different moments in time and for me life is one eternal moment that is one hundred and ten years long. . . .

So this awful moment is invariant, inescapable.

March 4, 2060. I reach down, pluck the Temp plant. I pull off a broad green leaf, put it in my mouth. It tastes bittersweet, woody, unpleasant. I chew it, bolt it down.

The Temp travels to my stomach, is digested, passes into my bloodstream, reached my brain. There changes occur which better men than I are powerless, will be powerless to understand, at least up till December 2, 2150, beyond which is blankness. My body remains in the objective timestream, to age, grow old, decay, die. But my mind is abstracted out of time to experience all moments as one.

It is like a *déjà vu*. Because this happened on March 4, 2060, I have already experienced it in the twenty years since my birth. Yet this is the beginning point for my Temp-consciousness in the objective timestream. But the objective timestream has no relevance to what happens. . . .

The language, the very thought patterns are inadequate. Another useful lie: in the objective timestream I was a normal human being until this dire March 4, experiencing each moment of the previous twenty years sequentially, in order, moment, after moment, after moment. . . .

Now on March 4, 2060, my consciousness expands in two directions in the timestream to fill my entire lifespan: forward to December 2, 2150, and my death, backwards to April 3, 2040, and my birth. As this timelocus of March 4 "changes" my future, so too it "changes" my past, expanding my Temp-consciousness to both extremes of my life-span.

But once the past is changed, the previous past has never existed and I emerge from my mother's womb as an infant-child-youth-man-ancient in a government cell a mental hospital dying in clean white sheets. . . . and—

I, me, the spark of mind that is my consciousness, dwells in a locus that is neither place nor time. The objective duration of my life-span is one hundred and ten years, but from my own locus of consciousness, I am immortal—my awareness of my own awareness can never cease to be. I am an infant am a child am a youth am an old, old man dying on clean white sheets. I am all these me's, have always been all these me's will always be all these me's in the place where my mind dwells in an eternal moment divorced from time. . . .

> ". . . The fond Voyeur and Narcissist alike
> devoutly peer into Disorder, . . ."
>
> Lines 2-5, Stanza 5,
> "Dance of the Solids"
> John Updike

Night and the Loves
of Joe Dicostanzo

SAMUEL R. DELANY

—

She was weeping, banally, in the moonlight.

He was annoyed, but contented himself with taking her luxuriant red hair (really rather mousy before the huge ivory disk balancing on the carbon-paper forest) and changing it to black. Then he coughed.

She turned from the balustrade. Tears rolled under her jaw. Two, like inexhaustible pearls, reappeared from the shadow on her neck. She *was* beautiful.

"Joey . . . ?" she whispered so softly he recognized his name only because that was what she must say.

He looked at his dirty knuckles against the top of the wall, then stepped forward, letting his fist roll. The open zipper on his sleeve jingled.

The breeze cast her hair forward from her shoulder, and her eyes (he would leave them green; green in the moonlight. Stunning) flicked down to perceive the change. "Oh, Joey . . ."

He wondered if she appreciated it. No matter. He

stuck his hands into his back pockets. The left one was torn.

"You're getting . . . tired of me, aren't you?"

"Jesus, Morgantha—" he said.

The breeze, for a moment, became a wind, and his chin and toes got cold. He curled his toes through the dust. He couldn't curl his chin, so he dropped it into the collar of his turtleneck.

She wore only the green gossamer, fastened at her shoulder with a cluster of gold scorpions. Her left breast, bare, taunted the moon.

He said, "Morgantha, you know you're a real—" and then just chewed on his back teeth and made fists inside his jeans.

"Joey—" She spoke with sudden eagerness, backing to the edge of the puddle so that her heels touched the heels of her reflection. "You know, I could be an awful lot of help to you. I really could, if you'd let me. I could tell you so much, about things you'd really like to know. Like why the clocks in the East Wing never read later than three. Or what's in the locked chamber that grumbles and thumps so. Joey, there's a little one-eyed boy coming to try and—"

"Oh, cut it out, Morgantha!" and felt his anger surge. He tried to stop. But it was too late because the emotion was what did it; there was no ritualized gesture, no motion of control.

Morgantha stepped backwards. Not a ripple: she fell straight down while her reflection shot up. For one moment reality and image were joined at the waist like a queen on some grotesque playing card. Then, there was only the green gauze settling, darkening here and there.

Regret had grown to pain in his belly and along the back of his neck, even before the anger peeled away. He lunged forward, grabbed up the wet shift, as if he might somehow retract, retrieve, recall. . . .

Gold insects scurried from the dripping folds, splashed through the shallows to trail dark curves over the flags. He danced back from their scrabblings. A baker's dozen of them, at least!

As he pranced from the largest, he saw the smallest stop beside his other foot, curl its tail, and deliver its sting straight into his instep.

He howled and hopped.

Satisfied, the vengeful beasts scurried away, disappearing into the crevices of the masonry, climbing over the wall, or merely flickering out in the shadow.

With a bellow he flung the wet cloth. It stuck on the wall, or seemed to. Fold on fold it opened down the rock. He turned and hobbled across the stone, the dust first softening under his wet feet, then gritty, then just cool and dry. And throb, throb, throb.

When he got to the doorway, he dug out his crusty handkerchief, pawed through for a clean spot, took off his rimless glasses, and scrubbed at the lenses (jingle, jingle, jingle; the zipper fasteners on his leather jacket). When he slipped the wire hooks back under the hair clutching his ears, he realized he'd only managed to fog one of the lenses so that the moon and the few lit windows in further towers had all grown luminous penumbras. And his foot hurt.

He picked up his unicycle and kicked unenthusiastically at the starter. The third time, which hurt the most, the motor coughed its hot breath against his pants leg. He manhandled it around toward the dark portal, put one leg over the seat, folded his arms, swayed a bit for balance. Then he picked up his other foot, leaned forward, and caromed down the spiral steps. At each turn, as he racketed around the tower, a narrow window flung a handful of moonlight in his eyes.

Between, was all darkness and thunder.

Joey halted halfway along the East Wing's northwest corridor on the seventh floor.

The motor stopped roaring; purred instead. He got off, and frowned at the line of depressed piling that ran back along the maroon carpeting into the lithic dark.

He dragged the unicycle over to lean it on the wall. "Hey!"

"Joey?"

"I'm coming in."

"I'll be there in a minute if you'll just—"

But Joey strode up the three steps in the narrow alcove, punched the wooden door with both fists: it flew in.

The grandfather clock in the niche in the floor-to-ceiling bookshelf said twenty to three.

"You know, you're a real pain," Maximillian said. "If I were only a fraction meaner than I am, I'd drop you back into whatever bad dream you came out of."

"Try it." Joey sat in the leather wing chair in front of the desk.

Maximillian pushed aside two mounds of books and regarded Joey through his black plastic frames. His fingers meshed into a big, veined knot between olive corduroy. "What's the matter now? And get your feet off my desk."

Joey put his feet on the floor again. "I just got rid of Morgantha."

"Why don't you go somewhere else and complain about your love life?" Maximillian leaned back and put his own loafers up. Two volumes dropped. And his heel had tapped the crystal paperweight which rolled forward and nearly—

Joey caught it.

"Thanks," Maximillian said.

Before he put it back, Joey looked into the flashings and crystal glister. Below the reflected points from the candles set about the room, there was a rippling as of water, cut by a darkness that could have been the edge of a bridge; also, something that might have been shrubbery, and in it: a face under lots of hair with a . . . black rag over one eye.

Joey's attention was broken by a rumbling below that ended in a double thump. The flames in their luminous waxen collars shook.

Maximillian put his own feet down. Both he and Joey looked at the floor.

A gold scorpion ran from beneath the desk, dodged about one of the fallen books that stood open on its spine and disappeared behind a pedestal on which sat the stained bust of a nameless patriarch.

"Eh . . . what's this?" Joey asked, hefting the crystal.

"Oh." Maximillian's eyes came up. His brows lowered. "Usually it shows the view through the front gate over the bridge."

"That's what I thought it was." Suddenly Joey turned and hurled the crystal.

It *thwumped* the thick hanging, which expelled a wall of dust that broke apart: great gray dragons fragmented into medium-sized vultures that finally vanished as small bats. The crystal thudded to the two-foot mound of tapestry on the floor and *churrrrred* across the planks to the side of the desk.

Maximillian picked it up and leaned on the front corner to examine it. After a while he said, "You really are upset about this Morgantha business, huh?" He put down the crystal, took out his meerschaum, and tamped it in the baboon's-head humidor beside him. The yellow eyes glanced up, blinked twice, then crossed again to contemplate the flat black, perpetually damp-looking nose. Actually, Joey knew, it was shellac. "Well go on, Joey. Talk about it."

"Max," Joey said, "you are a figment of my imagination. Why don't you admit it?"

"Because you are a figment of mine." Maximillian sucked the flaming flower from the match. After several bubbly explosions he caressed the ocher bowl with his thumb. "I'd rather talk about Morgantha. You're not really going to go through this again?"

"Yes, I am."

"Joey, look—"

"Max, I've finally got it figured out. One day, a long time ago, I decided to make something I couldn't unmake. I was very lonely. I wanted someone around as different from me as possible. So I made a Maximillian; and I made one I couldn't destroy. Then I made myself forget having made it. . . ."

"Oh, really, Joey! I made you. And I remember perfectly well making you. I remember before you were here; and I remember even before that."

"Because I *willed* you to have those memories, don't you see?"

"Joey, look: everything about you is preposterous. The way you clatter up and down the steps, and that outlandish outfit. How could you possibly be real?"

"Because you could never conceive of making anything that preposterous, Max. You've told me so a dozen times. How could you?"

"That is a very good question."

"If you made me like you say, then why can't you unmake me, the way I unmade Morgantha?"

"I have more self-control than you, for one thing."

"Because you can't! You can't! You can't! I get you furious a dozen times a week. Believe me, if you could unmake me, I'd have been gone long ago." He sat forward energetically. "I make and unmake things all the time. But I've never actually seen you make anything at all."

"I've told you before, I don't think it's something to be abused."

"You're just trying to keep me from getting really mad and unmaking you."

"Quote you back at yourself," Maximillian said dryly: "Just try."

"I have. It never works."

The hands on the grandfather clock had swung around with amazing stealth to two minutes of.

"What's more, I've given you the only explanation that accounts for why it doesn't."

Maximillian sighed. "I remember distinctly making you. You have no memory at all of making me. By all the laws of economy and logic—"

Joey flung his hand out. "Do you see anything around here either logical or economical?"

"That's not the same—"

"Could you make a rock so heavy you couldn't lift it?"

"Of course I could. And that's not the same thing at all as making a rock I couldn't unmake if I happened to see it falling toward me from a balcony."

"Max—" Joey clapped his hands in frustration. "Do you realize I've never seen you outside this *room?*"

"All my needs are provided for here or in the chambers adjoining."

"Come out with me now."

"I'm busy."

"You can't come out. I made you so you'd always be in this one room."

"Absurd. Every couple of days I go for a walk in some of the lower corridors."

"And every time I come here, you're always sitting behind that desk, no matter what time of the day or night. I've never caught you out. Not even to take a leak."

"All the more reason to believe I made you. I never summon you—I suppose I do it unconsciously, because I must admit I occasionally develop a certain fondness for you *in absentia*—while I'm taking a walk, a nap, or a . . . leak."

Joey just grunted. "What are you reading anyway?"

"*Puffins.*" He picked up his current volume. "M. R. Lockely. Perfectly delightful book. If you promise to take good care of it, I'll lend it to—"

"Max, you've got to come with me! There's something outside. Morgantha told me just before I got rid of her. There's something outside that's trying to get *in!*" He lowered his voice theatrically: "Over the moat!"

Maximillian's laughter burst out with an introductory sound Joey would have sworn was a "pop." "Go fight your own delusions."

"It's not one of mine; it's one of yours!"

"Cut it out," Maximillian said and picked up Lockely. "You really do make me angry sometimes, you know? You've got to learn to take the responsibility for what's yours and stop trying to assume the glory for what's not."

"Such as?"

The book flapped down on the table. "*You,* for one thing. *Me,* for another!"

"Damn it, Max—" In frustration Joey stalked across the room. He turned back, but his outrage was trapped by an occasionally recurrent stutter.

Maximillian had folded his arms and was glaring. The hands on the grandfather clock had crept back to quarter of.

Joey slammed the door.

The direct way to the moat took Joey roaring and bouncing down another flight of steps and off through a stone corridor whose ceiling was so low he had to hold his head down.

Fires flickered behind iron cages set in niches to the left. As he passed the flat, black, studded door of the locked chamber on his right—a five-by-five metal square recessed in the rougher wall—he could not be sure (it may have been vibrations from the engine, as his muffler had fallen off two weeks before) but he thought the door rattled as he shot by. He swung his vehicle around into another stairwell.

Fists bagging his jacket pockets even further, and meerschaum chirping, Maximillian shortly went for a walk in the remoter levels to ponder his origin. His certainty over the matter, alas, could only be assumed in the security of his study. The further away he wandered (and he did take at least one goodly stroll every other day) the greater grew his doubt. What he talked of to Joey—and he was fairly certain Joey knew it—was a period some years back when through overwork, fatigue, and the ever mounting pressure from the discovery in one of the lumber rooms of a slightly damp eleventh edition of the *Encyclopaedia Britannica* which threatened to decompose before he got all thirty-seven volumes read, he had hallucinated a time in which he had created not only Joey, but all the rooms, books, staircases, and chambers vacant, furnished, or locked, as well as the briny water around them and the brackish woods beyond. Before that, his memories were a little hazy. The only thing certain about that time was that Joey had been there, and the castle, and the wood.

He had been walking in darkness for some time when he became aware that the echo of his footsteps was returning over a very long distance.

Far above him and fifty feet to the right was a small rectangle of moonlight cut by bars. Equally far below him, and left, a luminous pearl flickered on shifting waters. And there was the distant plash, plash, plash. He had wandered onto one of the stone arches that spanned the castle's immense cistern. As he came down the steps (there were no rails on either side) a dim light ahead resolved into one of the iron cages where the oil still flickered, lighting the wet, high wall as though it were made of mica.

He reached the crumbling ledge, and entered a very narrow corridor, where more fires were caged by the doorway. After thirty feet the rough walls gave way to dressed stone. And the ceiling was a little higher. A little further and the dirt floor slipped beneath plank.

A chair had been placed at a bend. The carved black rungs had nearly pulled from their pegs. The leather cushion had cracked away at the corners and seemed to be stuffed with cardboard. But it was a chair.

A little further still, and the corridor had heaved itself out to respectable breadth and width. There were, irregularly, doors on the left and, quite regularly, windows on the right.

One reason Maximillian did not venture from his study more frequently was the feeling of being observed that grew with the distance. Joey must be spying on him—that was his rationalization. Alas, Joey had never given Maximillian the slightest inkling that he had observed any of his wanderings. Both spying and reticence were entirely alien to Joey's character as Maximillian perceived it. But Maximillian still nurtured the possibility as a hope.

Between dark drapes a wing of moonlight fell over an immense painting. The surface was nearly black with dirt and overvarnishing. The frame was an eight-inch width of gilded leaves, shells, and birds. Max stopped to gaze into the murky umbers stained to teak.

Behind the frame the canvas had come loose from its stretchers at one corner. A texture here from a brush stroke, there something that was either color or glare from the moon: was that a pale highlight, or a scar where the underpainting and layered glazes had cracked from the white-lead sizing?

Maximillian looked left where a crystal candelabra rewired for electricity had about half the bulbs working. He looked to the right where the chair sat in the corridor's dim elbow.

He faced the canvas again and cleared his throat:

"Agent XMQ7-34, calling Supervisor 86th Sector, Precinct B. Please come in. Please come in. This is Agent, eh . . . XMQ7-34 calling Supervisor of the—"

"Supervisor here. What's the report?"

"The experiment is progressing nicely, sir. The subject is responding well to the evocation of paranoid projection."

"Good."

"He's moving through the proscribed stages exactly on schedule."

"Very fine."

"The psychic tensions have practically webbed in the life force; it awaits only your orders before we move to the final phase."

"Oh, yes. Excellent. Splendid. But tell me, Agent XMQ7-34, how do you find yourself holding up under all this?"

"To tell the truth, it's a little hard on me, chief. You

know, it's funny, but I'm really becoming sort of fond of the subject . . . I mean, in a way."

"I'm afraid, Agent XMQ7-34, it's a process I'm familiar with. They try so hard, put up such a battle, that you can't help developing a certain respect for the little buggers."

"That's it, chief." Maximillian began to laugh. "That's it exactly. . . ." Laughter from the canvas joined his, merged with it, was absorbed by it, till Maximillian's rang alone. He was unable to keep up the charade any longer.

He glanced down the hall hoping to catch sight of Joey's head pulling back around the corner. But the audience for whom he conjured his voices was, as usual, absent.

As Maximillian turned from the painting, for one moment the vast surface cleared of moon glare.

A small window near the top: on a narrow stone bridge two figures struggled in the shadow of the wall, high above black water. One of the figures was naked.

But Maximillian had already taken another step; again reflected light blotted the surface. Frowning, he moved to one side, forward, back again, but could not find the spot again where the subject cleared.

Finally he turned and walked toward the chandelier.

Through blue hangings that curtained the open door came the sound of gentle converse. Occasionally a man's or woman's laughter segregated itself.

Maximillian frowned again.

It had been almost a year since he had been in this hall. His last visit had been on an evening when he had been particularly depressed. A disastrous idea, he had known it wouldn't work; still, he had made a party.

He had left early, fleeing back to his study and his books. As he stood here now, he realized he could not recall ever consciously unmaking the gathering. The voices chattered on.

He looked at the electrified chandelier. The black extension cord he had run to the other chandelier inside to light the party room still hung down to the rug, curled twice, and snaked off between the hangings.

His apprehension deepened. The party had been formal. He was wearing only his baggy corduroy. Suddenly, perhaps too suddenly, he pushed through the drapery onto the small balcony.

"Maximillian! Oh, there, I told you he'd be back. Steve, Bert, Ronny, Max is back. Didn't I say he wouldn't run off and just desert us forever?"

"Well, you certainly took your time, boy. It's almost twenty-five to three."

"Come on down from there and have a martini."

"Oh, Karl, it's much too late in the evening for martinis. Max wants something stronger than that."

"Are you feeling any better, honey? You looked a sight when you ran out of here."

"Oh, Max was just having one of his moods, weren't you, Max darling."

He held the railing and gazed down into the room.

"I think he still looks sort of green around the gills."

"All he needs is a drink. Max, come on down here and have a drink."

He opened his mouth, his tongue stumbling; he tried to think of something witty to toss before his descent.

"Max? Max! I *am* glad you came back, really. It wasn't something I said, was it? Tell me it wasn't something I said. I was only kidding, Max. Really I—"

"Come on, Sheila. Let it go—"

"Max, Ronny just told me the funniest story. Come on, Ronny, tell Max the one you just told me. The one about—well, you know!"

"Oh, yes, you've got to hear this one. Gracie laughed so much she lost her shoe. Gracie, did you ever get your shoe back? I saw Oliver doing something with it over there behind the piano."

"Max? Oh, come on, Max! You're not going to run out on us again, are you?"

"Of course he's not. He just got here; right, Max? Max . . . ?"

"Oh, don't pay him any mind. You know how Max is. He'll be back."

Maximillian stopped in the corridor. His palms were moist. As he opened his fingers, they cooled. For one moment he tried to summon up the will to unmake what was inside.

The hangings swung. The conversation burbled and wound. A woman laughed. More conversation. A man laughed.

He felt terribly drained. The necessary anger that would erase it all was stifled in him. He swallowed, and was surprised by the breaking sound from his throat.

Hands in his jacket pockets, he hurried down the hall.

The gate's beams, vertical and cross, creaked up into the stone. Joey looked out on the bridge. The trees beyond the shrubbery wrinkled and rolled. A moment later the surface of the water reticulated like foil. And terror divided the focus of his senses into some great fly's eye through which the whole vision before him was suddenly fragmented and absurd. Then the ordinary fear with which he could cope returned.

He stepped from the stone floor to the wooden bridge, paused for a moment with his hand on the seven-inch links of the draw chain, till he remembered it was caked in grease. He looked at the black smears on his fingers, wiped them on his jean thigh, and put both hands in his back pockets without checking again: it would take soap. And water . . .

Something moved in the shrubbery at the head of the bridge. Squinting through the fogged lens, Joey stepped forward. The forest roared softly. The wind flattened the leather jacket to his side; zippers tinkled.

A figure darted forward, gained the boards, and came up short as though it had expected no hindrance.

Joey snatched his hands from his pockets so fast his knuckles stung: he heard more threads go.

The boy was naked.

Crouched.

Balanced on the balls of his feet.

Hands to the side.

His hair, black as rags of the night itself, whipped and snapped at one shoulder.

". . . What do you want?" Joey demanded over the wind.

A black cloth was tied down around the left eye.

The right one, huge and yellow, blinked.

"Come on," Joey said. "What do you want?"

The boy blinked again. Then he laughed, a skinny sound that twisted out like barbed wire through dry pine needles. His arms came back to his sides. He took another step.

Joey said, "You better get away from here."

The boy said, "Hello, Joey."

"You better get away from here now," Joey repeated. "What do you want?"

There were cuts and scratches on the boy's shins and feet. He held his head slightly to the side in order to see. "Can I come inside, Joey?" and the following laughter was all breath. It sounded terribly wet.

"No. You can't. What do you want?"

"Aw, come on." Another step. The boy stuck out his hand. "I'll tell you when we get inside."

Joey took the hand to shake. "You can't come in." Joey's hand was thick, dry, and gritty.

"Yes I can." The boy's was long and moist. And he was still laughing.

"You get on out of here." But physical contact, unpleasant as it was, made the child less threatening. The eye-rag was knotted across his left ear. A splatter of acne wounds made their red galaxy on his jaw. "Get off the bridge." Joey tried to pull his hand away. The fingers stiffened around his own. "Now come *on*—" He shook his hand. The hand holding his swung with his shaking. "Hey—!" Now Joey pulled back in earnest.

The boy laughed and pulled against him. He was very strong.

Joey leaned back and grabbed his own wrist with his free hand. The boy leaned too. His free hand waved behind him. The boy's foot touched Joey's; his toes were wet and cold with night water.

The boy grinned.

Joey jerked, slipped, yanked.

Then the boy released all pressure.

Joey staggered backwards, almost tripped on the sill, went back three more steps, and sat down.

The boy stood over him, his grip still firm.

The gate creaked down. The splintered stumps of the vertical beams thudded into puddles that had collected in the worn depressions, sending dark rills through the checkered moonlight.

"Told you I could get in."

Something ran out into the pale square where the boy stood, paused to raise its glittering barb, thought better, and scurried off. Joey felt a sympathetic throb in his instep.

"You know what I want?"

As Joey pushed to his feet, the boy helped him with a tug. Joey narrowed his eyes; the boy released his hand.

"I'm going to unlock that room upstairs. I'm going to push back the door, and whatever is inside is going to come out."

"Huh?"

"What do you think will happen once it's let out?"

"What out?"

The boy suddenly giggled and rubbed his wrist across his mouth. "Joey, you know . . ." He looked around the dim hall. ". . . Maybe the clocks in the East Wing will get on with their business at last. Perhaps you and Maximillian will decide you don't want to live here anymore, and move away into the forest. Interesting to think about, isn't it?"

Joey tried to focus his discomfort.

The boy's vocal expression suddenly changed. "I've got to try and unlock it. Take me up there, Joey. All you have to do is show me the door. I'll do the rest. I'll let it out, and then I can go. It'll be simple. Show me where the chamber is. Once I open the door, I'll go away and leave you alone. . . ."

"*No* . . . !" Joey wanted to give his refusal full voice. But it came out in a rasping hiss. He turned in the echoing hall (the discomfort focused was terror) and ran through the nearest doorway.

"Joey . . . !"

He scrambled down the ill-lit steps. At the bottom he turned to see the silhouetted figure, a hand on either wall, starting after him.

Joey missed the next step. His heel struck full on the stone and jarred him to the head. But he was running again.

He swung under an archway, knowing steps would take him shortly up, up where the locked chamber waited. Desperately he tried to think of somewhere, place, direction to—

He crossed a grate and felt his feet press momentarily between cold bars. The steps were close.

"Joey . . . ?"

He practically fell up them, trying to recall some turn-off, some cross-passage to take him away. He scrambled over the length of the hallway in his memory. It opened directly into the low, stone corridor not three yards away from the recessed square of black metal, five by five.

He remembered the conduit the same moment he passed it. And he was on his knees, lugging away the heavy cover. He shoved the circular hatch from him and heard it clanging down the steps, *ka-tang, tang, tang,* for all the world like his unicycle.

"Hey, what the—" from behind him.

Joey lunged through the opening. His back and shoulders scraped the sides and roof.

"Joey, you shouldn't have done that—"

He had to crawl with his forearms flat. His own breath raged in echo around his ears. There was water

on the floor. And much more softly, at a distinctly different rhythm, somebody else was breathing.

His head tapped the plate on the other end in blackness. He shoved with his shoulder. For a moment it
stuck—

". . . Joey?"

—and that was terrible.

It pushed away. The *thud* of the fall was duller than
he expected. He scrambled out over the metal plate,
and crouched on all fours on a rug.

As he stood he saw a sideways H of light between the
double doors just ahead of him. Behind him was the
sound of scrabbling. He pushed the doors apart, lurched
out, and was practically blind after his crawl through
the darkness.

"Oh, I say there—"

"I told Sheila. I told her, I don't think anyone could
have blamed her. I mean, after all—"

"Oliver! Come out from under there!"

"Leave him alone, Bert. You know how Oliver is—
Oh, pardon me!"

"Hey, I didn't see you come in! Are you all right?
Here, let me get you a martini."

"For God's sake, Steve, it's too late in the evening
for—"

"Dreadfully sorry. Did I bump into you?"

". . . Joey?"

"Say, I bet you haven't heard this one. Ronny, tell
this young man here that story about—"

As he pushed forward, Joey felt the electrical cord
catch around his ankle. The chandelier shook overhead.

"—Hey, watch it there! Better keep your eyes in
front of you, young fellow."

The cord pulled free: the room dropped into darkness
deep as the conduit's.

"You're sure I can't get you something? If not a martini, perhaps—"

"I think you're terribly hard on him, Karl."

". . . after all, he has been under a great deal of pressure, you know."

"All *I* know is that if anyone had said that to me, I would have scratched his eyes out!"

"Joey?"

"Oliver? Is that you under there? Hey, are you all right? Oliver?"

Joey was clambering up the steps toward the little balcony.

"After I've gone and mixed this, doesn't anybody want it? Would you—"

"Joey . . . ?"

He beat at the hangings. Then, suddenly, he was through and into the hallway.

He stepped over the extension cord and hurried up the corridor. The air was dusty with moonlight.

By a huge gilt frame he turned to look behind him. For a moment the glare cleared from the blackened varnish: two figures struggled through a richly appointed room filled with men and women in evening dress. One of the figures was naked.

And someone was pushing aside the blue hangings back in the doorway.

Joey turned again and ran down the hall. At the bend, he punched the wall by the chair. Again he looked back.

"Joey, are you taking me in the right direction? You're sure now this is the way? If you take me there, then I can let it out and leave you alone. You know, you can't lose me. You think you'll just take me around in circles, don't you? But that's not going to work. You'll make a mistake, turn down the wrong hall, and there we'll be, won't we?"

Joey felt the arm of the chair move under his hand. He glanced down: the whole frame swayed, about to collapse.

"Lead on! Right this way to the locked chamber. Is it down there, Joey?"

Joey started along the hall again. He was holding his

breath, he realized. He let it out with an aching gasp and sucked in another.

"Right behind you, Joey."

The walls were no longer paneled, but merely dressed stone. And there were no more windows. He had barely noted this when the ceiling dropped to within a foot of his head.

"This long-way-around business is a real waste of time, Joey. Why don't you just give up and show me the quick way, nice and simple?"

The walls were closer too. He moved forward in slow-motion hysteria. Pebbles chewed the soles of his feet. The niched flames flickered. For a moment he had a vision of the hall diminishing to the size of the conduit.

He stopped, because suddenly he was standing in an echoing hollow that stretched out and up into dimness that became blackness and still went on.

"Which way do we go now?"

Joey jumped, because the voice was practically at his elbow. He was thinking about running, was running—

A weight landed on his back. Joey staggered forward, all zippers jangling like chimes. There was the sound of breath, roaring loud: then a sharp pain below his ear.

Joey's shriek vaulted about the echoing cistern. The boy had bitten. Joey went forward, clawing up the stairs. The weight released, and Joey ran ten more steps before he realized he was on one of the bridges. He turned to see the boy, again in silhouette from the fires on the ledge.

"Go on, Joey." The boy was breathing hard. "That was just to show you I'm losing patience, though."

Joey backed up another step.

The boy came on two.

At the next step pale light caught in Joey's eyes. High, very high above was a window, broken by bars and filled with moonlight. The beam lit three of the chipped steps before falling over the edge to flicker on the misty ripplings so far, so terribly far below. Joey backed up another four steps.

"You know I really am losing my taste for all of this crawling around in the dark." The liquescent breathing lisped among the sounds of dripping. "When are you going to cut this out and show me the chamber? I think I'm going to have to teach you another lesson." Then the figure was racing forward.

Joey saw him pass through the shaft. The face was creased with rage about the yellow eye. Joey whirled, started up, stumbled immediately. He went down on his hands.

At the same time he heard a high shriek. And something struck his back, slipped to the side— It jerked him hugely to the side. Joey went flat, clutching the edge of the steps, his cheek pressed against the crumblings.

And the shrieking.

Joey bit the corner of the stone and cried and kicked violently. An amazing weight was hanging from below his waist. There was the sound of ripping cloth. And then there wasn't any more weight.

The splash cut out the body of the sound. The echo grew quieter, and then even quieter. It may have been the reverberations from his own sobs, but the echo still went on.

After a while he pushed himself up. He stopped at the beginning of the moonlight's wash.

On the top step was a dark smear to the stairway's edge. At one end the golden carapace was crushed flat along with clotted maroon.

Stung and slipping, the boy must have leaped for Joey, only to catch his back pocket. Joey ran his hand over the stubble of threads on his buttock. Then, jingling softly, he stepped around the moonlit stain.

When he reached the ledge, he was holding his breath again. When he let it out, the echo still came back like shrieking.

The grandfather clock showed less than a minute to three.

The baboon's eyes uncrossed from the gleaming nose, rolled to the left, then to the right. The lips lifted from the yellow teeth. The humidor gave up a sound for all the world like someone clearing his throat:

"Agent XMQ7-34, calling Supervisor 86th Sector, Precinct B. Please come in. Please come in. This is, eh . . . Agent XMQ7-34 calling Supervisor of the—"

"Supervisor here," the marble patriarch announced from his pedestal. "What's the report?"

"The experiment is progressing nicely, sir. The subject is responding well to the evocation of—"

"Yes, of course," interrupted the bust. "I know, I know: but you just can't help respecting the little buggers. Oh, yes, yes. I know all about that."

Their mounting laughter was cut off by a sudden rumbling from the chamber beneath, punctuated by three distinct *thwumps*, the second much louder than either the first or third.

The baboon rolled his eyes around to observe the grandfather clock just as Maximillian opened the door: seventeen minutes past two.

Maximillian had been back from his walk almost half an hour, and was making fair progress in his comparison of Apollinaire's *Le Poète Assassiné* with the Padgett translation when the whine of Joey's unicycle came shuddering through the door.

I tell you truly, brethren, Padgett had rendered, *there are few spectacles that do not put the soul in danger. I know of only one place. . . .* Maximillian looked up, frowning. The familiar whine became a familiar roar. *. . . one place you can go fearlessly and that is—* Maximillian closed the book as the motor coughed to silence.

"Max!" The door banged back against the bookshelf as Joey bounded forward. "Max, it almost got in! But I

led it on a wild goose chase! Into the cistern. And it
tripped and fell into the— Oh, Max!"

"What are you talking about?"

Joey was gasping between each clutch of words. "It
wanted to open the locked chamber! Let it out! But I
wouldn't let it." He grabbed the edge of the desk.
"Max, don't make any more of those! Please, Max,
please don't ever make any more."

Maximillian shook his head. He wished Joey
wouldn't barge in on him. He was beginning to wish it
more than anything else. "Make what?"

"Ones like *that!*"

"God damn it, Joey, will you get *out* of here!" and
he was standing now, astounded at his own anger,
aware that the tics in the muscles of his face were his
own winces at the volume of his voice.

Joey backed to the door. He made three forays into
some word or other but kept jamming on the letter "b."
Then he fled the room.

Maximillian sat down while the unicycle thundered
outside, and couldn't find his place in Padgett at all.

Clacketing up the tower steps, he didn't care if Max
didn't know what he had just saved them from. And he
didn't care if Max never lent him another book forever
and ever. And he didn't care if Max never went out of
his old study anyway. And if he got mad enough, Max
better watch out, because he *would* unmake him.

He reached the sill and rolled out on the tower roof.
He caught himself on the stone wall as the cycle sagged,
got off, and positioned his machine against the door
jamb.

A small moon winked overhead between running
clouds. The puddle rippled by the balustrade as the
wind unrolled across the roof and swayed through his
hair so that it tickled his forehead.

He didn't care if he never saw Max again. He would
make a beautiful, sweet, interesting girl who would do
everything he said, and would never talk back to him,

and be very much in love. With him. He'd make this
one colored. And maybe she'd be able to play songs on
the autoharp. Yes, she'd have a nice voice, and would
sing to him after dinner and be as dark and as warm as
the shadows in the hallways in the remoter levels.

He picked the green shift off the wall. Then he sat
down and leaned against the rock. He held the gauze
around his fists, bent his face to touch his chin to it. It
was practically dry now, and cool.

He tried to think about the interesting colored girl.
But it was chilly, and his thoughts kept drifting. The
flags were cold on his feet and through the seat of his
pants (he didn't wear underwear any more), and soon
he would zip his jacket closed over his sweater. When
he squinted, the stuff on his right lens made the reflected moon explode on the waters beside him in a
shower of silent, silver needles. And he was tired, almost tired enough to sleep, right there, but first
he would think some more about the girl until he
would hear her voice behind him, calling him, *Joey?
Joey . . . ?*

In another tower a clock chimed three. He started to
his knees, looked out over the wall. But the chimes had
sounded from the West Wing where the clocks were all
perfectly normal anyway.

"Joey?"

Ah, what frightening Alchemy is worked here
To make Horror of the kind familiar.

Come Up and See Me

DAPHNE CASTELL

—

The hedge girdling Dupaman's garden began to lend a
different facade to the rest of the village. Small stone
cottages that had been plain, and uncompromisingly
stitched before and behind with border flowers in bla-
tant pink and blue, looked at last cunning and significant, crouching behind privet and box. They gave the
effect of peering.

Shops—not many of them—might have sold anything, from mercury to mandragora, and tins and pack-
ets disappeared from their windows.

The garage went out of business. The cute ring of
stone mushrooms that had for so long trimmed Miss
Aynard's displayed lawn were chipped and tumbled on
one night, and the next, had vanished to lurk near over-
grown hedgerows in various fields. The village had
never had much in the way of street lighting. Now it
had none, and local lovers pressed and squealed and
whispered in dank corners with more urgency than ever.

The great hedge had grown so fast, it would have astonished them all, if they had not been past surprise.
The hot, wet, seething summers of the last three

years—had it been that first season when Dupaman came?—had drained them and left their capacity for surprise or fear languid. Normal quicknesses of mind or movement were stifled in them and overlaid by garlands of hesitation first, then of lazy capitulation.

It was a pity, though, as far as any of them could feel pricks of anything like regret, that the hedge had grown so fast. You could not see the garden. It was worth seeing, the rumour went, if you were asked in by the right gate, at the right time of day.

And that, of course, was enough for Dupaman to hear, and begin cutting the hedge, a very little at a time. It meant a renewal of life to them. The juices began to flow again in their languid drying veins, and their actions began once more a fierce vendetta with environment.

Phyllis Aynard had abandoned her morning walk—lack of observation and encouragement. A hedge of admiring faces, as thick as the branches of Dupaman's hedge, should have escorted her manorial progress, in her arrogant muddled mind. The house was the oldest in the village, was in a sense its source. Without the efforts of the house to attract tenants, servants, neighbours, there would have been no village. All wills, obediences, skills, knowledge, had once been at its service.

But a foreign shoot, thrusting fiercely aside the clammy English undergrowth of her usual conclusions, told her that she might walk again in the mornings without loss of dignity.

"Because everybody is really so odd now," she said aloud, "and you can't expect them to behave as they should. Evan and Ron have always been queer"—here a spiteful mental titter—"and nobody ever knows what they're going to do next. But I did think Mr. Atkins had a proper sense of his position."

But Desmond Atkins' position, as he slumped over his counter to reach a piece of bacon that should not have been dropped, was not happy in any sense of the word. A great lardy broad-shouldered man, humped upwards like a reversed pear, he had a small miserable thoughtful face, as intelligent as a man had any right to be and still remain the keeper of a general store.

As Miss Aynard went her artful way, any definite purpose being disguised by a self-conscious humming, he stood still and mourned. Not for the bacon, which Meg Emmets would never buy now. If she had not been in the shop when he dropped it, he would have sent it to her, and she would never have known any better, would-be wise woman or not.

"Come to life, Mr. Atkins, and stop worrying your head over something that can't be helped," she mumbled at him, chewing her long lips into a drawn thread line. She'd be wanting to read his palm next. What made her think she could deal with other people's joys and miseries better than, or even as well as, anyone else? As well as Dupaman? Did he even read what folk had written on their faces? No-one knew; and no-one was likely to give Meg Emmets a chance of finding out that she might be successful.

Madam Emmets, the panderess to the sub-conscious. Desmond Atkins tried to twist this round into something that might replace his lost paper sheets. Why in God's name had he left them out last night? And the trouble was, other people wrote, too. Mean swine, all of them; he had an unmatchable glory of his own that their very breath would swoon at, if only he could get it to issue forth. Hadn't Eliot done something like that? He seemed to remember "madam." He looked painfully out into what should have been space, but was smeared by the progress of Phyllis Aynard.

There was the very incarnation of all madams, for you. Taking her walk again in the morning. When he came to think of it, he hadn't seen her lately—the weather, as it was for all of them. Perhaps things were brisking up again. She would walk in the mornings, to show that she wasn't hoping to be dragged into the bushes and raped. Rosie walked in the evening, not caring who knew that she was hoping to be dragged into

the bushes and raped. Oh, the pity of Rosie! Lush and
plushy and cuddlesome as a naughty nineties belle,
sparkling with golden hair and big white teeth, there
was somehow just too much of her for a carefree lad to
ruin. Like a peony whose petals have been trimmed by
earwigs, she invited, but on closer inspection, not delighted. You would have been worried to take on the
responsibility of the lust of so much flesh.

And all she wanted was to be a poor man's Amber,
Moll Flanders, Fanny Hill, not such a stupidly ambi-
tious peak to mount. The boys fought shy, however, and
shunned Lovers' Lane, except in the safe company of
other girls less willing to surrender.

"Don't blame them," muttered Desmond Atkins.
"Wouldn't myself, even if I hadn't my number of
blessed burdens, the last leaving school next year.
There's the last of Miss Aynard, too, heaving out of
sight beyond the bend. Wonder Rosie doesn't go that
way sometimes, make a change for her. Dupaman will
be leaning through his hedge now, if he's still trimming
it, just as Miss Aynard comes his way. She'll pretend
not to see him, same as we've all done in the past. Has
he been here for ever, or am I getting old? Easy come,
easy go." He said it with sudden viciousness, and a
weight of indigestion hit him beneath the heart and
alarmed him terribly.

But today was Miss Aynard's day for not ignoring
Dupaman. As he leant out at her, and smiled tiredly
and insolently, and went on silently clipping, she had to
stop and look, for the first glimpses were setting themselves into place. It was difficult to decide what Dupaman looked like since one never saw the whole of him;
and sometimes he was clean shaven, sometimes not.
Sometimes his chin was prickled all over by a fretful
thrust of frowsy beard, sometimes it was smooth and
young and impeccable. One never saw as far as his
eyes, for the conversations began with the mouth that
guarded them.

"I haven't seen any of your garden before," Phyllis

Aynard said primly. If there was doubt about Dupaman, there was none about the garden, even the little bit
of it she saw prudishly through the guardian teeth of
ragged snipped branches. It was surely the wonder of all
wonders. She couldn't imagine that anything had been
left out of it. But he had found it so and not made it,
for he had not been here long enough to establish such
a garden.

"It had potentialities. I found it, yes, and improved
it." Today was certainly Miss Aynard's day for talking
to Dupaman. She had not known it was her day for
seeing the garden, too, but she opened the gate dreamily
and went in.

At this time, Desmond Atkins was sharpening a knife
or two and laying them down, and reaching desperately
for a pencil, and thinking, "Today, some time today, I
ought to walk along up there and have a chat with
Dupaman."

For Ron and Evan there had never been a day for
not talking with Dupaman. But now they were having a
late breakfast and quarrelling, as they did sometimes, in
spite of loving one another.

Ron's lint-coloured hair bristled with annoyance, his
old-young worried face following his own hands as they
made their ineffectual gestures of complaint. Evan, the
little dark Welsh vixen of a person, shot and spat anger
at his target, vicious in anger as in love, so that you
could only tell whether he loved or hated people by the
way they behaved with him.

They knew, nowadays, less about the reasons they
quarrelled for, than they had done before Dupaman
came. For he had shown each of them in turn their own
side so clearly that the issue as a whole was obscure and
in doubt. So, Ron made little private hoards of sleeping
tablets and medicines, and Evan sharpened knives and
razors and blades of various sorts. And in between
cooking meals and loving and hating, they went up, sep-
arately, of course, and talked to Dupaman. They would
do that later today.

No, that was wrong. Only Ron would do that. For Evan, for the last time, had left a word and a knife in the wrong place. And, because of the weather, or for some other cause, the breach became complete scission, and Evan quiet for once in his life, or out of it. Ron, being the man he was, scrubbed up, and laid the furniture out neatly, and Evan between it on the floor, with his hands tidily clasped, and went off, almost whistling on a breath of relief, for a word or two with Dupaman.

Miss Aynard was not finding it easy to understand Dupaman, and imagined to herself that even that old crazy would-be witch woman Meg Emmets could be more at home with him. He had said to her, "You were born to rule, born to the purple, don't you feel it?" Well, she felt that without his telling her. But what did he mean by "Choose your subjects, since they won't choose you. Judge, condemn, mutilate, behead. Like a fairground—fun, isn't it!" She sat between the goldfish pond and the aviary and felt her sharp senses swooping around her, carrying her wits into all sorts of wrong places.

"A garden needs guests," said Dupaman. "Enjoy it, before the others come."

The enjoyment came to her as she sat, blind. She was in the movement of the dozen gross feathered things, joined by a pipeline of flesh, that huddled on a crusted part of the dark benches behind her and shared the intuitions of a single mind. Now her eyes darted behind the glaze of whatever swam in scales beneath the rotting water; or her body crouched, tenuously shuttered by skeleton bars of bones in a dead creature. She marched, one of an army of motelike symbiotes, round the veins of something that lay with its tail thrust everlastingly down its throat. She had power of a sort, but it was involuntary. She was the network of tissues across which all decisions made their way, from cruel chance or kind fortune.

The things of which she was a part took their life or

death from her, and could exist only in this hang-fire
continuum of the garden.

At last she ran with mouselike squeaks through the
mouth of her own body, to be trapped in Dupaman's
hairy hand; and the cycle began for her again.

Decaying and increasing constantly in her fury of living, she saw nothing of Meg Emmet's arrival. Meg crept
through the hedge at the other side, thinking that Dupaman would not see her. She clucked her tongue pee-
vishly, thinking how like Rosie this action of hers had
been. But Rosie was at home, damply and beatifically
sleeping away the hot hours in a medley of feverish
dreams. She had no spare thoughts to share with Meg
Emmet. Meg saw Miss Aynard, but garden-party guests
did not necessarily recognize one another, did they? and
in any case, she could now see the maze.

Into its wise intricacies she darted, like a bit of mag-
netized filing. The dewy, delicious entrance entranced
her, so cool and solemn, as if it were built of books.
Then the fluted joined trunks of tiny trees enmeshed
her, unevenly twisted and transparent, coloured like
Venetian glass. There was no choice of openings. She
could go only where she must, and the path to the
centre, though serpentine, was beautifully clear. All the
time, mirrored about her, were endless repetitions, a little distorted perhaps, of her private visions. Meg the silver and serene, sapient and timeless, a mother-goddess
hatched about by a litter of owls, lion cubs, cats and
distaffs.

At each turn she took, a sheet of glass rose up behind
her. At first, she turned and regarded this uneasily, but
by and by she grew used to it, and began to ignore it.
After all, she was interested only in seeing the centre.
Once she thought Desmond Atkins accompanied her for
a short way, his mouth open as if he were singing.

Dupaman, mounting a pair of step-ladders, took the
trouble to lean over the hedge to reassure her.

"It's only a mirage," he said. "He is somewhere else,

quite near, and you see his reflection, as in the desert. Many people, after all, are mirages." · · ·

Mr. Atkins, who would have been insulted to be considered among the mirages, was in fact at the moment in the conservatory, an ideal place for a reading, as he had told Dupaman.

Dupaman had courteously agreed. "I might have designed it myself. I almost feel that I did. And the poor things have so little in the way of relaxation."

The audience were most attentive. He knew they had never heard any other poet.

They were rapt and motionless. He thought that they talked admiringly out of perfectly still lips. They were as quiet and unmoving as if they grew there. He wished that Meg would not move so quickly, for she made the audience and the wall reflect her passage in the same way that polished railings reflect a cat going behind them, until one thinks they are completely transparent. She might as well have run a stick across them too, he thought despairingly. Their heads remained turned to one another and the inaudible whispers continued. It would have been more pleasant if once, only just once they would have looked at him.

And if Desmond Atkins had not been so busy, thought Meg crossly, he would not have been so distracting and kept her mind from the essential search for the centre, that remained as aloof as ever. To look for a centre is like going upon a pilgrimage—one must have complete concentration of thought.

Rosie had to be invited. Dupaman had to actually step outside the hedge to explain to her that she was welcome. For a moment, she misunderstood him hopefully, but not for long. He was extremely chilly, and if he had not wanted to tidy everything up, he might not have repeated his invitation. Of all his guests, he liked Rosie the least. The things she needed were so much too easy to supply. As, of course, with Ron. But Ron was an old friend, he had been that way so many times, though never before actually inside the garden. He should see it all, see the best of it. But meanwhile, a quiet sunny corner for Rosie. Not far from the compost, in a spot where everything thrived more than ordinarily, there was a carpet of fat, ivy-green grass for her to finish her interrupted sleep.

"I can recommend the pitcher-vine," said Dupaman, as he left her. The pitcher-vine sprawled its blossoms, sticky and enticing, at Rosie's small feet. It seemed to pant with the constant opening of fat buds all along its stem. They became enormous blossoms, wicked white, red-tipped, collapsing in a fragrant ruin of petals over a pocked yellow centre. It drew Rosie so gently forward that she yielded delightfully to the warm cocoon-like embrace. She lay quite content and flaccid, smelling the placid rich smell of over-populated soil, feeling the grains slip and crawl away like ants under her cheek.

There were no ants, but in the sheath-like leaves of her host were swarms of small creatures, half-human, half-beast. They ran out on the turf, performing a whole ballet of lustful actions before her wide startled eyes, actions she had never dreamed of in her wilder transports. She twitched a little in her prison, and heaved a sigh of anticipation, but the cocoon held her more sternly, and she had a moment's anxiety for the wrinkles she would find in her clothes when she got up. If she got up. Or perhaps Dupaman would be watching her watching these antics, for ever and a day. If there was to be anything more fretful than lying here, her eyes held prisoner as well as her body, it would be the knowledge of being looked at while looking. Anyone should be able to consider their own transports in privacy; and she was in a sense the creator of these small gymnasts, for they would not have emerged for anyone else. It was a pity that she possessed no power over them, not even as much as Miss Aynard did in the sharp flicker of her multiplicity of anguished existences. The dances of life became wilder, and she moaned indignantly.

Muted sounds of dusk struck the garden, and the guests paused momentarily in their quests; and saw, tiny and new, the altered stars, as if through the wrong end of a magnifying glass.

"The best time of day to visit," said Dupaman to Ron, leading him easily inwards. The fountains bent silently towards them, and the statues were almost invisible, mere traceries of reflection, but Ron admired everything with great earnestness, if a little absentmindedly. It seemed to him a particularly appealing place, and so many of the corners held puzzlingly familiar glimpses. There were echoes of quietly flying, authoritative footsteps and a droning voice. The glint of something white, like a gesture, held his attention, and was replaced by movements that recalled someone he had known well, now anxious not to wake him.

"I feel the statues were a mistake, perhaps. Not one I should have made, but I am merely a tenant." The words were surprising. Everyone had taken it for granted that Dupaman was simply a former owner, returned after long absence. "I am not an admirer of these sloppy-breasted, slab-haunched goddesses. They lack the admirable clean tensions of male flesh."

The anguish of this well-aimed thrust was so keen that for a moment Ron felt it as purely enjoyable. It reminded him, however, that he had left the rest of his life sealed in the neat white envelope of Evan's cold clasp; and he turned his back on the statues. Dupaman had evidently become tired of suggesting, pointing out, gently directing, and had gone away, leaving the intaglio of a series of dark footsteps in the grey dew on the lawn. The sword-plants were Ron's own discovery.

The air, relieved of the weight of day, rang in his dulled ears like bells, and he trod in and out of the ranks of great upthrust leaves, with their bare central spike, wondering if they flowered once in a hundred years, like some cactus he had heard of. His walk hurried and became a rhythm, to match the currents of scent and sound drifting, now evenly, sometimes in ed-

dies, through the maze of plants. Only one plant had a
bud, against the shelter of the blade. It was smaller than
the others, only a little taller than he was.

The currents of sound identified themselves as the
rustle of wings and paws, then as the clicks of a vexed
tongue. The scents became a girl's hair, too cloying to
allure, or the odour of stale incense, burnt too long before the wrong altar. The feet paused in their rhythm,
sensed an objective, and resumed in a much stronger
measure. Wings, claws, tongues, moans, took on a beat
too delicate to be tangible. Scent became so many
strands, as to lose all identification. Rhythm and coun-
terpoint became solely the realities.

When dawn reared an angry crest up, her giant
bloodstream ejected Phyllis Aynard, the glass maze
snapped and splintered round Meg Emmet, into pa-
thetic shards. Desmond Atkins stumbled through a haze
of dissolving audience into the presence of broken flow-
erpots and an old bench, warped by sun. The pitcher
plant flicked out Rosie in one orgiastic heave, drew itself together, and seethed away into rottenness.

The sword-plants, the fountains, and the statues, un-
affected by change of time or climate, assumed the rule
of the garden. They had an emblem of their own, now,
to match the anxiously-watched bud of the smallest
sword-plant. Flowering is always a chancy, uncertain
business. It is better to have a second string. And so
beautifully had the task of mounting Ron upon the
blade of the second smallest sword-plant been achieved,
that he might well have been still alive. There was an
air of satisfied restfulness in the garden.

After the sun had risen, Dupaman laid down his
shears with a grunt of accomplishment, and went out
into the road. There was a heavy cart trailing through
the recently laid dust, as the sounds of running water,
and the nostalgic scent of smoke became clearer.
"D'you want a lift?" called the driver, as Dupaman
walked along on the grass beside the road.

Dupaman considered. Why not? He had been here

long enough. There were other things to do, and people to meet. The night's resolutions had left everything exceedingly dull. He accepted. Climbing the cart, he sat down at the tail, as the driver whistled to the horse, and, facing backwards, contemplated his dangling legs.

> "And, lost each human trace, surrendering up
> Thine individual being, shalt thou go
> To mix forever with the elements . . ."
> "Thanatopsis," William Cullen Bryant

Shut the Last Door

JOE HENSLEY

—

The night was gentle and so Willie sat out on the combination fire escape and screened play area that hung in zigzags from the north side of the government-built, low-rent apartment building. He stayed out there in his wheelchair for a long time watching the world of lights from the other buildings around him. He liked the night. It softened the savage world, so that he could forget the things he saw and did in the day. Those things still existed, but darkness fogged them.

He reached around, fumbling under his shirt, and let his hand touch the long scar where it started. He couldn't reach all of it for it ran the width of his back, a slanting line, raised from the skin. Sometimes it ached and there was a little of that tonight, but it wasn't really bad any more. It was only that he was dead below the scar line, that the upper half of him still lived and felt, but the lower felt nothing, did nothing.

Once they'd called him Willie the Runner and he had been very fast, the running a defense from the cruel world of the apartments, a way out, a thing of which he'd been quite proud. That had been when he was thirteen. Now he was fifteen. The running was gone forever and there was only a scar to remind him of what had been once. But the new gift had come, the one the doctors had hinted about. And those two who'd been responsible for the scar had died.

A cloud passed across the moon and a tiny, soft rain began to fall. He wheeled off the fire escape and into the dirty hall. It was very dark inside. Someone had again removed the light bulbs from their receptacles. Piles of refuse crowded the corners and hungry insects scurried at the vibration of Willie's wheelchair. In the apartment his mother sat in front of the television. Her eyes were open, but she wasn't seeing the picture. She was on something new, exotic. He'd found one of the bottles where she'd carefully hidden it. Dilaudin, or something like that. It treated her well. He worked the wheelchair over to the television and turned off the late-night comic, but she still sat there, eyes open and lost, looking intently at the darkened tube. He went on into his own bedroom, got the wheelchair close to the bed, and clumsily levered himself between the dirty sheets.

He slept and sleeping brought the usual dreams of the days of fear and running. In the dream they laughed coldly and caught him in the dark place and he felt the searing pain of the knife. He remembered the kind doctor in the hospital, the one who kept coming back to talk to him, the one who talked about compensation and factors of recovery. The doctor had told him his arms might grow very strong and agile. He'd told him about blind men who'd developed special senses. He'd smiled and been very nice and Willie had liked him. The gift he'd promised had come. Time passed in the dream and it became better and Willie smiled.

In the morning, before his mother left for the weekly ordeal with the people at the welfare office, Willie again had her wheel him down to the screened play area and fire escape. In the hall, with the arrival of day, the smell was stifling, a combination of dirt and urine and cooking odors and garbage. The apartments in the building were almost new, but the people who inhabited the apartments had lived in tenement squalor for so long that they soon wore all newness away. The tenants stole the light bulbs from the hallways, used dark corners as toilets of convenience, discarded the leftovers of living in the quickest easiest places. And they fought and stole and raped and, sometimes, killed.

Sometimes, Willie had seen a police car pass in the streets outside, but the policemen usually rode with eyes straight ahead and windows rolled up tight. On the few times that police came into the apartment area they came in squads for their own protection.

Outside the air was better. Willie could see the other government apartments that made up the complex and if he leaned forward he could, by straining, see the early morning traffic weaving along the expressway by the faraway river.

His mother frowned languidly at the sky, her chocolate-brown face severe. "It'll maybe rain," she said, slurring the words together. "If it rains you get back in, hear?"

"Okay," he said, and then again, because he was never sure she heard him: "Okay!" He looked at her swollen, sullen face, wanting to say more, but no words came. She was so very young. He'd been born almost in her childhood and there was within him the feeling that she resented him, hated caring for him, abominated being tied to him, but did the dreary duty only because there was no one else and because the mother-feeling within warred with all the other wants and drives and sometimes won an occasional victory. Willie remembered no father and his mother had never spoken of one.

"None of them bad kids bother you up here, do they?" she asked, always suspicious.

He smiled, really amused. "No," he said.

She shook her head tiredly and he noticed the twitch in the side of her dark face. She said: "Some of them's bad enough to bother around a fifteen-year-old boy in a wheelchair. Bad enough to do 'most anything I guess. When we moved in here I thought it would be better." She looked up at the sky. "It's worse," she ended softly.

Willie patiently waited out her automatic ministrations, the poking at the blanket around his wasting legs, the peck on the forehead. Finally, she left.

For a while then he was alone and he could crane and watch the expressway and the river and the downtown to the north. He could hear the complex around him come to angry life, the voices raised in argument and strife. Down below four boys came out of a neighboring building. They were dressed alike, tight jeans, brown jackets, hair long and greased to straightness. He saw them gather in front of the building and one of them looked up and saw him watching. That one nudged the others and they all looked up, startled, and they went away like deer, around the far corner of their building at a quick lope. Willie only nodded.

A block away, just within his vision, a tall boy came out of the shadows and engaged another boy in a shouting argument. A small crowd gathered and watched indolently, some yelling advice. Willie watched with interest. When the fight began they rolled out of sight and Willie could only see the edges of the milling crowd and soon lost interest in watching.

The sun came out and the sky lightened and Willie felt more like facing the day. He looked down at his legs without real sorrow. Regret was an old acquaintance, the feeling between them no longer strong. Willie leaned back in the wheelchair. With trained ears alert to any sudden sound of danger, he dozed lightly.

Memory again became a dream. When he had become sure of the gift he had followed them to their clubhouse. It was in a ruined building that the city was tearing down to build more of the interminable housing units. He rolled right up to the door and beat on it boldly and they came and he saw the surprise on their faces and their quick looks to see if he'd brought police along.

"Hello, Running Willie, you crippled bastard," the one who'd wielded the knife said. The one who'd held him and watched smiled insolently.

He sat there alone in the chair and looked back at them, hating them with that peculiar, complete intensity, wanting them dead. The sickness came in his stomach and the whirling in his head and he saw them move at him before the sunlit world went dark brown.

And they died.

A door opened below and Willie came warily awake. He looked down and saw Twig Roberts observing the day.

"Okay to come on up, Willie?" Twig asked carefully.

"Sure," Willie said negligently.

Twig came up the stairs slowly and sat down on the top one, looking away into the distance, refusing to meet Willie's eyes. He was a large, dark boy, muscled like a wrestler, with a quick, foxy face. He lived in the apartment below Willie's.

"What we goin' to do today, Willie boy?" Twig asked it softly, his voice a whine. "Where we headin'?" He continued to look out at the empty sky and Willie knew again that Twig feared him. A small part of Willie relished the fear and fed on it and Willie knew that the fear diminished both of them.

Willie thought about the day. Once the trips, the forays, into that wild, jackdaw land below had been an exciting thing, a thing of danger. That had been when the power was unsure and slow, but the trips were as nothing now. Instead of finding fear below he brought it.

He said softly: "We'll do something, Twig." Then he nodded, feeling small malice. "Maybe down at Building Nineteen. You been complaining about Building Nineteen, ain't you?" He smiled, hiding the malice. "You got someone down there for me?"

Twig looked at him for the first time. "You got it wrong, Willie. I got relatives in that building. I never even taken you around there for fear . . ." He stopped and then went on. "There's nothing wrong with Nineteen." He watched earnestly until Willie let his smile widen. "You were puttin' me on, Willie," Twig said, in careful half-reproach.

"Sure, Twig," Willie said, closing his eyes and leaning back in the wheelchair. "We'll go down and just sort of look around."

The fan in the elevator didn't work and hadn't worked for a long time, but at least today the elevator itself worked. The odor in the shaft was almost overpowering and Willie was glad when they were outside in the bright sun that had eaten away the morning fog.

Twig maneuvered him out the back entrance of the building. Outside the ground was covered with litter, despite the fact that there were numerous trash receptacles. A rat wheeled and flashed between garbage cans and Willie shivered. The running rat reminded Willie of the old days of fear.

Twig pushed on into the narrow alley between the trash cans. The sound of their coming disturbed an old white man who was dirtily burrowing in one of the cans. He looked up at them, filthy hands still rooting in the can. His thin, knobby armed body seemed lost in indecision between whether to dig deeper in the muck or take flight. Hunger won.

"What you doin' there, man?" Twig demanded, instantly pugnacious at the sight of the dirty, white face.

The old man stood his ground stubbornly and Willie felt an almost empathy with him, remembering hungry days. The man's old eyes were cunning, the head a turtle's head, scrawnily protruding up from its shell of filthy clothing. Those eyes had run a thousand times from imagined terror, but they could still calculate chances. Those eyes saw only a boy in a wheelchair, a larger boy behind.

The old man reached in his pocket. "Ge' away, you li'l black bassurds. Ge' away fum me." The hand came out and there was a flash of dull metal. A knife.

Willie saw Twig smile triumphantly. Those who stood their ground were hard to find in these days of increasing fear.

"Hate him, Willie," Twig said softly. "Hate him now!"

Willie smiled at the old man and hated him without dislike. He had to concentrate very hard, but finally the wrenching, tearing feeling came in his head and the brownout and the sickness became all. He faded himself into the hate and became one with it and time stopped until there was nothing. When it was done and he was again aware he opened his eyes.

The old man was gone. There was nothing left to show he'd ever existed, no clothes, no knife.

"Did he run?" Willie asked.

Twig shook his head. "He smoked," he said, smiling hugely. "That was the best one yet. He smoked a kind of brown smoke and there was a big puff of flame and suddenly he ain't there any more." He cocked his head and clapped his hands in false exuberance. "That one was good, Willie. It was sure good." He smiled a good smile that failed to reach his eyes.

They moved on along the sidewalks, Willie in the chair, Twig dutifully behind. Ahead of them Willie could almost feel the word spread. The cool boys vanished. The gangs hid in trembling fear, their zip guns and knives forgotten. Arguments quieted. In the graveled play yards the rough games suspended. Small children watched in wonder from behind convenient bushes, eyes wide. Willie smiled and waved at them, but no one came out. Once a rock came toward them, but when Willie turned there was no one to be seen. There was a dead zone where they walked. It was always like that these days.

A queer thought came to Willie as he rode along in solitary patrol. It was an odd thought, shiny and unreal.

He wondered if someplace there was a someone with the gift of life, a someone who could set stopped breath to moving again, bring color back to a bloodless face, restart a failed heart, bring thought back to a dead mind. He rather hoped that such a gift existed, but he knew that on these streets such a gift wouldn't last. In this filth, in this world of murderous intent the life-giver would have been torn apart. If the life-giver was Willie—if that had been the gift—they would have jerked him from the moving casket he rode, stomped him, mutilated him. And laughed.

There were other worlds. Willie knew that dimly, without remembrance, without real awareness. There was only a kind of dim longing. He knew that the legs were the things that had saved him from a thousand dangers. He remembered the leering man who'd followed him one day when he was twelve, the one who wanted something, who touched and took. He remembered the angry ones with their knives and bicycle chains, the gangs that banded together to spread, rather than absorb, terror. He looked at his world: the ones who'd roll you for the price of a drink and the ones who'd kill you for a fix. It was the only world he knew. Downtown was a thing of minutes spent. It wasn't life. Life was here.

The legs had been survival. A knife had taken them. The doctor had promised something and Willie had believed. Survival was still necessary and the world savage.

So was the compensating gift.

His mother was back and she was also high when he returned to the apartment. Willie fought the hate very hard and was successful. She had an immunity to the gift, but the gift grew stronger.

She waved an exuberant, drugged hand. "Welfare office all closed," she said. "Flowers on the door. Someone said another rent collector died."

Willie nodded. Rent collectors were very easy to hate. They came and brought nothing, but they demanded a taking away. It seemed to make little difference how many he hated. There were always more.

His mother nodded solemnly and watched him with happy, pinpoint eyes in which there was no love and no hate and he rolled away from those eyes and on down to his favorite spot on the fire escape. Down below games were going again and he envisioned what it would be like to play again, to be all normal, to be afraid again.

The sun was warm and he sat there and knew he'd been alone for all fifteen of his years and now, with the gift, that he would remain alone and that he was quite sanely mad.

He looked down again at the children playing their rough games in the measured gravel and he knew he could explode them all like toy balloons, but the insanity he owned, he realized, should be worse than that.

The sun remained warm and he contemplated it and thought about it and wondered how far the gift extended. *If I should hate the sun* . . .

There was another thought. He worked it over in his head for a long time, while his fingers absently reached and stroked the long scar on his back.

There was a way out, a possible escape.

Tomorrow he might try hating himself.

However, some changes are both chemical and alchemical.

Big Sam

AVRAM DAVIDSON

—

Ellen heard Big Sam before she ever saw him—but not much before. He was one of the group of men standing around the aluminum keg of draft at a wedding (Jinny MacKew to Lew Harris) and she, moving around with an air of being less alone than she actually felt, passed by as a deep voice was saying, "No, I don't believe in that. I wouldn't do any asking and I wouldn't do any telling." Something made her give a quick glance around just before the deep voice had finished, and so she saw him. He was big and hulking and he looked just a bit sleepy. But he looked nice. Later on she was to say that she drew a circle around him with an imaginary finger and told herself, *That one is mine.* It was early spring.

The mountain county had a smaller population than it had had a hundred years ago, which hadn't been many even then, but the modern world kept catching up with it at intervals; isolated as it was, still, it couldn't escape that. A new office machine had just lately been installed at the phone company and as nobody already living in the county knew how to operate it, Ellen—who had begun to feel bored and out of things where she was—had been persuaded to accept a transfer, even though it meant giving up her share of the pleasant-enough three-girl apartment and moving two hundred miles north. "Two men to every female up there," the personnel man said, smiling to show he wasn't being offensive, and, "Well, I certainly can't pass up a chance like *that*," Ellen answered, almost without reflecting, but also smiling not seriously.

Afterwards, when her roommates asked her how come, she only said, "It's time for a change." So here she was, in this country hotel, which the wedding party had all to itself, the start of the summer season still a couple of months away.

"Yeah, but suppose there *is*, well, *some*thing, I don't just mean like, other guys, other women before. But something else," an older fellow, probably the one who'd first asked the question at the beer keg, went on.

"Like what?" the tall and husky one wanted to know. He sipped at his glass.

"Oh . . . I don't know . . . maybe a baby . . . maybe an old trouble with the law. . . . . Hasn't the other person got a right—"

"Yeah, how about that, Sam?" asked a third man.

Sam shrugged. "Marriage looks tough enough—from all I *hear*, I mean—" They laughed. "Maybe nobody ever finds out about this premarital whatever-it-was. Maybe by the time they do, they wouldn't care all that much."

Then a fourth man said, "Okay, Sam, you persuaded us: you get married, don't tell her you had a baby." Everybody burst out laughing, Sam with a great big *ha ha!* and Ellen walked calmly on her way to get a ginger ale and a sandwich. This was not a canapé and cocktail kind of wedding party.

By and by Ellen said to the other girl from the office who was at the table, "Who's the guy with the red tie back there? The one who's standing by the beer?"

Mrs. Bartlett, who was a girl by courtesy only, pushed back some gray hair, looked, and said, still chewing, "Who, Sambo? Sam Bock, I call him Sambo, everybody else calls him Big Sam. He's got that gas station out on the South Road. I think he goes to L.A. or somewhere in the winters, just keeps open for the summer trade, hunters, tourists, *you* know. Not enough business, hardly, in the winter, to pay both the stations here in town to stay open. Nice guy. You tried this liver sausage? It's *good*." Mrs. Bartlett was kind of slow, but she always managed to get there, and after a while she introduced them, she called to him—he was off standing by himself by that time—and he shambled over and she introduced him to Ellen. Then she said, "Don't they *feed* you down there in L.A., Sam? You always turn up thin as a rail. Ellen, fix him a sandwich, *I* am going to get some *beer*." Then she went over to the keg herself, leaving the two of them more or less alone.

After a while Sam, who hadn't been very talkative, said, "You like drunk parties?"

"Not very much."

"Didn't think so. This one's about to start." So they went out and went for a ride and he showed her a lot of places she hadn't yet seen out in the country and even the crumbling old joss house from the gold rush days, on the other side of town, when the coolies used to wash the leftovers the American miners wouldn't bother with. Then he drove down the South Road and showed her his gas station and the house behind it.

"I turn up in plenty of time each year to get things ready for the season," he said. "I like to do things slow and easy. But I have to be quick in the summers, you bet."

He already had an arm around her shoulders. Nothing offensive, just friendly in an awkward but nice way. She thought he was moving just fast enough right now. "That's an odd-looking house," she said. "Is it historical too?" He said, well, it was old, but in good shape—roof would hold up a whole winter's snow. He didn't ask her in then, just drove back to town and they had coffee and they made a date for later in the week.

The manager was a little annoyed at first when Ellen quit. "Have to go through that all over again . . . new girl," he said. But wasn't really angry. "Lots of women keep on working after they're married," he pointed out. Ellen said she didn't believe in that. She believed that a woman's place was with her husband. "Will wonders never cease," the manager said, rubbing his hand over his bald spot. So there was another wedding and another wedding party and once more Sam and Ellen left before it got drunk. They drove down to Sacramento and got on a plane and had a short honeymoon in Mexico, in a place called Rosarito Beach. The nice old lady who ran the motel had a parrot who walked around in the yard like a chicken and there were horses galloping in the sand. Ellen loved it, but she understood that they could stay only a few days, and so back they came.

It surprised her to learn how domestic she could become; in fact, after a while the sight of Sam shambling around made her a bit impatient. "Shoo!" she said. "Scat! You take care of getting the station ready, and the outside of the house. *I'll* manage the inside, all by myself." He laughed but did as she said, and everything worked out fine. She swept and she sewed and she did some painting and she aired the linens and the huge piles of thick blankets and, observing how he liked things, she canned and jarred and preserved a mountain of food. She wondered about a few things, but didn't ask. She trusted Sam.

Gradually Ellen came to pick up the rhythm of the way things went on the long summer days. There was a busy time early in the mornings with hunters and fishermen going farther back into the mountains. The tourists and family vacationing groups would be along later. Now and then she looked out of the window and saw Sam's big form shuffling along from gas pumps to car front windows, then to the cash register in the tiny "office." Kids trotting out to the bathrooms. Sometimes nobody at all, just Sam sitting slouched in a chair. Sometimes horns would blow. And blow. Gradually she learned to ignore that. If it went on *too* long, she might throw up a window and yell, "Closed!" If, as it seldom was, a real emergency, she would sell the people the contents of one of the cans of gasoline Sam had filled. "My husband had to go someplace and I don't know how to work the pump. This will get you into town, anyway."

Once . . . the first time . . . she did ask him, "How come you just took off to go hunting and fishing?"

He smiled, stretched hugely. "Felt like it," he said. And gathered her into an enormous hug.

"Stop it," she said. "You'll crack my ribs. *Sam!*" But wasn't angry. Everybody had to have *some* fault or funny way. After all, he put up with her when she chased him outside. "I have *work* to do," she'd say. "Men get in the way."

The summer passed so quickly, and one day the CLOSED sign went up and stayed up. Now Ellen began to wonder about the winter in L.A. or wherever it was. Would Sam expect her to pack and move? What, exactly, or even approximately, *were* they going to do? But he didn't say and she didn't ask, determined not to be one of those suspicious or even nosey wives. Just went on with her work about the house. She cooked. And Sam tucked it away appreciatively, as though he was able now for the first time to sit back and really enjoy it. They had few visitors on the South Road nowadays, few cars even went by. Sometimes Ellen wondered about her husband's background. He never mentioned any family. Never one to talk your ear off, he was talking even less. After supper, dozing by the radio, he might snap awake and ask, "Any more chops left?"

"I'll heat them, they're all greasy by now—"

Down they went, grease and all.

"You're putting on weight, Sam."

He just smiled. She just smiled back. It was very nice, way out alone there, just the two of them. They were both sleeping longer, going to bed earlier, relaxing after the short but busy season. There was a limit, however, to how long Ellen could remain in bed. She had to be up and doing after a while, fixing huge breakfasts of bacon and eggs and steak and pancakes. "Where do you *put* it all?" she asked, curiously. He yawned, held out his plate for more. Lunch had become dinner and supper was immense. "You better take some exercise," she said, just a bit critically. "Look how your belt is digging in." Sam's only answer was to open the belt and lie down on the sofa for a nap. She managed without him, doing the dishes, a million of them though there seemed to be. It was nice being by herself in the kitchen. In fact, afterwards, when she sat down in the living room with one of the piles of magazines which, bought out of habit when in town, she'd had no time to really read till now—in fact, Sam snoring on the sofa seemed a bit . . . well, more than a bit . . . in the way.

"Shame on you," she told herself.

It was becoming a nuisance to tug him awake to shamble off to bed. One morning he didn't get up for breakfast. She called him softly a few times. He didn't answer, then he just mumbled, turned over, snored. It was well after dinnertime when, following many peeps into the bedroom, she saw him open his eyes a little way and look at her. "Ellen . . ."

"Yes, Sam?"

He almost closed his eyes all the way shut again, but he didn't, quite. "You *know* . . . don't you?"

It was like something from one of the magazines, one of the stories, only different, his asking it like that. She *did* know, and in that minute she realized that she had known for quite a while now. She understood now just what the pile of thick blankets and the well-filled shelves, the stout snow roof and thick walls, were for. She knew there wasn't going to be any L.A. for them, and never had been for Sam. "Yes, Sam," she said.

He gave a deep sigh of contentment. His eyes slipped shut and in another minute he was sound asleep again. She quietly closed the door of the darkened room and went away. After all, there were all kinds of marriages. After all, she had a lot of work to do. She had to get all kinds of stuff ready for the freezer and for the preserving kettle. After all, Sam would be hungry, he would be very hungry, when he awakened in the spring.

"The play's the thing . . ."
Wherein to change the frame of everything.

More Light

JAMES BLISH

—

1.

I have never trusted Bill Atheling. Like me, he has a mean streak in him (and I don't say so just because he once tore a story of mine to shreds in a review; that's what critics are for). But perhaps for the same reason, I also rather like him. Hence when I first saw him again in New York—after I'd spent two years in exile, lobbying before Senate committees—I was shocked. My instant impression was that he was dying.

I thought at first that it was only the effect of a new beard, which was then just two weeks old and would have made any man look scruffy. And in part it was, for surprisingly, the beard was coming out white, though Bill is only forty-seven and is gray only at the temples.

But there was more to it than that. He had lost some twenty or thirty pounds, which he could ill afford, since he never weighed more than 150 at his best, and stood 5' 10" or so. His skin was gray, his neck crepy, his hands trembling, his eyes bleached, his cough tubercular; he stared constantly over my shoulder while we talked, and his voice kept fading out in the middle of sentences. If he was not seriously ill, then he had taken even more seriously to the bottle, which wasn't a pleasant thought either.

This was hardly the shape in which I had expected to find a man with a new young wife (the artist Samantha Brock) and a fine new house in Brooklyn Heights (it had once been a Gay Nineties house of ill fame, and Samantha had decorated it in that style: red plush, beaded curtains, crystal light fixtures, gold spray on the capitals of Corinthian wooden pillars, an ancient Victrola with a horn in the parlor—all *very* high camp). But I made as light of it as I could manage.

"You look terrible," I told him over the brandy. "What in God's name have you been doing to yourself? Reading the *Complete Works* of Sam Moskowitz? Or have you taken up LSD?"

He came back with his usual maddening indirection; at least *that* hadn't changed. "What do you know about Robert W. Chambers?" he said, looking off to the left.

"Damn little, I'm glad to say. I read some of his stuff when I was in college. As I recall, I liked his stories about his art-student days in Paris better than the fantasies. But that isn't saying much."

"Then you remember *The King in Yellow*."

"Vaguely. It was one of the first semi-hoaxes, wasn't it? An imaginary book? People who read it were supposed to go mad, or be visited by monsters, or things like that. Like the *Nekronomikon*."

"As a matter of fact, it was supposed to have been a play," Atheling said. "But go on."

"You're a pedant to the last. But there's nothing to go on about. Nobody can believe any more that a book could drive anybody mad. Real life's become too horrible; not even William Burroughs can top Dachau." Suddenly, I was overcome by suspicion, and something very like disgust. "Sour Bill Atheling, are you about to tell me you've found the play in your cellar, and that you've been haunted ever since? And then pony up a concocted manuscript to prove it? If that's the case, I'll just throw up my dinner and go home. You know damn well it'll never sell, anyhow."

"It was you who asked me what was wrong with me," he said, reasonably enough. "Simmer down. If you don't want to credit my explanation, then the burden of concocting another one falls on you."

"Concocting—!"

"If you can't stop squeaking, you might as well go home."

"All right. Observe me; I am breathing evenly. Now, is this honestly the explanation you're about to offer me?"

"Yes," Atheling said. "I do in fact have the play."

I sat back, completely at a loss. Nobody peddles such nonsense any more. At last I said: "I think the decor around here has gone to your head. Well, go on, I'll listen. Just don't expect me to be taken in. Who wrote this Dreadful Work—as if I didn't know?"

"You don't know, and neither do I, but I'm pretty sure it was Chambers himself. It's interesting that you mentioned the *Nekronomikon* without any prompting, because it was through Lovecraft that I got the play in the first place—which also explains why I hadn't read it until last year. But I'd better give you the story in sequence. Come upstairs with me."

He got up and I followed him, not failing to pick up the Grand Marnier bottle as I passed it. Atheling's office was as always almost pathologically neat—another trait that, in a writer, automatically inspires mistrust in me—but it had been recently painted a brilliant chrome yellow with a faint, bilious trace of green in it, a scheme which would have driven me out of my mind in short order, with no help needed from any imaginary play. There was a Vermeer reproduction on one wall which, against all that flat yellow paint, looked almost exactly like a window, except that it had in it a window of its own which looked even realer. I was surprised; in this atmosphere I would have expected a Parrish, or maybe even a Bok.

Atheling pointed me to a straight and inhospitable-looking chair, and then produced from a four-drawer file cabinet a fairly thick folder which he brought back to his desk. From this, in turn, he extracted two small sheets of blue paper closely covered with tiny handwriting in dark blue pen.

"Is that it?" I said. "Or are those just the commercials?"

"No, that's not it," he said in a rather dangerously flat tone of voice. "Just shut up for ten seconds and listen, Jim, will you? If you keep on nattering, I may run out of guts. I'm none too sure as it is that I ought to be talking to you."

"Then why do you bother? You know damn well I won't believe a word you say."

"Because you're just slightly less stupid than anybody else I know, and once upon a time knew something about magic. Now are you going to listen?"

"Fire at will," I said, with spurious resignation. I really could not imagine how even Atheling could make a good story out of such a stock opening, but I was thoroughly interested in hearing him try it—as of course he knew as well as I did.

"All right. I was a Lovecraft fan when I was a kid, as you probably know; so were you. And I believed devoutly in all those spurious books that he and the other members of the Cthulhu circle concocted to make their tales sound more plausible. I was completely taken in. I wrote to the Widener Library to try to borrow a copy of the *Nekronomikon;* I looked for it in secondhand bookstores; I tried to buy it in a plain sealed wrapper from Panurge Press. Nothing worked, so finally—this was when I was fifteen years old—I wrote to Lovecraft himself for help.

"Well, you can guess what happened. He politely told me that he had invented the book. But at fifteen I wasn't easily dashed. Instead I proposed that, since the book didn't exist, he should write it, and I would publish it. In installments, of course, in some sort of amateur magazine."

I laughed. "He must have gotten twoscore letters like that."

"I don't doubt it. In any event, he declined, very politely, of course. He said he had already quoted the *Nekronomikon* from pages well beyond nine hundred or a thousand, and he didn't really think he wanted to undertake writing a volume of that size. Well, I more or less took the hint. But I couldn't prevent myself from adding that I hoped he'd get around to writing at least a few chapters some day, and if he did, well, Willy Atheling hoped he would remember who stood ready to publish it. I was a terrible little snot in those days. Please don't add any footnotes, because here is one of my own."

He handed me one of the sheets of blue notepaper. I have seen Lovecraft holographs before; this one, with its tiny, utterly legible handwriting which looked as though it had been constructed along a straightedge, was either the real thing or it had been made by a master forger, a talent I was pretty sure Atheling lacked. Atheling pointed to one long paragraph, which read as follows:

Yr persistence is flattering indeed, but really I do think that for me to write more than a few sentences of the *Nekronomikon* here and there, would be folly. Were I to do so, I would most seriously risk spoiling the effectiveness of the stories I have based upon it. I have seen at least one writer of genius so stumble, namely Robt. Chambers, who actually sat down to write his infamous and horrible *King in Yellow* (I refer, naturally, to the play, not the existing book), whereas, he might much better have left it afloat in the imagination of the reader. The play is a fine work, but it could not possibly have been either as fine or as frightening as his stories adumbrated. It is his good fortune, and ours, that it has never been published, so that we are free to continue to dream of it fearfully and never know what it says or means.

I once exchanged a few letters with Lovecraft myself, as you may see in his volume of collected letters; I knew not only the handwriting and the letter paper, but also the epistolary style. This was authentic. I said, "I begin to see where this is going."

"Of course you do. But bear in mind that back in those days—you see the date, 1937—I had never heard of Chambers. I hunted down the short-story collection. Then nothing would prevent me from seeing the play. Conscienceless teen-ager that I was, I *demanded* that HPL send me a copy. And here's the reply."

Another sheet of blue notepaper was passed to me. It said:

I do not really know what disposal to make of the *King in Yellow,* for Chambers and I were never intimate and I was staggered that he sent me the play upon my own very tentative inquiry—so much like yours, and others', about the *Nekron.* etc. The MS. now in my hands is I think quite superb; yet, as I have already told you, I would be hesitant to see it used to destroy the effective hints of it in his stories. On the other side, it *is* an object lesson, in when *not* to follow up such hints; and contains much beauty, as well as much terror, that should not remain hidden. What therefore I have done is to have a typescript made by a young lady who has been trading me secretarial work for some small editing services of my own; and I send you herewith the carbon copy, with the injunction that *no* right of publication inheres in its transmission.

This too was an authentic letter, I was convinced. "All right," I said. "That was thirty years ago. And yet you didn't read the play then, if in fact you did get it. You say you hadn't read it until just a little while ago. Why not?"

"I was outgrowing Lovecraft and all that crowd. Also, I was ashamed to have been taken in by the *Nekronomikon,* and didn't want to be taken in again. I was having a fight with a fat boy down the block over an even fatter redhead. And a lot of other things intervened. In short, I put off reading it for a couple of weeks, and during those couple of weeks, Lovecraft died, before I had even had the courtesy to thank him for having sent me the play. After that, I was also embarrassed for my own thoughtlessness, and I put the play away, and soon after, Jim, I managed to forget all about it. No earthquake could have buried it more thoroughly than my own sense of guilt, plus my own contempt at myself for ever having been a fantasy fan at all. If you don't understand how that could have happened, then I will abort the rest of the story right here."

"No, I understand it well enough. I'm not sure I credit it, but I do understand it. Go on."

"I didn't think of it again until 1967, when Ace republished the short-story collection. Then of course I was reminded that, if indeed there had ever been such a play, I was the only one in the world who had a copy. At least, no such thing ever turned up in Chambers' own papers—he died in 1933—and Lovecraft's top typed copy and the manuscript must have been lost."

"What makes you think so?"

"Lovecraft's literary executors have been publishing every scrap of HPL they could find, including his laundry list. If they had found *The King in Yellow,* the world would know it by now. If my copy is real, it is the last one and the only one. So, I got it out of my safe-deposit box and read it."

"What does Samantha make of all this?"

"Oh," he said, "she knows most of what I've told you, but she just thinks I'm being more than usually neurotic—'You know how writers are.' These City College types have pat explanations out of Karen Horney and Erich Fromm for everything; it saves them the trouble of thinking. And I'm not about to change her mind, either. I certainly haven't shown her the play."

"Female common sense would blow the whole thing sky-high in a minute," I agreed. "And you're now about to tell me that you won't show it to me, either."

"On the contrary," he said, a malicious grin splitting his beard and mustache apart. "It's really not so terrible; I'm sure it can't hurt you a bit. As you said downstairs, life is more horrible than any possible book."

"Then what *is* the matter with you, Bill? You're a good deal more hard-nosed than I am; you're the *last* person I'd expect to be scared by Oscar Wilde or Lovecraft or Arthur Machen or any of the rest of that crowd. I can't imagine your trying to scare me, either; you know I know better."

"That's not the point," Atheling said. "As I've said, the play isn't very frightening. But I say that with reservations, because I have not read all of it, not even yet."

"I don't follow you."

"I have not been able to finish reading it," Atheling said, with a kind of sad patience. "There is a point in the play at which I have to quit. It varies, from reading to reading, by a line or so to one side or the other, but I do know the place that I haven't yet been able to get beyond.

"Now, I know from another Lovecraft letter, which I'll show you *after* you've read the play, that he also found this to be the case for him—but that he had to quit several whole pages before I did. I find this curious and I have no explanation for it at all. I want to know when *you* have to stop—if you do."

"May I suggest a very simple expedient?"

"Oh God, sure. Turn to the last page. I've done that. I know how it ends. I know every line of it. I could set it to music if I had to. That's not my point. I'm talking only about the cumulative *effect,* not the state of the text. I want to know how far you get, the first time through."

"I'll finish it," I said. "Have you messed with the typescript at all, Bill?"

"No. There were notes at the back that evidently were intended to be put into a later draft, and I've prepared a version into which I've incorporated them—or those I could understand. But this in the folder is the original."

He handed the folder to me. Well, I was hooked—or, anyhow, prepared to be amused, and, if possible, admiring of Sour Bill's ingenuity. "Okay. Where do I sleep?"

"You can have our room. Samantha's with her mother for the whole week to come—some psychiatric casework sort of chore—so you can rattle around at will. I'll use the guest room. Take the bottle, I don't need it—but don't tell me in the morning that you had to quit reading because you got fried. I want a complete report."

"You'll get it." I opened the folder. Inside it was what would have been the most brittle sheaf of yellow, brown-edged second sheets in the world, had they not each been carefully cased in plastic. I bore them off.

2.

The bed was a magnificent old four-poster, quite in keeping with the house, and it had a small, projector-style reading lamp fastened to the headboard. I washed up and settled down. Just as I did so, either Atheling's furnace or his refrigerator went on and all the lights in the house dimmed momentarily—evidently his wiring needed tending to, which wasn't unusual in these old brownstones either. It was a nice coincidence and I relished it. Then I poured myself a sizable slug of the brandy and began to read.

And this is what I read:

ACT ONE

(*A balcony of the palace in Hastur, overlooking the Lake of Hali, which stretches to the horizon, blank, motionless and covered with a thin haze. The two suns sink toward the rippleless surface.*

(*The fittings of the balcony are opulent; but dingy with time. Several stones have fallen from the masonry, and lie unheeded.*

(CASSILDA, *a Queen, lies on a couch overlooking the Lake, turning in her lap a golden diadem set with jewels. A servant enters and offers her a tray, but it is nearly empty: some bread, a jug. She looks at it hopelessly and waves it away. The servant goes out.*

(*Enter* PRINCE UOHT, *a portly man in his early millions.*)

UOHT:	Good day, mother.
CASSILDA:	Good-bye, day.
UOHT:	You have been looking at Carcosa again.
CASSILDA:	No. . . . Nobody can see Carcosa before the Hyades rise. I was only looking at the Lake of Hali. It swallows so many suns.
UOHT:	And you will see it swallow so many more. These mists are bad for you; they seep into everything. Come inside.
CASSILDA:	No, not now. I am not afraid of a little mist; nor, of a little time. I have seen quite a lot of both.
UOHT:	This interminable siege! Would that the Lake would swallow Alar for once, instead of the suns.
CASSILDA:	Not even Hali can do that, since Alar sits upon Dehme, which is quite another lake.
UOHT:	One lake is like another: water and fog, fog and water. If Hastur and Alar changed sites between moons, nobody would notice. They are the two worst situated cities in the world.
CASSILDA:	Necessarily, since they are the only ones.
UOHT:	Except Carcosa. . . . Well?

CASSILDA: I am not sure, my Prince,
            that Carcosa is in the world. In any event,
            it is certainly fruitless to talk about the matter.

            (CAMILLA, *a Princess, enters, then hesitates.*)

CAMILLA: Oh. I—
CASSILDA: Come ahead, Camilla, hear us.
            There are no secrets any longer. Everything
            has been worn thin, and Time has stopped.

            (*Enter* THALE, *the younger Prince.*)

THALE: Nonsense again, mother?
CASSILDA: If it pleases you
            to call it that, Prince Thale. As for me,
            I am only a Queen; I can be mocked at will.

THALE: But no, I didn't mean—
UOHT: Mockery or no,
            Prince Thale is right. Time does not stop.
            It is a contradiction in terms.

CASSILDA: Time stops,
            my Uoht, when you have heard every possible banality
            every possible number of times. Whenever
            has anything happened in Hastur, please?
            Any new word, or any new event? The siege,
            as you very justly and repeatedly observe,
            is right flat-out interminable, and that's that.
            Neither Hastur nor Alar will ever prevail.
            We shall both just wear down into dust—
            or boredom, whichever arrives first. Ah,
            I am sorry for you, Uoht, but I'm afraid
            you only remind me now that there's no future
            in being human. Even as a baby,
            you were a little dull.

UOHT: You may say
            what you please of me, too, for royalty
            of course has its privileges. All the same,
            not all time is in the past, Cassilda.
            It lies in your power to change things,
            were you not so weary of us—and of yourself.

CASSILDA: Oh, are we to talk of the Succession again?
Nothing is duller than dynasties.

THALE: Mother, must the Dynasty die only because you
are bored?
Only a word from you, and the Black Stars
would rise again. Whatever your soothsaying,
Alar could not stand against them; you know that.
It would be—it would be an act of mercy,
to the people.

CASSILDA: The people! Who are they?
You care as little for the people as Uoht does.
Thale, I know your heart, and his as well.
All the diadem means to either of you is your sister.
There's no other reward now, for being a king
in Hastur. As for black stars, enough!
They radiate nothing but the night.

THALE: Camilla loves me.

UOHT: Liar!

CASSILDA: Camilla?

UOHT: Ask her, if you dare.

THALE: Who would dare,
without the diadem? You're not so bold, Uoht.
Have *you* found the Yellow Sign?

UOHT: Stop your mouth!

CASSILDA: And stop your bickering,
you two frogs! . . . *I* will ask her.

CAMILLA: I am not ready to be asked, mother.

CASSILDA: No? Camilla, *you* could have the diadem.
Then you could take your pick of your brothers,
and we'd have an end to all our problems.
See how I tempt you. The Dynasty would go on,
and you'd be free of all this conniving.
Perhaps, even, the siege would end. . . .
Well, Camilla, speak!

CAMILLA: No, no. Please.
You cannot give the diadem to me.
I will not have it.

CASSILDA: And why not?

CAMILLA: Then *I* would be sent the Yellow Sign.

CASSILDA: Possibly, if one can believe the runes.
But would that be so very terrible?
Tell us, Camilla, what, after all, does happen
when one receives the Yellow Sign?

CAMILLA (*whispering*): It . . . It is come for.

CASSILDA: So they say.
I have never seen it happen. But suppose
it does. Who comes for it?

CAMILLA: The Phantom of Truth.

CASSILDA: And what is that?

CAMILLA: Please. I do not know.

CASSILDA: No more do I. But suppose, Camilla,
whatever it is, that perhaps it's real.
What then? Does it frighten you?

CAMILLA: Yes, mother.

CASSILDA: All right. If that's the case,
then I shall give the diadem to one of your brothers,
and end this steamy botheration in some other way.
You have only to choose between them, as they ask.
I would be delighted to give you a marriage
in the utmost of state. At the very least,
it would be a novelty, in a small and noisy way.

VOHT: A wise decision.

THALE: And not a small one, mother.

CAMILLA: But mother, there *is* something new;
we do not need a stately wedding yet.
That's what I came to tell you, just before
the old quarrel started up again.

CASSILDA: And what is that?

CAMILLA: Mother, there's a stranger in the city.

CASSILDA: A stranger! Now living god, hear that.
You all have the mists of Hali in your brains.
I know every face in Hastur, and in Alar, too.
Camilla, how many people do you think there are
in the living world? A spate of handfuls,
and I've seen them all.

CAMILLA: This one is new in Hastur.

CASSILDA:	Nobody, nobody these days goes about Hastur but the hearse-driver. Sensible people hide their faces even from themselves.
CAMILLA:	But that's it. You can't see his face. He's walking masked.
CASSILDA:	Oh, covered with a veil? Or is he hooded?
CAMILLA:	Neither, mother. He wears another face. A white mask—whiter than the mists. The eyes are blank, and it has no expression.
CASSILDA:	Hmm . . . In all conscience, strange enough. How does he explain it?
CAMILLA:	He speaks to no one.
CASSILDA:	I will see him. He will speak to me. Everyone does; and then he'll be unmasked.
UOHT:	But mother, this is only a conceit. It is of no moment in the tree of time. If Camilla will but choose—
THALE:	And bring back the Succession—
CASSILDA	*(placing the diadem upon her head)*: We will talk of that some other time. Send me now Noatalba, and the man in the pallid mask. Camilla does not wish to choose now, and no more do I.
UOHT:	Time is running out. There has been no king in Hastur since the last Aldones—
CASSILDA:	Do not tell me again the story of the Last King! Oh, I am so sick, so sick of you all! I tell you now, do you goad me further, there will be no other king in Hastur till the King in Yellow!

(There is a long, shocked silence. CAMILLA, UOHT and THALE go out, stunned and submissive. CASSILDA lies back, exhausted and brooding.

(Enter A CHILD, with jeweled fingers, wearing a small duplicate of the diadem.)

CHILD:	Tell me a story.
CASSILDA:	Not now.

CHILD: Please, tell me a story. Please.
CASSILDA: I do not feel like telling you a story now.
CHILD   (*menacingly*): Grandmother?

(CASSILDA *sits up resignedly. She does not look at the*
CHILD.)

CASSILDA: Once upon a time . . .
CHILD: That's better.
CASSILDA: . . . there were two lakes in the heart of
Gondwanaland, called Dehme and Hali. For millions of years they
lay there with no-one to see them, while strange fishes bit their sur-
faces. Then, there appeared a city by the Lake of Hali—

(*During the course of this scene, the suns set. Across the
water, the Hyades come out, slightly blurred by the mists.*)

CHILD: That's not a story, that's only history.
CASSILDA: It is the only story that there is.
              Besides, if you'll be quiet, I shall tell you
              the rest that's in the runes. Is that agreed?
CHILD: Oh good! I'm not supposed to know what's in the runes.
CASSILDA: That doesn't matter now. But to go on:
This city had four singularities. The first singularity was that it appeared overnight. The second singularity was that one could not
tell whether the city sat upon the waters, or beyond them on the invisible other shore. The third singularity was that when the moon
rose, the towers of the city appeared to be behind it, not in front of
it. Shall I go on?
CHILD: Of course, I know all the rest.
CASSILDA: Misfortunate prince. Well then, the fourth singularity
was that as soon as one looked upon the city, one knew what its
name was.
CHILD: Carcosa.
CASSILDA: Even as today. And after a long time, men came to the
lakes and built mud huts. The huts grew into the city of Hastur,
and soon a man arose who proclaimed himself king in Hastur.
CHILD: Aldones. My grandfather.
CASSILDA: Yes, some ages back. And he decreed that all the kings
in Hastur thereafter should bear his name. He promised that if his

Dynasty be maintained, then someday Hastur would be as great as
Carcosa across the waters.

CHILD: Thank you. That's enough.

CASSILDA: No, it is not enough. That night some one heard him.
You have asked, and must hear the end.

CHILD: I have to leave now. I forgot something.

CASSILDA: (*her eyes closed*): And that same night,
he found the Yellow Sign.

(*The* CHILD *runs out.* CASSILDA *opens her eyes and re-
sumes watching across the Lake. A page enters with a
torch, fixes it in a sconce, and goes out again.* CASSILDA
does not stir.)

(*In the near-darkness,* NOATALBA, *a priest, enters.*)

NOATALBA: My Queen.

CASSILDA: My priest.

NOATALBA: You forgot the fifth singularity.

CASSILDA: And you are an incurable eavesdropper.
I am not surprised. In any event,
one does not mention the Mystery of the Hyades
to a child.

NOATALBA: No. But you think of it.

CASSILDA: No. Everyone today imputes philosophy to me.
I'm not so thoughtful. It is only that
the shadows of men's thoughts lengthen commonly
in the afternoon. Dusk is dusk.

NOATALBA: Long thoughts cast long shadows
at any time of day.

CASSILDA: And no news is good news. Noatalba,
must you wash me clean with banalities too?
Next, you will be speaking of the Succession.

NOATALBA: As a matter of fact, nothing was farther from my mind.

CASSILDA: A good place for nothing.

NOATALBA: I am pleased to hear you jesting. Nonetheless,
I have something else to tell you.

CASSILDA: The man in the pallid mask?

NOATALBA: You have heard.
Good. Then I will be brief.

CASSILDA: Good.

NOATALBA: I think you should not see him.

CASSILDA: What!
Nothing will prevent me! Do you think
I will refuse the only novelty in human history,
such as it is? You know me little.

NOATALBA: I know you better than you know yourself.

CASSILDA: And nothing is certain but death and . . .
Oh living God!

NOATALBA: You spoke?

CASSILDA: Ignore me.
Why should I not see this man?

NOATALBA: It is by no means certain that he is a man.
And if he is, at best, he is a spy from Alar.

*(There is a very long silence, as if something had inter-
rupted the action; both* CASSILDA *and* NOATALBA *remain
absolutely immobile throughout it. Then their dialogue re-
sumes, as if both were quite unaware of the break.)*

CASSILDA: A poor spy then, to be so conspicuous.
And in any event, poor priest, what is there
that Alar does not know about us? That is why
we are in this impasse in the war: We know
everything. Were one stone to fall in Alar
that I did not hear about, the war would be over;
and Aldones, poor man, is in the same whale.
But he knows me, and I know him, and that's
the end of the matter. We shall die
of this glut of familiarity, he and I,
lying in the same tomb, measuring away
at each other's hair and fingernails
in the hope of some advantage even in death.
Why would he send a spy? He is the father
of my tiresome children, and the architect
of my miserable city. Oh, Noatalba, how
I wish I could tell him something he does not know!
He would die of joy, and Alar would sink
into the Lakes—Hastur thereafter!

NOATALBA: Perhaps. You think more highly of novelty than I do;
it is a weakness in you. But I myself
do not think this creature in the pallid mask
to be a spy. You are surprised? But no;
I only said of that possibility: "At best."

CASSILDA: (*with a short chopping gesture*):
All right, I yield you that. The worst, then?

NOATALBA: This thing may be the Phantom of Truth.
Only ghosts go about in white.

CASSILDA: (*slowly*):   Oh. Oh.
Is that moment come? I see. Then I was wise
to abort the Dynasty, after all. I am not often wise.
But perhaps any end is a good end . . . if it is
truly an end. But . . . Noatalba—

NOATALBA: Speak.

CASSILDA: I have not found the Sign.

NOATALBA: (*indulgently*): Of course not, or you would have told
me.
But we cannot be sure that the Sign is always sent.
The sender—

(*He falls silent.* CASSILDA, *perceiving that she has the
upper hand again, grins mercilessly.*)

CASSILDA: —is the King in Yellow.

NOATALBA: Well . . . yes. The King . . . warns . . . as he warned
the first Aldones. We know nothing about him
but that. And should not know.

CASSILDA: Why not?
Perhaps he is dead.

(NOATALBA *abruptly hides his face.*)

Or too busy in Carcosa, so that he has forgotten
to send the Sign. Why not? We are well taught
that with the King in Yellow, all things
are possible.

NOATALBA (*unmasking his face slowly*):
                    I have not heard you.
You did not speak.

CASSILDA: I only spoke to your point, my priest . . .

that this man in the pallid mask may indeed
be the Phantom of Truth, though I
have not found the Sign, no more than you.
That was what you were saying, was it not?
Be silent if you wish. Well, I'll chance it.

NOATALBA: Blasphemy!

CASSILDA: Is the King a god? I think not.
In the meantime, Noatalba, I would dearly love
to see the face of Truth. It must be curious.
I have laid every other ghost in the world;
send me this man or phantom!*

(*Exit* NOATALBA.

(*The* STRANGER *enters. He is wearing a silken robe on
which the Yellow Sign is embroidered: a single character
in no human script, in gold against a circular black ground.
The* QUEEN *turns to look at him, and then with a quick
and violent motion, plucks the torch from the sconce and
hurls it from the balcony into the Lake. Now there is only
starlight.*)

CASSILDA: I have not seen you! I have not seen you!

STRANGER: You echo your priest. You are all blind and deaf—
obviously by choice.

CASSILDA: I . . . suppose it is too late
to be afraid. Well then; I am not.

STRANGER: Well spoken, Queen. There is in fact
nothing to be afraid of.

CASSILDA: Please,
phantom, no nonsense. You wear the Sign.

STRANGER: How do you know that? You have never seen
the Yellow Sign.

CASSILDA: Oh, I know. The Sign
is in the blood. That is why

---

* Here indeed I did have to stop for a moment—not because
I was in the least frightened, but because my eyes were tiring
after so many pages of dim-rubbed, time-browned carbon copy;
and just at this instant, the *Queen Mary* or whatever it was
Atheling kept in his basement got under way again and dimmed
the lights, too, to the point where the letters swam in front of my
eyes. Then the light came up again. I took another pull at the
brandy and went on.

I aborted the Dynasty. No blood should have to carry
such knowledge through a human heart;
no children's teeth so set on edge.

STRANGER: You face facts. That is a good beginning.
Very well; then, yes, in fact this is the Sign.
Nevertheless, Cassilda—

CASSILDA: Your Majesty—

STRANGER: —Cassilda, there is nothing to fear.
You see how I wear it with impunity.
Be reassured; it has no power left.

CASSILDA: Is that . . . a truth?

STRANGER: It is the shadow
cast by a truth. Nothing else
is ever vouchsafed us, Queen Cassilda.
That is why I am white: in order to survive
such colored shadows. And the Pallid Mask
protects me—as it will protect you.

CASSILDA: How?

STRANGER: It deceives. That is the function of a mask.
What else?

CASSILDA: You are not very full of straight answers.

STRANGER: There are no straight answers. But I tell you this:
Anyone who wears the Pallid Mask need never fear
the Yellow Sign. You tremble. All the same,
my Queen, that era is over. Whatever else
could you need to know? Now your Dynasty
can start again; again there can be a king
in Hastur; and again, Cassilda, the Black Stars
can mount the sky once more against the Hyades.
The siege can be lifted. Humankind
can have its future back.

CASSILDA: So many dreams!

STRANGER: Only wear the Mask, and these are given.
There's no other thing required of us.

CASSILDA: Who tells me this?

STRANGER: I am called Yhtill.

CASSILDA: That is only Alaran for "stranger."

STRANGER: And Aldones
is only Hasturic for "father." What of that?

CASSILDA: Your facts are bitterer than your mysteries.
And what will happen to you, Yhtill,
you with the Yellow Sign on your bosom,
when the Sign is sent for?

STRANGER: Nothing at all.
What has Carcosa ever had to do
with the human world, since you all lived in mud huts?
The King in Yellow has other concerns, as is only
    supernatural.
Once you don the Pallid Mask, he cannot even see you.
Do you doubt me? You have only to look again for
    yourself
across the Lake. Carcosa does not sit upon the Earth.
It is, perhaps, not even real; or not so real
as you and I. Certainly, the Living God does not
believe in it. Then why should you?

CASSILDA: You are plausible, you in your ghost face. You talk
as if you know the Living God. Do you also hear
the Hyades sing in the evening of the world?

STRANGER   (*shortly*): No. That is strictly the King's business.
It is of no earthly interest to me.

CASSILDA   (*once more recovering a little of her aplomb*):
I daresay. How can I trust any of these answers?
Do we indeed have to do nothing more to be saved
than don white masks? It sounds to me
like a suspiciously easy answer.

STRANGER: Test it then.

CASSILDA: And die. Thank you very much.

STRANGER: Not so fast.
I would not kill you, or myself. I propose a masque,
if you will pardon me the word-play. All will wear
exactly what they choose, except that all will also wear
the Pallid Mask. I myself shall wear the Yellow Sign,
just as I do now. When you are all convinced,
the masks will be doffed; and then you may announce
the Succession, all in perfect safety.

CASSILDA: Oh, indeed.
And then the King descends.

STRANGER: And if the King
should then descend, we are all lost, and I have lost
     my bet.
I have nothing to lose but my life. You have more.
And if the King does not descend, what then?
Think! The Yellow Sign denatured, human life
suddenly charged with meaning, hope flowering every-
     where,
the Phantom of Truth laid forever, and the Dynasty
free of all fear of Carcosa and whatever monsters live
     there,
free of all fear of the King in Yellow and his tattered,
smothering, inhuman robes!

CASSILDA: Oh Living God!
How would I dare to believe you?

STRANGER: You do not dare not to . . .

*(During this conversation, the moon has been rising
slowly, contrary to the direction of sunset, and the stars
fade, though they do not quite disappear. Long waves of
clouds begin to pass over the surface of the Lake of Hali,
which begins to sigh and heave. Spray rises. The STRANGER
and CASSILDA stare at each other in a dawn and sunset of
complicity and hatred.)*

CASSILDA: Why would I not dare?
I who am Cassilda, I, I who am I?

STRANGER: Because, Cassilda, risk nothing, and you risk it all.
That is the first law of rulership. And, too,
because, Cassilda, in your ancient heart
you love your children.

CASSILDA: Oh, you are a demon!
You have found me out.

STRANGER: That is what I came for.
Very well. I shall see you tomorrow, after sunset.
Wear the Mask, and all eyes will be opened,
all ears unstopped. Good night, my Queen.

CASSILDA: If you are human, you'll regret this.
STRANGER: Utterly.
            And so, good night.

(The STRANGER goes out. CASSILDA puts her hand to her head and finds that she is no longer wearing the diadem. She gropes for it, and finally locates it among the cushions. She starts to put it on, and then instead stands at the balcony rail, turning the crown in her hands. The lights go down into semidarkness.

The fog rises in the moonlight: the stars disappear. On the horizon, seemingly afloat upon the Lake of Hali, appear the towers of Carcosa, tall and lightless. The center of the city is behind the rising moon, which seems to be dripping white blood into the lake.

Enter NOATALBA.)

NOATALBA: And so, good night, my Queen.
            You saw him?
CASSILDA: I . . . think so.
NOATALBA: And—?
CASSILDA: He says . . . he says the King in Yellow
            can be blinded.
NOATALBA: And you heard him out.
            Now, very surely, we are indeed all mad.

(Curtain)

Right while I was in the middle of that last long stage direction, the damned lights flickered again, and this time they did not come all the way back to full brightness. Sour Bill really ought to have that wiring checked, or someday soon his fine old Victorian bagnio was going to burn down.

However, this was a natural place to pause and ponder. The text thus far at least settled one suspicion that I had not mentioned to Atheling: that if Atheling himself hadn't written it, perhaps Lovecraft had. Having already invented a number of imaginary literary works, HPL was in theory quite likely to have concocted still another one.

In theory; but Lovecraft never wrote more than a few fragments of his own imaginary reference works; why should he attempt to create the whole of one imagined by another author? Moreover, a play in blank verse was not a likely sort of production for Lovecraft, whose poetic gifts were feeble at best; whereas Chambers, I seemed to recall, had not only published several volumes of verse, but several plays and even an opera libretto. Also, the text thus far already showed a few flashes of humor, a trait not at all characteristic of Lovecraft.

Of course, none of this ruled out Atheling as the probable author, despite the aged paper, but I was pretty sure it did rule out the Spook of Innsmouth.

What about the play proper, then? Horrifying it was not; it was not even as evil as a seventeenth-century "tragedy of blood." Also it was pretty derivative, chiefly of Wilde and of Poe's "The Silence" and "The Mask of the Red Death." And it was terribly dated. I suppose no man living today is in a position to understand why so many of the writers of the 1890's thought that yellow was an especially ominous color.

Grumbling about the light, I brought the smudged pages closer, wondering why I was bothering at all. By this time, I was tired as well as impatient, and, I am afraid, in fact a little drunk, despite Atheling's warning.

Then I discovered that the next page was a misplaced one. Instead of the first page of the second act, it was the "Dramatis Personae" page, which should have been all the way at the front. With one exception, it was nothing but a list of the names—including Aldones, who so far hadn't appeared at all. But the exception was this notation:

"*N.B.* Except for the Stranger and the King, everyone who appears in the play is black."

Nota bene, indeed. It would be hard to imagine another single instruction which could so completely change the whole apparent thrust and effect of what I had read so far. Or did it? Perhaps I was only projecting our current racial troubles into the direction; Chambers may merely have meant to suggest (if he had been

that much of an anthropologist) that after all, all our
remote prehistoric ancestors had been black. But then I
remembered, too, that in the very first story about *The
King in Yellow,* Chambers had proposed banishing all
Negroes to a "new free state of Suanee."

Now both wider awake and a great deal more dis-
oriented, I put the misplaced page aside and plunged on:

ACT TWO

(The CHILD appears before the curtain.)

THE CHILD: I am not the Prologue, nor the Afterword;
            call me the Prototaph. My role is this:
            to tell you it is now too late to close the book,
            or quit the theatre. You already thought
            you should have done so earlier, but you stayed.
            How harmless it all is! No definite
            principles are involved, no doctrines
            promulgated in these pristine pages,
            no convictions outraged . . . but the blow has fallen,
            and now it is too late. And shall I tell you
            where the sin lies? It is yours.
            You listened to us; and all the same you stay
            to see the Sign. Now you are ours, or, since the runes
            also run backwards, we are yours . . . forever.

*(The stage is in darkness when the curtains part. After
a pause, there are a few soft spare chords of music, and the
voice of CASSILDA is heard singing.)*

CASSILDA: Along the shore the cloud waves break,
            The twin suns sink behind the lake,
            The shadows lengthen
                        in Carcosa.
            Strange is the night where black stars rise,
            And strange moons circle through the skies,
            But stranger still is
                        Lost Carcosa.
            Songs that the Hyades shall sing,
            Where flap the tatters of the King,
            Must die unheard in
                        Dim Carcosa.

Song of my soul, my voice is dead,
Die thou unsung, as tears unshed
Shall dry and die in
Lost Carcosa.*

(A murmur of voices and music rises under the last verse. The lights go up to reveal that the front of the stage has become a crowded ballroom, with the balcony at its back. The STRANGER and all the Hasturites are present; all the latter wear white masks with the visage of the STRANGER, to which individual taste has added grotesque variations. The result is that each mask looks like a famous person. The costumes are also various and fantastic. The STRANGER still wears the silken robe with the Yellow Sign, and CASSILDA, though masked, still wears the diadem, as does the CHILD. Many are dancing to a formal measure, something like a sarabande, something like stalking.

CAMILLA is talking to the STRANGER, front left. CASSILDA watches the masque from the balcony, Carcosa and the Hyades behind her; the moon has vanished.)

STRANGER: There, Princess, you see that there has been
no sending, and there will be none.
The Pallid Mask is the perfect disguise.

CAMILLA: How would we know a sending if it came?

(CASSILDA descends and joins them.)

STRANGER: The messenger of the King drives a hearse.

CASSILDA: Oho, half the population of Hastur does that.
It is the city's most popular occupation,
since the siege began. All that is talk.

STRANGER: I have heard what the Talkers were talking—the talk
of the beginning and the end;
but I do not talk of the beginning or the end.

CAMILLA: But—the sending? Let us hear.

STRANGER: Also,
the messenger of the King is a soft man.
Should you greet him by the hand, one of his fingers
would come off to join yours.

---

* If this is the correct text of this song, all the others are corrupt in the last verse.

(Camilla recoils in delicate disgust. Noatalba, who has been circling closer and closer to the group, now joins it.)

NOATALBA: A pretty story.
You seem to know everything. I think perhaps
you could even tell us, given gold,
the mystery of the Hyades.

STRANGER: He is King there.

NOATALBA: As everywhere. Everyone knows that.

STRANGER: He is not King in Aldebaran. That is why
Carcosa was built. It is a city in exile.
These two mighty stars are deep in war,
like Hastur and Alar.

NOATALBA: Oh, indeed.
Who then lives in Carcosa?

STRANGER: Nothing human.
More than that, I cannot tell you.

NOATALBA: Your springs of invention run dry
with suspicious quickness.

CASSILDA: Be silent.
Stranger, how did you come by all this?

STRANGER: My sigil is Aldebaran. I hate the King.

NOATALBA: And his is the Yellow Sign, which you mock him
by flaunting before the world. I tell you this:
he will not be mocked. He is a King
whom Emperors have served; and that is why
he scorns a crown. All this is in the runes.

STRANGER: There are great truths in the runes.
Nevertheless, my priest, Aldebaran
is his evil star. Thence comes the Pallid Mask.

NOATALBA: Belike, belike. But I would rather be
deep in the cloudy depths of Dehme
than to wear what you wear on your bosom.
When the King opens his mantle—

(Somewhere in the palace, a deep-toned gong begins to strike.)

CASSILDA: Have done . . .

* * *

Now is the time I never thought to see:
I must go, and announce the Succession.
Perhaps . . . perhaps the world itself
is indeed about to begin again. How strange!

(*As the gong continues to strike, everyone begins to unmask. There are murmurs and gestures of surprise, real or
polite, as identities are recognized or revealed. Then there
is a wave of laughter. The music becomes louder and in-
creases in tempo.*)

CAMILLA: You, sir, should unmask.
STRANGER: Indeed?
CAMILLA: Indeed, it's time. We have all laid aside
disguise but you.
STRANGER: I wear no mask.
CAMILLA: No mask? (*To* CASSILDA): No mask!
STRANGER: I
am the Pallid Mask itself. I, I, I
am the Phantom of Truth. I came from Alar.
My star is Aldebaran. Truth is our invention,
it is our weapon of war. And see—
By this sign we have conquered, and the siege
of good and evil is ended. . . .

* * *

(*On the horizon, the towers of Carcosa begin to glow.*)

NOATALBA (*pointing*): Look, look! Carcosa—Carcosa is on fire!

(*The* STRANGER *laughs and seizes* CAMILLA *by the wrists.*)

CAMILLA (*in agony*): His hands! *His hands!*

(*At her cry the music dies discordantly. Then a tremen-
dous, inhuman voice rolls from Carcosa across the Lake of
Hali.*)

THE KING: Yhtill!
Yhtill!
Yhtill!

(*The* Stranger *releases* Camilla, *who screams wordlessly and falls.*)°

THE KING:	Have you found the Yellow Sign?
	Have you found the Yellow Sign?
	Have you found the Yellow Sign?
STRANGER	(*shouting*): I am the Phantom of Truth!
	Tremble, O King in tatters!
THE KING:	The Phantom of Truth shall be laid.
	The scalloped tatters of the King must hide
	Yhtill forever. As for thee, Hastur—
ALL:	No! No, no!
THE KING:	And as for thee,
	we tell thee this; it is a fearful thing
	to fall into the hands of the living god.

(*The* Stranger *falls, and everyone else sinks slowly to the ground after him.*

The King *can now be seen, although only faintly. He stands in state upon the balcony. He has no face, and is twice as tall as a man. He wears pointed shoes under his tattered, fantastically colored robes, and a streamer of silk appears to fall from the pointed tip of his hood. Behind his back he holds inverted a torch with a turned and jeweled shaft, which emits smoke, but no light. At times he appears to be winged; at others, haloed. These details are for the costumer; at no time should* The King *be sufficiently visible to make them all out.*

Behind him, Carcosa and the Lake of Hali have vanished. Instead, there appears at his back a huge sculptured shield, in shape suggesting a labrys, of onyx, upon which the Yellow Sign is chased in gold.

The rest of the stage darkens gradually, until, at the end, it is lit only by the decomposed body of the Stranger, *phosphorescing bluely.*)

* The light faded further with a distant mechanical rumble. My eyes ached abominably, and I realized that I should have had a bath; I felt itchy. The carbon by this time was so weak that the letters looked as though they had been typed in ashes; there were whole lines I simply could not read; and I was developing a clamorous headache. God damn Atheling and his hypnotic tricks!

THE KING: I have enfolded Yhtill, and the Phantom of Truth
is laid. (*More quietly*): Henceforth, the ancient lies
will rule as always. . . . Now. Cassilda!

(CASSILDA *rises mutely to her knees.*)

THE KING: Thou wert promised a Dynasty by Truth,
and in truth shalt thou have a dynasty.
The Kingdom of Hastur was first in all the world,
and would have ruled the world, except for this;
Carcosa did not want it. Hence, thereafter,
Hastur and Alar divided; but those in Alar
sent you from Aldebaran the Phantom of Truth
and all was lost; together, you forgot
the Covenant of the Sign. Now there is much
which needs to be undone.

NOATALBA (*faintly*): How, King, how?

THE KING: Henceforth, Hastur and Alar will be
divided forever. Forever shalt thou contend
for mastery, and strive in bitter blood
to claim which shall be uppermost;
flesh or phantom, black or white. In due
course of starwheels, this strife will come to issue;
but not now; oh, no, not now.

CASSILDA (*whispering*): And—until then?

THE KING: Until then,
Carcosa will vanish; but my rule, I tell you now,
is permanent, despite Aldebaran. Be warned.
Also be promised: He who triumphs in this war
shall be my . . . can I be honest? . . . inheritor,
and so shall have the Dynasty back. But think:
Already you own the world. The great query is,
Can you rule it? The query is the gift.
The King in Yellow gives it into your hands,
to hold . . . or to let loose. Choose, terrible children.

NOATALBA (*faintly*): You are King, and are most gracious.
We thank you.

THE KING: *You* thank *me*? I am the living god!
Bethink thyself, priest. There is a price,
I have not as yet stated the half of it.

(*Everyone waits, petrified.*)

THE KING: The price is: the fixing of the Mask.
                          (*Silence.*)

THE KING: You do not understand me. I will explain
              it once and then no more. Hastur, you
              acceded to, and wore the Pallid Mask.
              That is the price. Henceforth all in Hastur
              shall wear the Mask, and by this sign be known.
              And war between the masked men and the naked
              shall be perpetual and bloody, until I come
              again . . . or fail to come.

                   (Noatalba *starts to his knees.*)

NOATALBA: Unfair, unfair!
              It was Alar invented the Pallid Mask!
              Aldones—

THE KING: Why should I be fair? I am
              the living god. As for Aldones, he
              is the father of you all. That is the price:
              the fixing of the Mask.

ALL: Oh!

CASSILDA   (*bitterly*): Not upon us, oh King; not upon us!

ALL: No! Mercy! Not upon us!

THE KING: Yhtill!
              Yhtill!
              Yhtill!

              (The King *vanishes, and with him his throne. The Hya-
              des and Carcosa are once more visible over the balcony
              rail. The mass of corruption that had been the* Stranger
              rises slowly and uncertainly. The Child *runs out from the
              crowd, and seizing the* Stranger *by one mushy hand, leads
              him shambling out across the balcony in the wake of* The
              King. *There is a low, composite moan as they exit.*)

CASSILDA   (*standing and throwing her arms wide*):
              Not upon us! Not upon us!

THE KING   (*offstage, remote, diminishing*):
              What! Did you think to be human still?

                   (*There is a long pause.*)

NOATALBA: And if we now . . .

The light faded out entirely . . . and high time,
too. . . . I was so exhausted I was outright sick. Odd

noises rang through my pounding head; sometimes I thought I could hear lines from the play being spoken, as if in an echo chamber, or, sometimes, even being sung. Occasionally, too, there was a spitting howl which seemed to come from behind the house; I remembered that the Athelings kept cats, though I had not seen any during this visit. And the rumbling below ground was now continuous, like stones being slowly and mindlessly crushed to powder.

Atheling had won . . . whether by suggestion or by alcohol I could not tell, but I could not finish *The King in Yellow* . . . and worse, much worse, was that I felt so dirty that I could hardly bear to touch myself; I was a blackened man lying in a pool of soot; my rings were cutting off my fingers, there were maggots feeding in my ears, and deaf, dumb, blind, anosmic, numb and convicted, I came apart into a universe of slimy saffron rags.

3.

I awoke in a blast of painful yellow sunlight, with that lowering feeling of being about to be Found Out which is for me the most intolerable symptom of a hangover. There were neither curtains nor shades on the windows, which made it worse; no matter how recently *I* had moved into a new place, curtaining the master bedroom would have been the first thing I'd have done.

Then I realized that Atheling was standing over me, in that holier-than-thou pose he assumes when he thinks he's about to lose an argument, looking absurdly knobby in a short red flannel nightshirt and a tasseled red nightcap, and holding out to me a tall red drink.

"Bloody Mary," he said tersely. "Breakfast below in a while. Where did you stop?"

I looked around confusedly. The pages in their plastic sheaths turned out to be all over the floor on the window side of the bed. Getting up, I risked dizziness to pick them up and align them on the bedside table, wincing a little at the sharp *cracks* the plastic edges made against the wood.

"Never mind that, I'll do it later," he said. *"Where did you stop?"*

"Uh . . . let me think a minute, will you? I hate people who expect me to be awake before noon. I stopped at—at Noatalba's speech, just after The King's."

"Which speech of The King's?"

"The off-stage one, where he asks, 'Did you think to be human still?' "

"Damn you," Atheling said. "That's farther than I ever got. You were almost, almost at the end."

"What does happen at the end?"

"Nothing. The Child comes back on stage and draws the curtain."

"That's all?"

"That's all. I can't understand it. You were so close. Only one line short. There must be *somebody* who can get to the end by first intention. What stopped you?"

"The simplest thing in the world, Bill: your damned wiring. The lights kept fading on me. Eventually my eyes wore out and I fell asleep. No mystery. Just eye-strain." I added honestly, "Probably the brandy helped."

"Oh," he said. And then again, "Oh. No more than that. Evidently it doesn't matter who reads it, after all. . . . Leave the play on the nightstand. I'll put it in my wall safe and forget about it. Samantha won't have any trouble forgetting about it, she thinks it's all psychosomatic anyhow. And you might as well forget about it too."

"It's not the most memorable thing I ever read, that's for sure."

"No." He stood silent for a moment. Then he said: "But I'll tell you something irrelevant now."

But he didn't. He just stood there.

"Well?"

"When I first bought this place," he went on in a remote voice, "I planned to have air conditioning installed—mainly to keep the soot out of Samantha's studio. And off the windowsills. You know how filthy this town is."

This seemed irrelevant indeed; but knowing Atheling, I waited.

"So," he said, "I had the house converted to two hundred and twenty volts. Top to bottom. All in BX cables. We had to rip out half the walls to do it. It cost a fortune, but I could run a machine-shop in here now if I had to."

"Then—" I swallowed and started again. "Then what the hell is that grumbling in the cellar? That couldn't have been only eyestrain."

"You've been out of town too long," he said. "The Seventh Avenue IRT goes by only two blocks from here. I don't own any heavy machinery, and there is nothing wrong with the wiring. Nothing."

He continued to hold out the drink to me over the bed, but I was no longer in the bed—hadn't been for at least five minutes. The raw sunlight beat upon the blind and pallid mask of his face through the naked, dirty windows. He went on looking over my shoulder, or where my shoulder would have been, had I been where he thought I was.

I left the house as quickly as I decently could. I hear lately that the Athelings have given it up and moved to England. I should worry about them, I suppose, and I would if I had not just broken my fourth pair of new glasses, right in the middle of a long novel project.

I do sometimes wonder what he did with the play, but not often. The old adage is sadly true: Out of sight, out of mind.

Are "devils" academic, or terribly, terribly real?
Depends, doesn't it, on your point of view.

The Man Who Could
Not See Devils

JOANNA RUSS

—

My father, who saw devils at noonday, cursed me for a
misbegotten abortion because I did not see them. But I
saw nothing. Incubi, succubi, fiends, demons, were-
wolves, evil creatures of all sorts might do what they
pleased for all of me; I could not eavesdrop on them
and holy water turned only to water in my hands,
though I have seen the victims carried in, bloodless, the
next day, and indeed I carried one home myself, a boy
with his throat cut from ear to ear, and that was the
only time I got gratitude out of the pack of them. And
for nothing.

My neighbors, I mean. "There! There! Don't you
see?" they'd cry, the girls tumbling to get away from the
hearth, the houselady fainting, "Don't you *see?*" But I
saw nothing. Cats were possessed, strange shapes hovered in the air; in broad daylight one head turned, and
then another, and then another, as I tried in vain, always in vain. "Don't you *see?*" Until I was twelve I
lived terrified that I might bump into something some
broad morning, out of sheer ignorance, and was never
let abroad by myself. Then, when I was twelve and a

138

half (if I had not been an only son, they might have let me alone, but I was too precious) a neighborhood conjuror tried to de-hex me of what he assured my parents was a particularly virulent curse—and failed—and I spent a night alone, by pure mistake, in a haunted ravine, trembling at every sound but emerging whole, and then repeating the experiment with a growing conviction that if I could not see the devils, perhaps it was because they could not see me.

When I told my father, he beat me.

"Those who cannot see devils, cannot see angels!" he roared.

I replied in a desperate fury that I should be glad enough to see some human beings, and when he reached for the poker I asked him, with mad inspiration, if he would like to spend the night in the ravine with me.

He turned pale. He said I was probably crazy and ought to be put to bed.

I said he would have to chain me up; but he could not do that every night; and as soon as I was free I would spend every night out in the woods and tell him about it in the daytime.

He said suicide was a sin.

I said I did not care.

"My poor boy," he said, trembling, "my poor boy, don't you see? Satan is deceiving you and giving you a false sense of security. Some day—"

"Show me Satan," I said.

"A ghost passed through this room three nights ago," he said, getting down on his knees, his beard wagging. "A ghost shaped like the body of a drowned girl, shining with a green light and we all saw it."

"I saw *you*," I said. "And pretty fools you looked too, let me tell you, gaping at nothing."

"And it was wearing a white dress covered with seaweed," he went on in a singsong, "that shone in the darkness, and it passed through the candles and one by one they went out" (I had not seen that either) "and when it passed them they sprang up again and we saw each other's faces and we were all pale, all, all, except you" and to my amazement he burst into tears.

"I can't help that," I said, feeling uncomfortable.

"Didn't you see anything?" he said.

"Nothing."

"Anything?"

"Nothing."

I had never seen my father cry before, or since; in fact, this incident is my one even vaguely pleasant recollection of him, for the next day he was altogether himself. He thrashed me, thoroughly and formally, for no particular reason, and began that monotonous series of cursings that I have mentioned before. The story of the ghost (a distant cousin of my mother's) went the rounds of the village but with improvements—she had hovered over me, calling me by name; she had passed right through me; she had apostrophized me as one deaf and blind—

In three days no one would speak to me.

When I was sixteen, I ran away, got caught, and was brought back. They could beat me as much as they liked in the daytime, I said furiously, but they knew what would happen at night.

When I was seventeen, I ran away again, this time compounding the offense by stealing six silver pennies which is no more than the price of one-quarter of a not very good horse. I had the money wrested out of my hot hand (actually it was tied up in a tree and someone found it) and was set hoeing beans as a penance.

At nineteen I ransacked the house in a long, leisurely afternoon's search (by now they were terrified of me), locked one cousin securely in a closet (into which he had fled at the sight of me), pinned another to the wall with an old rapier I had found in the attic, stuffed the price of three farmhouse estates into the front of my shirt, and rode off humming to myself bitterly between my teeth. I had escaped for good—or so I thought.

It was the money, of course. It had to be the money.

It was too much to lose, even with ten thousand imps clinging to each coin. I was thirty-five miles away, eating my soup like a peaceable citizen in a neighborhood inn, when I felt a hand descend on my shoulder and sprang to my feet to see—my uncle! the most tough-minded of the lot, who always said, "A good man need fear nothing," though in what his goodness consisted, his wife—God help her!—and his maidservants and his black-and-blue children did not seem quite able to tell. But here he was with twenty men with him, and a priest. It was the priest that made them so brave.

"Be careful," I said. "You don't know what may happen."

"My boy, my boy," he said, excessively kind, "we've had enough of this."

"Not half as much as you will have," I said while I tried to size them up and remembered bitterly that the money was still on me and so I was in a bad bargaining position—also there was no back door. "Not half as much," said I, "as—"

"You shall come home at once," said my uncle softly, "and we will find a way to cure you, my dear boy, oh we will."

"With my allies?" said I. He was moving closer.

"You have no allies, poor boy," said he, sweating visibly. "Poor boy; they are only the deceitful fancies of the—" But I, knowing them by now, made for the priest, and then there was a frightened row, with much cursing and screaming (though the money made them desperate) and in the end the poor holy man was sitting in a chair having his bleeding head bathed with vinegar and water, and there I was under a heap, or rather clump, of relatives. They found the money immediately and my father (who had hidden behind them in his fright) began sobbing and saying "Praise be to God" for his estate come back.

I told them fervently what would happen to them.

"Let him up, let him up," said my father, and they let

me scramble to my feet, each retreating a little as the heat of the fight wore off.

"Give me a tenth and let me go," I said, out of breath.

"A tenth is for the church," said the priest, uncommonly keen all of a sudden, "and it would be blasphemous to do anything of the kind."

"I'll break your neck," I said intently, looking from one man to the other, "I'll break your spine, I'll make you die in slow torments, I'll—"

"Give it him, give it him," said my father, shaking all over, and he began to fumble among the money which my uncle immediately snatched away from him with the stern reminder that some people were too weak-minded for their own good.

"There is only one way to deal with this," said my uncle importantly, "and that is to take the boy home and exorcise him" (here his eyes gleamed) "and thrash him" (he tucked the money up neatly and buttoned it into the inside of his coat) "and make sure—sure" (said my uncle, hitting one fist into the other with slow relish) "make sure—sure, mind you—that this spell or devil or whatever it is, is driven out. Driven out!" added my uncle, loudly, to everyone's approbation. "Driven out! If we let him go, heaven only knows what may become of us. We may die in our sleep. Othor." Here he pushed a reluctant kinsman forward. "Tie him up." And, seeing that I was not to get away, not even penniless—I drove my head into the nearest stomach and called down such imprecations on them that they begged the innkeeper for a blanket to throw over me, the way you'd bag a cat, for my prophesying and cursing (as I could do nothing else) became every moment more frightful to their ears, seeing that I cursed them in curses they had never even heard before—as indeed they never had for I was making them all up.

"My God!" cried my uncle, "shut the boy up before it all comes true!" and as the innkeeper refused to interfere, someone went outside and got a horse blanket and it was with that abominable smell in my nose and throat that I stumbled blindly outside where I threw myself forward, I cared not where, and struck somebody's boots—or strongbox—or wall.

And that was the end of that, for the time.

I woke up sitting bolt upright on a stool set in the center of a room that looked vaguely familiar—it was my uncle's small estate—with a vague memory of riding dizzily in, saying, "That's right, that's right, I'm only a servant"—and then a blur in one corner resolved itself into a small, redheaded cousin of mine, a brat so ugly and unpleasant that even his own mother disliked him, God help him.

"What?" I said stupidly. I saw the imp jump a little, and then settle back onto his feet. He was watching me suspiciously. He was hung all over with charms: bangles, crosses, hearts, lockets, medals, rings, bells, garlands and staves, until he looked like a dirty, decorated Christmas tree; I suppose they had put him to guard because he was the most expendable member of the clan, for he was only thirteen and very scrawny.

"Well, they've got *you*," he said, with a certain satisfaction. "They're inside, deciding what to do with you." I shut my eyes for a few minutes, and when I opened them he was lounging against the wall, picking his teeth. He sprang to attention.

"What time is it?" I said, and he said, "Late," and then colored; I guessed that he was not supposed to talk to me. I had not thought I had slept when I shut my eyes and my head was still ringing; it occurred to me that I was perhaps still a little out of my mind, but that seemed quite all right at the time; I took out of my shirt one coin they had not found, a gold piece given me by my nurse when I was a child, and I held it up and turned it round so the candlelight made it twinkle. I could see my little cousin licking his lips in his corner.

"This could be yours," I said. He looked doubtful.

"Nyah," he said, and then he said, "is it real?"

"It won't disappear," I said, "if that's what you mean. It's not bewitched."

"Don't believe it," he said, standing virtuously upright, on guard again.

"Then don't believe it," I said, and I tossed it on the floor in front of him. It rang on the stones and lay, winking.

After a short hesitation he picked it up. He whistled ecstatically. ·

"Say, you don't want this," he said.

"Yes I do; give it back," I said. He snorted.

"Nyah! Nyah! Feeble-mind!" he crowed. "Feeble-mind! Now I have it," and he tossed it up and caught it deftly backhand, as if to prove that it was real.

"You don't have it," I said.

He stuck out his tongue at me. I got off the stool and was at him in two strides; I covered his mouth and plucked the coin out of his hand; then I put it back, went back to my stool, and sat down. He stared at me dumfounded.

"Do you really think," I said, "that they would let you keep it, if I told them about it?" (He thrust it into his coat.) "And do you think I wouldn't tell, if I felt like it?" (He threw it on the floor.) "No, no, keep it," I said carelessly. "Keep it. For a favor."

"Wouldn't do you a favor," he muttered, patting his magical garlands that encircled each wrist in the manner of a sacrificial lamb. "Wouldn't be right."

"Bah! nonsense," said I.

"*I'm* safe," he said, shaking his garlands, and tinkling all over. "Pooh," he added. He began to recite under his breath, imitating his father's nasal twang to perfection, a poor persecuted man whose crops always failed, whose babies always had the croup, whose attic leaked—

I took the boy by the arms and shook him till his teeth rattled.

"He—he—hel—" he said.

"Listen," I said, shaking him, "you numb-headed,

misinformed baboon! You've known me all of your wretched life, you beast!" He began to cry. He stood there in the rags and tatters of his charms, bawling.

"Oh for God's sake," I said in despair, "shut up." And I sat back down on my stool and put my head between my knees.

He stopped crying. I said nothing. Then, after a considerable silence, he said: "You stole all that money?"

I nodded.

"Boy!" he said. There was a further silence.

"Hey, you wanna get out?" he said. I shook my head. "Sure you do. You wanna give me that gold money and get out?"

I shook my head again.

"Ah, come on," he said, "sure you do." And he sidled up to me and stood there in friendly fashion, his bells and jingles bumping lightly against me.

"Ah, come on," he said. I held out my hand with the coin in it. He took it and sprinted to the door, clanging; he flung open the door with spirit.

"I'm going to tell a story," he said. "I'm going to lie down and pretend to be dead."

"Bully for you," said I.

"I'll carry on," he said. "It'll be smashing. Shall I tell it to you?"

"No," I said, "and for God's sake, lower your voice."

"But it's *so* nice," he wheedled, "and it's—" So partly to shut him up and partly in a sudden liking for him (he was smiling a kind of gap-toothed, ecstatic smile and his orange freckles were aglow) I pulled off my ring—a cheap thing but my own—and gave it to him.

"Hide it," I said, and slipped out into the courtyard.

Now I had a rough idea of where I was, but only a rough idea; so I went to the stables by taking what proved to be the longest way, hugging the walls and stumbling now and again against household remnants left out to freeze or dry, with a noise that I thought must waken the dead. I even saw the council through a window, and stood horribly bewitched for a moment, as if at my own funeral, until the sight gave me the shivers and I crept on. At the deserted stable I slashed the reins of all the horses, searched through saddlebags with my heart knocking at my teeth, found a small moneybag (my uncle's, one-quarter of a sheep this time) and mounted, snatching a torch from the wall, spurring toward the farm gate, dashing at the two guarding it, and firing the thatch above their heads.

What a blaze in an instant! What an uproar! Behind me in the court the freed beasts dashed effectively back and forth, barring everyone from the gate and then (in the most sensible manner possible) streaming behind me, leaving their owners horseless and homebound until someone should round them up the next morning. No one—not even my little cousin—would go out *that* night! The picture pleased me. As I rode through the windy black night, I imagined uncles and cousins and grandfathers huddling uncomfortably in the dark of their charred and roofless rooms, seeing specters with every moan of the wind. It was damned cold. I was in my shirt. I stopped and searched the saddlebags again and heaven provided me with a jacket, knit by a suffering aunt. I became hysterical. The horse was stepping warily in the dark (we seemed to be traversing rocks) and we went around in circles until he simply stood still. I roared and rocked in the saddle. When I came to my senses, I headed south by the stars (who else but I even knew the stars? who else had spent nights in the open?) and saw the beautiful sun come up on my left, over gravelly hills, found a stream, washed and drank, and went on very much improved. But heaven proved to be remarkably improvident in the matter of food, and it was the next midday before I found a farm, stopped at it, and asked the hired girl—

She was off like a shot. I took advantage of my infamy and the sudden terror it produced to rifle the kitchen and change horses, leaving my uncle's to be dehexed, de-bewitched, have chants chanted over it and expensive charms hung upon it and finally (I hoped) adopted and fed. Very likely my uncle would have to pay to have it back. I rode on in better spirits, but miserably fed, and finally, my infamy running out and reduced from a werewolf to a beggar, I sold the horse, proceeded on foot, sold my clothes and bought others cheaper and lighter and found—to my distress—that I had no money. None at all. In the north, where there was no food, I could have lived half a winter on that little bag. In the south, where the ricks ran over, I starved.

I do not like to remember what happened to me then. It was the only time in my life I saw things in simple truth. It seemed to me that the country was feeding off me, for as I got sicker I walked farther south and the spring came, and I fancied the wild mallows and the roses got their color from my blood; I was very sick. If I had not walked into houses at night and stolen, I think I would have died; for the people of the south do not disbelieve in demons, despite their cultivation; oh no. They would watch me, trembling behind the wall, as I stared at their pantry shelves, stared at the loaf in my hand, even forgetting why I had come. Sometimes I would put it down like a sleepwalker; once I lay on the grass by the open highway and wept for no reason, looking up at the stars. Someone saw me then, at dawn; someone (once!) gave me good-day. It was as I walked up to the gates of my first city, low and gray in the wet dawn mist, that I knew I was going to die. As I went through the gates, they closed over me like the dull roar of water over one's head, and I lay down (as I thought) to quit this world.

But the world had other ideas.

I woke on a stone floor, with two faces bending over me, one thin, one fat; the fat man plump as a pig and oily, delighted, writhing, pious, all at once. I thought I had gone to heaven. Then he said, "My dear boy." He beamed. "My dear, poor boy, a treasure! A find! A find! What a find!"

"He needs some more," said the other face, laconi-
cally, and disappeared to fetch something. Somebody
put a pillow under my head and I tried to sit up.

"No, no, no, no," said the fat face, serenely, twid-
dling a finger at me. "Lie down. That's good. Here" (to
someone outside my field of vision), "here, help him
up," and they propped me against a wall. "Dear boy"
(someone drew a blanket over me), "dear foolish boy,
you didn't even have the sense to beg," and began feeding me something I could not taste, smacking his lips as
if I were a baby, and muttering to himself. I am seeing
visions at last, I thought, and they are angels, and with
this thought (which was rather distressing) I came bolt
awake.

"Who the devil are you?" I croaked. Fat-face
wreathed and writhed in delight and thin-face next to
him put hands together and cast eyes piously upward.
Then he scuttled out of my field of vision.

"Friends," said fat-face, beaming, "Orthgar, get me a
napkin" (presumably to someone in the room, for I was
lying on the floor of a kind of office, with ledgers open
on a table and parchments and such gear all about the
walls), and he began feeding me some more. Then he
stopped and, ecstatically shutting his eyes, kissed me on
the forehead.

"You," he said, "are going to make a lot of money."

"What?" said I. He patted my cheek, still beaming as
if I were a prize pig.

"Later," he said. "Do you think you can sit up?" and
I said possibly and they propped me in a chair where I
could see (wonder of wonders!) a garden, and a gardener clipping fruit trees.

"My dear fellow," said fat-face, "you must tell me
your name." And I did, and he said, "I am Rigg and
this is Orthgar. Orthgar, get me a brandy." Orthgar disappeared. I stared up at my fat host in bewilderment (it
grew no less in the next ten years!) and asked him—
well, asked him— He put up one hand for silence.

"You mustn't talk," he said fondly, "you'll exhaust

yourself. You sit there like a good little boy and *I*—"
(he heaved himself ponderously off the table, where he
had been perched like a great, fat finch) "and *I* will
explain everything." He smiled. "I am a banker," he
said, shutting his eyes, and then opening them, he added
delicately, "but not a banker," and looked modestly at
his hands, which were fastidiously picking up pages and
turning them over.

"Well?" said I.

He looked beatific. "I," he said, squirming with mod-
esty, "I—that is, we—all of us—we are Appropria-
tors."

"What?" I said. He shrugged.

"Thieves," he said. "But that's a nasty name. Call me
Rigg. Ah! the brandy," and he poured from his glass
into another and gave the second to me.

"I am not a good thief at all," said I.

"You will be," he said. "You will be. Besides, my
dear—" (and here he and Orthgar smirked at each
other) "think of your great talent."

"Talent?" I said dully.

"Oh yes," he said, sliding off the seat and walking
expansively around the room. "Orthgar found you at
dawn in the city cemetery. Orthgar is protected by very
strong charms. There you were, sleeping like a baby,
obviously unharmed except for semi-starvation, of
course, perfectly oblivious to the danger you ran. That
is, you didn't run. That's the point. It's a ghastly place;
people go mad there, cut each other's throats, hang
themselves on empty air, really dreadful."

"City ought to do something," interposed Orthgar.

"Certainly they ought," said my host emphatically.
"But they won't. Who can? Only our friend here." He
beamed. "And he won't, either. He'll be too busy. The
present administration," said Rigg heatedly, "is rotten!
Rotten! Luckily." He stopped. "Am I boring you?" he
said.

"How can I be useful?" said I.

"'The clever fellow reaches conclusions more

quickly than the stupid one,' " said Rigg, scratching behind his right ear and looking very piglike. "You ask good questions. Very. You see, when Orthgar brought you here—dear, brave fellow, Orthgar! I owe him a great deal—when Orthgar brought you here, we gave you all sorts of tests to see if you were suited to the job. We spoke Awakening Spells over you. You snored. We conjured up your spirit. You snored. Finally I had Thring—Thring's a friend of ours, very useful fellow, Thring—go out and get a priest to exorcise you, cleanse you and anoint you. Nothing. Finally we put you to the ultimate test, pronounced a frightful malediction upon you, several frightful maledictions, in fact—"

"It was a strain to be in the room," said Orthgar.

"But nothing happened," said Rigg. "In fact, you opened your eyes and said something unprintable about your uncle."

"Yes," said I, thoughtfully.

"So then," continued Rigg excitedly, drinking his brandy and mine too, "so then we *knew!* My dear fellow, we *knew!* One man like you is worth a hundred of us! Do you know how many lockmakers there are in this city? Well, there are twice as many magicians. And there you have it." They clinked glasses. At this I laughed, and then I said that I wanted some brandy, too.

"You'll throw it up," said Rigg warningly, "it's too soon," but he gave me some anyway and keep it down I could not, and made a mess that the landlady had to clean up.

"Beggars," she said, and then she said. "You owe three weeks' rent."

"Madam," said my host with dignity, "I shall give you six. Do you see this paper?" and he showed her a page of a ledger.

"I can't read," said the landlady sullenly, going out the door with the slop basin. "But I can count," she said, putting her head in at the door, and then vanishing.

"I feel sick," I said, and Rigg took from a pocket a small green vial with a brass stopper.

"Here," he said, smiling shrewdly. "Oil of peppermint. Good for the stomach." He gave it to me. "Even yours," he said, with meaning. I drank some and closed my eyes. It burned and numbed my mouth and it made me feel a little better that there was medicine in the world for me, for me, yes even me.

"Well?" he said.

"Well?"

"What share will you take?"

"One-quarter," I said.

"One-eighth," he said.

"One-quarter," I said. "You have to give me reasons for living."

He looked unhappy.

"One-sixth?" he said.

"Done."

"I told you," said Orthgar, and he cleared away the ledgers. "You'd best put them back on the shelves," he said. "They don't belong to us."

I laughed again.

"The unholy alliance," I said.

"Mm?" said Rigg, over his brandy.

"Nothing," I said.

"Well," said Rigg, "if you feel better, let's get you to bed. The proper soup and in three days you'll be on your feet."

"We'll have to travel," said Orthgar. "All six of us. His life won't be worth anything once they find out."

"Oh, it'll take time," said Rigg serenely, his eyes sparkling. "It'll take time. They'll try spells first" (and he giggled) "and by then we'll be somewhere else." He looked out the window and sighed. "I hate the provinces," he said. He strolled over and helped Orthgar get me to bed. "Wait," he said, patting my cheek. "Drink soup. Think of wine, women, and song."

"I have never heard songs," I said, "and I hate

women only a little less than men, I assure you." My
foster father patted my cheek again.

"You'll like music," he said. "It shows in the shape
of your ears." And waving gaily, he gathered up the
brandy, bottle, glasses, tray and all and strolled out.
Orthgar stood at the door for a moment.

"He's not too bad," said Orthgar. "You can trust
him." And then he too went out.

But I was not thinking of money. I was thinking
rather of the oddness of the world and how strange it
was that people bothered themselves with spells and
counter-spells and did not investigate the really compel-
ling questions, such as whether the sun's fire burned the
same material as ordinary fires, for anyone can look
into a wood fire, even a goldsmith's, but it is common
knowledge that the sun dazzles the eyes for even a moment. And the moon must burn still another thing, for
its fire in the daytime is pale white.

I remember my nurse, when I was little, asking me
whether when the sun rose I did not see a great company of the heavenly host all crying Holy Holy Holy
and I had said no, I saw only a round, red disk about
the size of a penny coin. And then I wondered, drifting
off to sleep to the sound of the gardener's shears,
whether it might not be an advantage not to see demons
and angels, and if it was, whether my children might not
inherit the trait and pass it on to their children; and
perhaps eventually (here the garden and its blossoming
fruit trees wavered in the undulations of drowsiness)
everyone would be like me, and if you asked people
about the afreets, the succubi, the vampires, the angels
and the fiends (very vaguely, far away, I could see the
gardener cry out and back away from something, yet I
knew I was safe; it might put its teeth into me and rage
and roar and stamp—all silently—but I could sleep
on), they would say *Those creatures? Oh, they're just
legends; they don't exist. . . .*

How do I get there from here?
Shall I count the ways?

The Key to Out

BETSY CURTIS

———

This character has been hanging around Mike's Bar for about a week, he's there every time you go in. You wonder if he even goes home at night. A character. He tells anybody who happens to be standing next to him that he's got the Key to Out, but when you ask him what that *means* . . . gibberish. So a couple of the guys decided to lead him on a bit. They got another guy, brother of one of them, to pretend he's a reporter, come to get the inside story. That's a laugh!

Well, anyhow, the fake reporter says the Key is already somewhat famous or notorious, and he wants the details from the man who can use it.

The character is so flabbergasted he almost sobers up. "Oho?" he says. "Can it be you they want?" Talking to himself about himself—oh, he was far gone, he was!

So it was drinks all around.

"Here's to you, Jake," says the character.

"Jake? My name's James," says the fake reporter. "James Malloy, at your service."

"Same thing," says the character.

"Not exactly," says James Malloy.

And he was stiff enough about it that it could have been an argument, and there's an end to our hazing the character. Except he says quick enough, "Where I came from, originally, I mean, Jacob means 'the supplanted.' And James is the Greek form of Jacob."

"Interesting," says James Malloy. "And what's your name then?"

"Then?" says the character, as if he's been stung by a hornet. "Well, now, I don't think that's pertinent. I'll tell you later, maybe."

Crazy. It took several more drinks and some blarney to get him talking, after he'd been speaking his piece all week to anybody that'd listen to him ten minutes running. Finally James must have asked the right question, though. . . .

. . . The closest I can come to describing it is that it's how it feels to your tongue. Like that cavity in this molar here . . . aaanh . . . feels very different in shape and size from the way it looks in the mirror when I look at it. Bigger, sure, but not exactly the same shape, either. There's this fellah has done some research I was reading about in, I think it was, uh, *Science,* says that when your hands tell you one thing about size and shape and your eyes tell you something else, you tend to trust your eyes. So the dentist trusts his and fills the cavity and you don't get into any hassles over the actual (whatever that means) size and shape of the thing, see? But what I'm telling you is about a sort of size and particularly shape that you can feel inside somewhere in connection with, well, a thought about something.

My Aunt Martha always gave me a feeling, a tongue sort of feeling, but more up right inside my hard palate, of a sort of double saucer shape, convex on both sides that is, but with the outside rim an equilateral polygon. Aunt Martha's a problem.

No, I can't explain it without that kind of hard

words. A polygon is a flat surface thing with lots of sides like a circle, maybe, with a lot of short straight edges instead of a smooth round edge. Equilateral just means that all the sides are the same length. Convex means it bulges out.

What's that all got to do with a Key? Well, it's the only way I can explain.

There are these universes.

Well, a universe is somewhere, somewhen that's not exactly like any other somewhere. No. The bathroom isn't one universe and the living room another . . . for me, that is. I suppose it might seem that way to a baby who can't go back and forth by himself to see that they're connected by the hallway into parts of the same universe.

Some universes are nice and some are nicer than that and magic, and some are pretty rough. Some are closed systems and some aren't.

Oh, a closed system is like a game where you have just so many pieces or cards and just certain rules and moves and that's all. Read a book review of a book about a closed-system society where they don't believe there's more than just so much good and evil in the universe . . . that universe. For anybody to get some good, well he's gotta take it from somebody else. And I suppose if anybody gets more than his fair share of hard luck then somebody else must be having it good. Author of the book called it a shared poverty system. Ugh. That's what I mean by closed system. Like conservation of matter and energy in a good many universes. Of course there are universes where you just make some energy or vanish some matter and nobody gets particularly shook. I been in that kind, too.

A Key is what I call the thing that gets you out of one universe and into another. And it's a shape feeling inside. I can't describe it in words because words generally show you how a thing looks and not how it feels.

Look. I keep this crystal in this plastic capsule that came out of one of those nickel or dime machines in the lobby of supermarkets and such. You have those here, I know . . . not the crystal, the capsule. It had little pieces of gum and a minibook in it once. The crystal is just a piece of quartz. Knocked it out of a bit of granite because it looked a little bit like that shape that's the Key I'm talking about. Here. Put it in your mouth and feel it with your tongue. Roll it around under your tongue and press it against the roof of your mouth. It's O.K. It's been boiled since anybody else had it. I can't explain without you get the feel of it. Oh go on, nobody's gonna notice. The boys are looking at the girls and the old men are looking at the girls and the women are looking at the men and boys and the younger . . . well, middle-aged men are looking into their drinks. That's right. Pop it in your mouth.

Now feel it around. Got it? Doesn't feel just the same shape as it looks but you get more shape feeling in your mouth than just looking at it, huh? O.K. Spit it back into the capsule again. Thanks.

Well, now, can you get the feel of that again but a lot bigger? So that it fills most of your throat and mouth and up a little bit into your head? That's what I mean by a shape feeling and that's about where you feel it to be a Key.

Now here is how you change universes.

Why? I couldn't say that, exactly, either. You like it here? Always? Just the way it is with just the rules this universe is run on? Like war is a good solution to being hungry or bored or mad at somebody? Or like some rules you learned as a kid, like: you're safe if nobody notices you, but if nobody notices you you're damn lonely? There are universes where you're safe only when somebody *is* noticing you and when nobody's noticing you the boogers'll mow you down without even noticing. Opposite rules. I'll bet you've been in both kinds of universes without even noticing they were different; but I'll bet you don't know how to get from one to the other. I know.

It's with a Key.

There are other types of Keys. There's some music notes or bits. There are smells. I'm not too good at making up smells so I don't try to use that. When I change universes because of a smell, it's an accident.

All in my mind? Brother, you haven't said a thing. Where is my mind? You can't see it and I can't see it and even if you try to tell me where it is, I can say I don't *feel* it that way. If my mind is in my throat and mouth and head, maybe it's in my mind, but anyhow it's real and it's definitely in one universe or another.

There are other shape feelings besides Keys, too. A problem has a shape if you take time to feel it. I know one that tastes like a sphere with frills. No, I'm not kidding. But a problem doesn't get you anywhere. It just sits there like this lumpy sphere with frills, maybe, and just is.

A Key does something. When you really feel it fully it takes you some other someplace from where you were before. Things may look just the same but the rules are different and the *feeling* of the place. As different as the feelings of different kinds of weather. Like rain in one universe is a nasty tiring drizzle and in another it's like a long drink of cold water when you're so thirsty and in another it's like the air full of crazy fairies.

No, I *don't* mean flipped homosexuals. You don't want to be that way about it. You want to know about this Key, or don't you? Well, does the *magazine* want the story about the Key, the one that sent you here to see me? I don't care if *you* don't really want to know. It doesn't matter to me. You obviously aren't the right James, James. I don't have to wait here. There are other universes where you aren't even around, I think. At least not for me.

No. What you think about me doesn't bother me a bit. You think however the rules are for you. Not much you can do about it, so why should I blame you?

You *do* want to know? O.K. Now listen carefully; of course maybe you'll have to practice a bit and come back and see me again when you've got the hang of it.

Yes, I'll wait around a few more days in this universe.
It's not exactly too bad to stand it here. For a while.
You know, like they say about New York. I wouldn't
want to *live* here.

Yes, I suppose you might find me . . . well, someone who looks like me, even next month if you know
where to look. *I* couldn't say. Yes, right in this universe,
but it won't be me. You don't leave a gap in the universe when you go into another one; but I don't know
too much about who or what you do leave because I'm
not here to know about it. Somebody or something else.
Maybe it goes home and puts itself away in a closet till
I get back, if I do. Or maybe it has a better job than
mine right here. I don't have to worry about that at all.
There's always a body waiting for me when I want to
come here.

You think I'm out of my head, don't you. Well, that's
the right way to put it, friend . . . I'm often out of *this*
head. And when I am, I'll bet this body doesn't even
recognize *you*. Well . . . anyhow . . .

Now what you do is, you get the feel of the Key to
whatever universe you want to get into. . . .

Yes, there are different Keys for different universes
and the one I'm gonna show you is just one and I
couldn't say which universe it might take you into because there are so many and I can't be sure of your
getting exactly the same feel that I do . . . but that
doesn't matter because once you get the hang of it you
can try different shapes and find the one *you* like. I
know mine.

As I was saying, you get the feeling of the Key, bigger than that crystal you had in your mouth . . . a
good deal bigger . . . so it fills most of your neck and
maybe a little way into your chest and up into your sinuses like just touching sort of inside the sides of your
nose. Yeah . . . about that big . . . big as a half-
gallon milk carton, sort of. And *then* you get the feeling
of a *cavity* in there that shape. The Key is . . . oh,

you don't have to believe it, just listen . . . the Key is an *empty* space of a certain size and shape.

Told me in high shcool geometry that a triangle is a plane surface bounded on three sides by straight lines which meet each other at the corners. Well, that defines two absolutely different triangles. The little one inside and the big one that's all the space there is in that plane *except* the little one. Infinite triangle, you could call it, except how can it be infinite when there's that little bit of the surface that it *isn't?*

So the Key is all of infinity in all directions at once *except* the little empty space about the size of a half-gallon milk carton.

That crystal you had in your mouth is *about* the shape of the Key except that all the surfaces of the crystal would have to be just a little curved and the bottom part where the crystal's sheared straight across is really concave . . . that means it curves in . . . sort of like the bottom of that brandy bottle on the end of the row over there, but it doesn't curve so deeply as that.

That curve should come just about the bottom of your esophagus. Huh? Well, say just at the bottom of your neck. Can you feel it? That curvy part makes it so that it doesn't get near your stomach or something. Get the feel? Those upper jaggy parts up in the top of your mouth and the sides gently curving out down through your mouth and throat with those sides out here and in there? Yeah, curved up at the bottom just below the base of your neck. *Now* remember that all that is empty . . . not part of the Key. The Key is the feeling of being on the outside of a that-shaped bubble. No, it took me quite a while to get the real feel consciously . . . on purpose. I imagine it would take you about ; . . .

"The idea is that a problem is a lump, specifically shaped, and a universe where the problem does not exist," says James Malloy suddenly, . . . "or where the negative-of-lump exists, is a different one from the universe where it does exist. Right?"

"Right," says the character, looking dazed and gratified. And startled.

"One more thing you have to get straight, Mac," says James Malloy. "In this universe, James means 'the supplanter.' "

"You may be sure, James, you'll get your just desserts, whatever." The character is all business now, very crisp. "I'll stand *you* the drinks next time. If you get back."

They went out the door together. The character turned around and smiled. "Drinks are better there than here."

James Malloy must have had quite a bit, all told. Says he doesn't remember much about the interview. Wishes that guy would drop around again, because he can *almost* remember how it felt, the Key, though.

One of the guys says, "That's just your this-universe body talking!" That's a laugh, huh?

Does the Future, itself a magical prospect to lure us unsuspecting to "live another day," offer hope to the hopeless, solution to the insoluble, or academic—and alchemical—justice?

Ringing the Changes

ROBERT SILVERBERG

—

There has been a transmission error in the shunt room, and several dozen bodies have been left without minds, while several dozen minds are held in the stasis net, unassigned and, for the moment, unassignable. Things like this have happened before, which is why changers take out identity insurance, but never has it happened to so many individuals at the same time. The shunt is postponed. Everyone must be returned to his original identity; then they will start over. Suppressing the news has proved to be impossible. The area around the hospital has been besieged by the news media. Hovercameras stare rudely at the building at every altitude from twelve to twelve hundred feet. Trucks are angle-parked in the street. Journalists trade tips, haggle with hospital personnel for the names of the bereaved, and seek to learn the identities of those involved in the mishap. "If I knew, I'd tell you," says Jaime Rodriguez, twenty-seven. "Don't you think I could use the money? But we

161

don't know. That's the whole trouble, we don't know. The data tank was the first thing to blow."

The shunt room has two antechambers, one on the west side of the building, the other facing Broadway; one is occupied by those who believe they are related to the victims, while in the other can be found the men from the insurance companies. Like everyone else, the insurance men have no real idea of the victims' names, but they do know that various clients of theirs were due for shunting today, and with so many changers snarled up at once, the identity-insurance claims may ultimately run into the millions. The insurance men confer agitatedly with one another, dictate muttered memoranda, scream telephone calls into their cuff links, and show other signs of distress, although several of them remain cool enough to conduct ordinary business while here; they place stock-market orders and negotiate assignations with nurses. It is, however, a tense and difficult situation, whose final implications are yet unknown.

Dr. Vardaman appears, perspired, paternal. "We're making every effort," he says, "to reunite each changer with the proper identity matrix. I'm fully confident. Only a matter of time. Your loved ones, safe and sound."

"We aren't the relatives," says one of the insurance men.

"Excuse me," says Dr. Vardaman, and leaves.

The insurance men wink and tap their temples knowingly. They peer beyond the antechamber door.

"Cost us a fortune," one broker says.

"Not your money," an adjuster points out.

"Raise premiums, I guess."

"Lousy thing. Lousy thing. Lousy thing. Could have been me."

"You a changer?"

"Due for a shunt next Tuesday."

"Tough luck, man. You could have used a vacation."

The antechamber door opens. A plump woman with dark-shadowed eyes enters. "Where are they?" she asks.

"I want to see them! My husband was shunting to-day!"

She begins to sob and then to shriek. The insurance men rush to comfort her. It will be a long and somber day.

NOW GO ON WITH THE STORY

After a long time in the stasis net, the changer decides that something must have gone wrong with the shunt. It has never taken this long before. Something as simple as a shift of persona should be accomplished quickly, like the pulling of a tooth: *out, shunt, in.* Yet minutes or possibly hours have gone by, and the shunt has not come. What are they waiting for? I paid good money for a shunt. Something wrong somewhere, I bet. Get me out of here. Change me.

The changer has no way of communicating with the hospital personnel. The changer, at present, exists only as a pattern of electrical impulses held in the stasis net. In theory it is possible for an expert to communicate in code even across the stasis gap, lighting up nodes on a talkboard; it was in this way that preliminary research into changing was carried out. But this changer has no such skills, being merely a member of the lay public seeking temporary identity transformation, a holiday sojourn in another's skull. The changer must wait in limbo.

A voice impinges. "This is Dr. Vardaman, addressing all changers in the net. There's been a little technical difficulty, here. What we need to do now is put you all back in the bodies you started from, which is just a routine reverse shunt, as you know, and when everybody is sorted out we can begin again. Clear? So the next thing that's going to happen to you is that you'll get shunted, only you won't be changed, heh-heh, at least we don't *want* you to be changed. As soon as you're able to speak to us, please tell your nurse if you're back in the right body, so we can disconnect you from the master switchboard, all right? Here we go, now, one, two, three—"

*

—*shunt*

This body is clearly the wrong one, for it is female. The changer trembles, taking possession of the cerebral fibers and driving pitons into the autonomic nervous system. A hand rises and touches a breast. Erectile tissue responds. The skin is soft and the flesh is firm. The changer strokes a cheek. Beardless. He searches now for vestigial personality traces. He finds a name, Vonda Lou, and the image of a street, wide and dusty, a small town in a flat region, with squat square-fronted buildings set well back from the pavement, and gaudy automobiles parked sparsely in front of them. Beyond the town the zone of dry red earth begins; far away are the bare brown mountains. This is no place for the restless. A soothing voice says, "They catch us, Vonda Lou, they gonna take a baseball bat, jam it you know where," and Vonda Lou replies, "They ain't gone catch us anyway," and the other voice says, "But if they do, but if they do?" The room is warm but not humid. There are crickets outside. Cars without mufflers roar by. Vonda Lou says, "Stop worrying and put your head here. *Here.* That's it. Oh, nice—" There is a giggle. They change positions. Vonda Lou says, "No fellow ever did that to you, right?" The soft voice says, "Oh, Vonda Lou—" And Vonda Lou says, "One of these days we gone get out of this dime-store town—" Her hands clutch yielding flesh. In her mind dances the image of a drum majorette parading down the dusty main street, twirling a baton, lifting knees high and pulling the white shorts tight over the smug little rump, yes, yes, look at those things jiggle up there, look at all the nice stuff, and the band plays "Dixie" and the football team comes marching by, and Vonda Lou laughs, thinking of that big hulking moron and how he had tried to dirty her, putting his paws all over her, that dumb Billy Joe who figured he was going to score, and all the time Vonda Lou was laughing at him inside, because it wasn't the halfback but the drum majorette who had what she wanted, and—

Voice: "Can you hear me? If there has been a proper matching of body and mind, please raise your right hand."

The changer lifts the left hand.

*

—shunt

The world here is dark green within a fifty-yard radius of the helmet lamp, black beyond. The temperature is 38° F. The pressure is six atmospheres. One moves like a crab within one's jointed suit, scuttling along the bottom. Isolated clumps of gorgonians wave in the current. To the left, one can see as though through a funnel the cone of light that rises to the surface, where the water is blue. Along the face of the submerged cliff are coral outcroppings, but not here, not this deep, where sunlight never reaches and the sea is of a primal coldness.

One moves cautiously, bothered by the pressure drag. One clutches one's collecting rod tightly, stepping over nodules of manganese and silicon, swinging the lamp in several directions, searching for the place where the bottom drops away. One is uneasy and edgy here, not because of the pressure or the dark or the chill, but because one is cursed with an imagination, and one cannot help but think of the kraken in the pit. One dreams of Tennyson's dreamless beast, below the thunders of the upper deep. Faintest sunlights flee about his shadowy sides: above him swell huge sponges of millennial growth and height.

One comes now to the brink of the abyss.

There hath he lain for ages and will lie, battening upon huge seaworms in his sleep, until the latter fire

shall heat the deep; then once by man and angels to be
seen, in roaring he shall rise and on the surface die.
Yes. One is moved, yes. One inclines one's lamp, hoping its beam will strike a cold glittering eye below. Far,
far beneath in the abysmal sea. There is no sign of the
thick ropy tentacles, the mighty beak.

"Going down in, now," one says to those above.

One has humor as well as imagination. One pauses at
the brink, picks up a chalky stone, inscribes on a boul-
der crusted with the tracks of worms the single word:

NEMO

One laughs and flips aside the stone, and launches
one's self into the abyss, kicking off hard against the
continental shelf. Down. And down. Seeking wondrous
grot and secret cell.

The changer sighs, thinking of debentures floated on
the Zurich exchange, of contracts for future delivery of
helium and plutonium, of puts and calls and margins.
He will not enter the abyss; he will not see the kraken;
feebly he signals with his left hand.

*

—shunt

A middle-aged male, at least. There's hope in that. A
distinct paunch at the middle. Some shortness of breath.
Faint stubble on face. The legs feel heavy, with swollen
feet; a man gets tired easily at a certain age, when his
responsibilities are heavy. The sound of unanswered
telephones rings in his ears. Everything is familiar: the
tensions, the frustrations, the fatigue, the sense of things
unfinished and things uncommenced, the staleness in
the mouth, the emptiness in the gut. This must be the
one. Home again, all too soon?

Q: Sir, in the event of an escalation of the crisis,
would you request an immediate meeting of the Security

Council, or would you attempt to settle matters through quasi-diplomatic means as was done in the case of the dispute between Syria and the Maldive Islands?

A: Let's not put the horse in the cart, shall we?

Q: According to last Monday's statement by the Bureau of the Budget, this year's deficit is already running twelve billion ahead of last, and we're only halfway through the second quarter. Have you given any concern to the accusation of the Fiscal Responsibility party that this is the result of a deliberate Communist-dictated plan to demoralize the economy?

A: What do you think?

Q: Is there any thought of raising the tax on personality-shunting?

A: Well, now, there's already a pretty steep tax on that, and we don't want to do anything that'll interfere with the rights of American citizens to move around from body to body, as is their God-given and constitutional right. So I don't think we'll change that tax any.

Q: Sir, we understand that you yourself have done some shunting. We—

A: Where'd you hear that?

Q: I think it was Representative Spear, of Iowa, who said the other day that it's well known that the President visits a shunt room every time he's in New York, and—

A: You know these Republicans. They'll say anything at all about a Democrat.

Q: Mr. President, does the Administration have any plans for ending sexual discrimination in public washrooms?

A: I've asked the Secretary of the Interior to look into that, inasmuch as it might involve interstate commerce and also being on federal property, and we expect a report at a later date.

Q: Thank you, Mr. President.

The left hand stirs and rises. Not this one, obviously. The hand requests a new phase-shift. The body is properly soggy and decayed, yes. But one must not be deceived by superficialities. This is the wrong one. Out, please. Out.

*

—shunt

The crowd stirred in anticipation as Bernie Kingston left the on-deck circle and moved toward the plate, and by the time he was in the batter's box they were standing.

Kingston glanced out at the imposing figure of Ham Fillmore, the lanky Hawks southpaw on the mound. *Go ahead,* Bernie thought. *I'm ready for you.*

He wiggled the bat back and forth two or three times and dug in hard, waiting for the pitch. It was a low, hard fastball, delivered by way of first base, and it shot past him before he had a chance to offer. "Strike one," he heard. He looked down toward third to see if the manager had any sign for him.

But Danner was staring at him blankly. *You're on your own,* he seemed to be saying.

The next pitch was right in the groove, and Bernie lined it effortlessly past the big hurler's nose and on into right field for a single. The crowd roared its approval as he trotted down to first.

"Good going, kid," said Jake Edwards, the first-base coach, when Bernie got there. Bernie grinned. Base hits always felt good, and he loved to hear the crowd yell.

The Hawks' catcher came out to the mound and called a conference. Bernie wandered around first, doing some gardening with his spikes. With one out and the score tied in the eighth, he couldn't blame the Hawks for wanting to play it close to the belt.

As soon as the mound conference broke up it was the Stags' turn to call time. "Come here, kid," Jake Edwards called.

"What's the big strategy this time?" Bernie asked boredly.

"No lip, kid. Just go down on the second pitch."

Bernie shrugged and edged a few feet off the base. Ham Fillmore was still staring down at his catcher, shaking off signs, and Karl Folsom, the Stag cleanup man, was waiting impatiently at the plate.

"Take a lead," the coach whispered harshly. "Go on, Kingston—get down that line."

The hurler finally was satisfied with his sign, and he swung into the windup. The pitch was a curve, breaking far outside. Folsom didn't venture at it, and the ball hit the dirt and squirted through the catcher's big mitt. It trickled about fifteen feet back of the plate.

Immediately the Hawks' shortstop moved in to cover second in case Bernie might be going. But Bernie had no such ideas. He stayed put at first.

"What's the matter, lead in ya pants?" called a derisive voice from the Hawk dugout.

Bernie snarled something and returned to the base. He glanced over at third, and saw Danner flash the steal sign.

He leaned away from first cautiously, five, six steps, keeping an eye cocked at the mound.

The pitcher swung into a half-windup—Bernie broke for second—his spikes dug furiously into the dusty basepath—

Out! Out! Out! The left hand upraised! Not this one, either! Out! Get me out!

*

—shunt
Through this mind go dreams of dollars, and the changer believes they have finally made the right match-up. He takes the soundings and finds much here that is familiar. Dow Jones Industrials 1453.28, down 8.29. Confirmation of the bear signal by the rails. Penetration of the August 13 lows. Watch the arbitrage spread you get by going short on the common while picking up 10,000 of the $1.50 convertible preferred at—

The substance is right; so is the context. But the tone is wrong, the changer realizes. This man loves his work.

The changer tours this man's mind from the visitors' gallery.

—we can unload 800 shares in Milan at 48, which gives us two and a half points right there, and then after they announce the change in redemption ratio I think we ought to drop another thousand on the Zurich board—

—give me those Tokyo quotes! Damn you, you sleepy bastard, don't slow me up! Here, here, Kansai Electric Power, I want the price in yen, not the American Depositary crap—

—pick up 22 per cent of the voting shares through street names before we announce the tender offer, that's the right way to do it, then hit them hard from a position of strength and watch the board of directors fold up in two days—

—I think we can work it with the participating preference stock, if we give them just a little hint that the dividened might go up in January, and of course they don't have to know that after the merger we're going to throw them all out anyway; so—

—why am I in it? Why, for the fun of it!—

Yes. The sheer joy of wielding power. The changer lingers here, sadly wondering why it is that this man, who after all functions in the same environment as the changer himself, shows such fierce gusto, such delight in finance for the sake of finance, while the changer derives only sour tastes and dull aches from all his getting. It's because he's so young, the changer decides. The thrill hasn't yet worn off for him. The changer surveys the body in which he is temporarily a resident. He makes himself aware of the flat belly's firm musculature, of the even rhythms of the heart, of the lean flanks. This man is at most forty years old, the changer concludes. Give him thirty more years and ten million more dollars and he'll know how hollow it all is. The futility of existence, the changer thinks. You feel it at seventeen, you feel it at seventy, but often you fail to feel it in between. I feel it. I feel it. And so this body can't be mine. Lift the left hand. Out.

*

"We are having some difficulties," Dr. Vardaman confesses, "in achieving accurate pairings of bodies and minds." He tells this to the insurance men, for there is every reason to be frank with them. "At the time of the transmission error we were left with—ah—twenty-nine minds in the stasis net. So far we've returned eleven of them to their proper bodies. The others—"

"Where are the eleven?" asks an adjuster.

"They're recuperating in the isolation ward," Dr. Vardaman replies. "You understand, they've been through three or four shunts apiece today, and that's pretty strenuous. After they've rested, we'll offer them the option to undergo the contracted-for change as scheduled, or to take a full refund."

"Meanwhile we've got eighteen possible identity-insurance claims," says another of the insurance men. "That's something like fifteen million bucks. We got to know what you're doing to get the others back in the right bodies."

"Our efforts are continuing. It's merely a matter of time until everyone is properly matched."

"And if some of them die while you're shunting them?"

"What can I say?" Dr. Vardaman says. "We're making every attempt."

To the relatives he says, "There's absolutely no cause for alarm. Another two hours and we'll have it all straightened out. Please be assured that none of the clients involved are suffering any hardship or inconvenience, and in fact this may be a highly interesting and entertaining experience for them."

"My husband," the plump woman says. "Where's my husband?"

*

—shunt

The changer is growing weary of this. They have had him in five bodies, now. How many more times will they shove him about? Ten? Twenty? Sixteen thousand? He knows that he can free himself from this wheel of transformations at any time. Merely raise the right hand, claim a body as one's own. They'd never know. Walk right out of the hospital, threatening to sue everybody in sight; they scare easily and won't interfere. Pick your body. Be anyone who appeals to you. Pick fast, though, because if you wait too long they'll hit the right combination and twitch you back into the body you started from. Tired, defeated, old, do you want that?

Here's your chance, changer. Steal another man's body. Another woman's if that's your kick. You could have walked out of here as that dyke from Texas. Or that diver. That ballplayer. That hard young market sharpie. Or the President. Or this new one, now—take your pick, changer.

What do you want to be? Essence precedes existence. They offer you your choice of bodies. Why go back to your own? Why pick up a stale identity, full of old griefs?

The changer considers the morality of such a deed.

The chances are good of getting away with it. Others in this mess are probably doing the same thing; it's musical chairs with souls, and if eight or nine take the wrong bodies, they'll never get it untangled. Of course, if I switch, someone else switches and gets stuck with my body. Aging. Decrepit. Who wants to be a used-up stockbroker? On the other hand, the changer realizes, there are consolations. The body he wishes to abandon is wealthy, and that wealth would go to the body's claimant. Maybe someone thought of that already, and grabbed my identity. Maybe that's why I'm being shunted so often into these others. The shunt-room people can't find the right one.

The changer asks himself what his desires are.

To be young again? To play Faust? No. Not really. He wants to rest. He wants peace. There is no peace for him in returning to his proper self. Too many ghosts await him there. The changer's needs are special.

The changer examines this latest body into which he has been shunted.

Quite young. Male. Undergraduate, mind stuffed full of Kant, Hegel, Fichte, Kierkegaard. Wealthy family. Curling red hair; sleek limbs; thoughts of willing girls, holidays in Hawaii, final exams, next fall's clothing styles. Adonis on a lark, getting himself changed as a respite from the academic pace? But no: the changer probes more deeply and finds a flaw, a fatal one. There is anguish beneath the young man's self-satisfaction, and rightly so, for this body is defective, it is gravely marred. The changer is surprised and saddened, and then feels joy and relief, for this body fills his very need and more. He sees for himself the hope of peace with honor, a speedier exit, a good deed. It is a far, far better thing. He will volunteer.

His right hand rises. His eyes open.

"This is the one," he announces. "I'm home again!" His conscience is clear.

*

Once the young man was restored to his body, the doctors asked him if he still wished to undergo the change he had contracted for. He was entitled to this one final adventure, which they all knew would have to be his last changing, since the destruction of the young man's white corpuscles was nearly complete. No, he said, he had had enough excitement during the mixup in the shunt room, and craved no further changes. His doctors agreed he was wise, for his body might not be able to stand the strain of another shunt; and they took him back to the terminal ward. Death came two weeks later, peacefully, very peacefully.

Pollution is not the only problem you can have with water and pipes and plumbing and bathing and exorcising. But is it a problem?

In a Quart of Water

DAVID TELFAIR

—

My name is Peter Thornton.

I was born and grew up in Setback, a small town in the Cumberland Mountains, the seat of the First University of the Confederacy. Throughout my early adolescence I was Yelling for Yale or Hoping for Harvard, but I matriculated at FUC, a sacrifice to economic necessity and appearances.

My father, a faculty fixture, insisted that I do so. My sole gesture of independence was to hold out for history, since any interest I might have had in the biological sciences had been decisively stifled when, at the age of six, I first encountered Dad's pickled squids.

Although my father was respected and admired, each year the chief allocation of funds was lavished upon the chairman of the Chemistry Department. This was one Langweilig Wassermann, brilliant and unorthodox. His assistant and wife, Trudl, was guided by a single idea: the success of her husband. As a result of her astute display of charm, my family and I lived rather on the shabby side, if not in actual poverty. I'm sure the Wassermanns held nothing against my father; there simply wasn't enough money available to all departments.

In 1958, shortly after I graduated, my parents were killed in a plane crash, and I was appointed to an assistantship in history. The house to which I had to move was owned by the University, and had previously been occupied by Doctor and Frau Wassermann. They had, perhaps ungratefully, certainly providentially, disappeared during the unusually hot summer. That their lease extended to another five years seemed to have no effect upon their scruples—to say nothing of Wassermann's lush and long-term contract.

I was left alone in a scrambly duplex bungalow and a dismal frame of mind. I had a job and a place to live, but I needed someone to share the rent. I had been fond of my parents, and I was lonely.

In spite of FUC being a church-directed institution, I had never taken much interest in such gaieties as the Eleven O'Clock Service, and I had usually mollified my parents by going at Easter and Christmas. However, after I was left alone—most of my close friends, male and female, were in other schools—I began to attend the Sunday services. My main objection to the production was the orgy of handshaking that went on at the south door after everything was over. It was during one of these sessions that I found myself murmuring something about my need for companionship—male. (Another kind of companionship had occurred to me, but I wasn't fool enough to think that I could get away with it in Setback.)

The University Chaplain was sympathetic. I think that everybody was disposed in my favor, thanks to the recent tragedy; they were certainly very kind. On this particular Sunday, Bishop Elgin and his wife were with the Chaplain, and through them I met the bishop's new assistant, Terry Shaw, who was staying with the Elgins until he could find suitable quarters. But before explaining Terry, however, I'd better try to explain the Elgins. Others have tried. I may be no more successful.

I never had much social intercourse with Bishop Elgin until I met Terry, although I saw rather more of him and his wife than I wanted to—and they of me—thereafter.

The bishop had confirmed me, of course, seven years earlier. I remember only that I couldn't make head or tail of the sermon he preached on that occasion. At the time I put it down to his being an administrator rather than a churchman, and to my being sixteen. That didn't explain his lack of conversation seven years later, however. Maybe his appearance did. Even his detractors admitted that the bishop was strikingly handsome: a fine crop of silver-white hair and a lean legal-looking face. His looks may have been such an asset that he'd never had to use his brain. It's hard to believe that he used it when he asked his wife to marry him. She may have had money. I don't really know.

The bishopess, the fag end of an old Memphis family, was convinced that she was psychic and had second sight. (Her idea of a quiet evening was to stick pins into wax images of her bridge opponents.) She reminded me of an untidy and harassed chipmunk, without a chipmunk's charm. She always looked as if she'd got dressed on the edge of a hurricane. Mrs. Elgin was her husband's intellectual superior. Most people were. Otherwise, they set each other off admirably. He was tall and silver, she was dumpy and dark. While Bishop Elgin looked very impressive in his episcopal vestments, his wife didn't look impressive in anything; she might have achieved a certain dignity in a coffin. Her chief advantage over the bishop was that when she wouldn't have known what she was talking about, she said nothing. Her one flight into irresponsible speech, perhaps, was her assent to the bishop's proposal of marriage. About four times a year she decided that the house was haunted and insisted that the bishop exorcise whatever was favoring them with its attentions.

The bishop got nowhere pointing out that the *Book of Common Prayer* doesn't contain a Rite of Exorcism.

He had the book; she provided him with candles, bought a bell, and told him to get to work. He did, each time more reluctantly, but I don't think he was especially successful. His wife continued to have stitches in her side and still complained of the milk's going sour. (Did I mention that Mrs. Elgin was fond of munching on raw kidneys?)

To get back to Terry Shaw. Newly arrived in Setback, seven years my senior, and even more handsome than Elgin, this blond and blue-eyed cleric moved in. He looked like the Pride of Stockholm. Actually, he was a hopeless playboy from Jasper, Tennessee, who had heard the Call.

The plan was that we'd have a Cozy Bachelor Establishment. The rental agent, one Gurgitt, got wind of this and came to reason with me. I wouldn't buy it. Gurgitt gave a deep sigh.

"My dear Mr. Thornton," he said, turning on all four watts of his charm, "please consider the matter more carefully. You would hardly believe me if I told you how much the University Rental Office spent on redecorating this house after the Wassermanns' sudden departure."

"I probably wouldn't," I said coldly.

Gurgitt winced but held on to his brave smile. He then explained that cozy bachelor establishments were frowned upon: too many wild parties. The Wassermanns, he added, had been *ideal* tenants.

My manner became even colder. I reminded him that I had seen the house before redecoration, and that some of those ideal evenings at home must have been pretty noisy in their way, judging from the spatters and stains, not only in the bedroom that Langweilig had equipped as a full-blown laboratory, but everywhere else. The ceilings—all the ceilings!—God alone knows what Langweilig had been up to, but I *did* happen to know that the tenants in the other half of the house had been plagued by stenches, whistlings, rattling pipes, and things that went boom in the night. My inside knowledge gave me the advantage, and Gurgitt could only bite his lips while still trying to smile. To clinch the matter, I pointed out that not only was the Reverend Terence Shaw a clergyman, but that he was Bishop Elgin's assistant. I could not, I said with considerable dignity, foresee any wild parties. Gurgitt sighed again and then left—to slow music, so to speak.

As it happened, Gurgitt was right. The parties were wild, although we made a real effort to keep the decibels to a minimum. Every weekend five or six empty fifths appeared in the trash barrels (which must have given the garbagemen food for thought) but life went merrily on with no complaints from the neighbors to bring Gurgitt back on the scene.

What Terry and I had in common I'll never know. His Simple Faith was enough to curdle Norman Blood. I heard him preach—*once*. Then there was the time that he played the entire album of *The Art of the Fugue* and complained that the "tune" never got anywhere. Furthermore, he actually *liked* carrots and peas cooked together. He used to ask his girl friends over. I wouldn't say they were frumps, but they didn't look like the Junior League, either. That was funny because most of them *were* in the Junior League, and as for those that weren't, it wasn't for lack of trying. Together, Terry and I set out to elevate Setback's tone.

I had a lot of inherited silver and china. We hired Della Bryant, an efficient part-time maid, and entertained with punctilio to the point of retching. We even had the bishop and his wife to dinner. They seemed surprised that they weren't required to eat from paper plates, but the occasion went off agreeably enough otherwise except for Mrs. Elgin's remarking of the house as they left that Something Was Wrong. At the time I paid no attention. Well, Terry wallowed in all this elegance. While I spent a good deal of time between festivities sending my card with "Regrets" scrawled in the corner, Terry's greatest effort was making out guest lists for more parties. These were parties *I* did the cooking for, understand, and it was Della who cleaned up afterwards. But on the whole, Terry and I got along well enough, though we had an occasional sharp exchange.

The first such was late one afternoon about three weeks after Terry moved in. I came home from a late class and found him constructing hors d'oeuvres that would have sent Escoffier screaming to the nearest hamburger joint. Terry was in the kitchen, a good fifty feet from the bathroom. The shower was on full, and the whole bathroom and the adjoining hall were so thick with steam that I thought the wallpaper would peel down in sheets.

"Did you forget that you left the shower on?" I asked.

Terry sampled some of the mess he was fooling with and said he hadn't left the shower on.

"Well, it's still running," I told him.

"Dripping, you mean? If it's leaking we'd better get a plumber."

"You go look at it. If that's what it does when it leaks, we don't need a plumber. We better call in the Coast Guard."

"Oh, quit bitching, and go turn it off!"

He had a number of expressions that I didn't expect to find used by the cloth.

"Turn it off yourself. *I* didn't turn it on. *I* just came home—to find the bathroom half-drowned and you in here lousing up cream cheese."

Terry slammed down the knife and walked out of the kitchen. The sound of running water ceased, and he was back.

"That's a pretty childish trick to pull!" he growled.

Well, there's no profit in relating our little discussion. Neither of us would believe the other wasn't lying—and we both got pretty sore about stupid practical jokes. Neither one would back down, but eventually it blew over.

In the next month each of us found the shower running full force four or five times, and our mutual recriminations and remonstrances built up to a three-dimensional row that had the elderly couple next door pounding on the party wall with their crutches. It wasn't until, having driven together to Lexington for the day, Terry and I returned to find Old Faithful roaring away in solitude, and then each was convinced of the other's innocence.

Time after time we'd get home and find that damned shower playing with itself, sometimes hot, sometimes cold, but always with the valve wide open. We tried tying the faucets together with piano wire. We even attacked it with a wrench—inexpertly, neither of us being what Della called "handy"—but at least we were *there* when it flooded, and the plumber never was.

The plumber was no help at all. Once we telephoned him when the shower was making such a racket that I could hardly hear the man. The cascade went on until the doorbell rang, and by the time the plumber was through the front door, the only disturbance in the bathroom was Terry: he was yelling things he normally wouldn't even spell. Remembering Mrs. Elgin's remark, I finally decided that we were haunted. But I said nothing to Terry.

Della said a good deal to both of us. She was good tempered, but I couldn't blame her for objecting to climbing a stepladder so often to mop up the condensation and water stains on the bathroom and hall ceilings. Della had worked for the Wassermanns for a time, and she said that she used to have the same trouble cleaning up after "them un-Christian goings-on" of the departed couple, only they were worse.

One Wednesday in November, Terry was supposed to go parish-hopping on some diocesan business. I left before he got up and got back home around 6 P.M. I was irritated but not surprised to find the shower going. I stuck my head in the bathroom, on the off chance that Terry had collapsed on the floor.

"You there?" I yelled.

There was no answer, so I looked around the stall.

He wasn't there. I turned the damned thing off and went to the kitchen to mix up a quart of stiff martinis. When I got back to the bathroom, all was quiet.

As I passed Terry's bedroom door, I noticed that his suitcase was still on the bed where he must have been packing that morning. I realized that he hadn't gone to Lynchbury after all. Just then the telephone rang. It was the bishop, and he wanted to know where Terry was. I told his nibs that Terry wasn't at home.

"Did he go to Lynchbury, do you know?" asked Elgin.

"I don't know, but his suitcase is still here. I thought he might be at your office."

The bishop sounded a little miffed and asked me to have Terry call him in the morning. I drank the martinis and went to bed looped.

At nine-thirty on Thursday morning I woke up wishing I were dead. On Thursday I had no classes, but I was never able to make much of it because of the things I did the night before. I lay a while in a sort of embalmed coma before I became aware of a watery bedlam in the bathroom. Swearing I'd wrench the pipes out of the wall, I lurched across the bedroom, managing to get the door open before I went through it. At that moment the water went off, and I heard Terry making those noises he called singing. I went into the bathroom. Terry stepped around the enclosure and reached for a towel.

"Be out in a minute. What're you doing home? You sick?"

"Merely dead," I answered. "Where were *you* all night?"

He was trying to mop his back.

"Where would I be? In bed, naturally."

He dropped the towel and flexed his biceps before the mirror.

"Are you off on Wednesdays now?" he asked, baring his teeth to admire their perfection.

"It must be wonderful to be beautiful," I said, "and for your information, this is Thursday."

Terry looked at me severely, his big-brother manner bulging out like his deltoids.

"If you must go to bed crocked, Peter, you could at least keep a calendar by the alarm clock."

This annoyed me, because though I *had* gone to bed crocked, I wasn't *still* crocked.

"*I* happen to know that today is Thursday. In the first place, I had to conduct that freshman seminar on the French Revolution at five o'clock Wednesday, which, thank God, is only once a week, and I did it yesterday. In the second place, the bishop called last night while you were helling around and asked if you weren't supposed to be in Lynchbury or some such God-forsaken spot on Wednesday, and why weren't you there. And in the third place—"

Terry interrupted, and we argued about what day it was until he thought of the morning paper, and stalked majestically to the front door. He remembered just in time that he was in no condition to appear in the full light of Johnson Street. He got his dressing gown. Then he got the morning paper. The *Post-Journal* was never up to much, but it did carry the day of the week. Terry stared at the front page.

"It says Thursday," he remarked, sounding quite aggrieved.

I said nothing, audibly.

"But this is *Wednesday!* It's *got* to be Wednesday," he said.

I was beginning to worry. It was plain he wasn't trying to be funny. Anyway, his sense of humor, such as it was, didn't run to that sort of thing. Jerking chairs from under people was Terry's idea of a *jeu d'esprit*.

I reminded him: "The bishop wants you to call him."

Terry looked confused, but he telephoned. The conversation at Terry's end was pretty monotonous. "Yes, sir," he said. "Yes, sir." And in a different key, "Yes,

sir." Then there was some burbling sort of assurance
that he'd be at the office within the hour. The poor guy
looked more worried than ever when he came back to
the sitting room.

"The bishop says it's Thursday," he complained.

"How clever of him! That's the sort of thing it takes
a prelate to grasp," I said.

Then I regretted my sarcasm. Instead of flaring up,
Terry just looked more miserable and sank down in an
armchair, his wet calves on the cushion.

"I don't understand it," he said. "I know exactly
what I did yesterday—*Tuesday*. I went to bed before
you did—about ten-thirty, right?"

I nodded.

"Then I got up this morning and packed my bag.
After that I got in the shower—and then you came in.
Isn't that right?"

I didn't nod. I didn't really know what to say. Finally
I told him what I've written down here. I told him I was
doubly sure because on Wednesday morning the car
wouldn't start and old Dr. Hendricks had come along
and given me a lift to the campus. I offered to call Hendricks for corroboration, but Terry didn't insist. He just
sat there for a time and looked at nothing. At last he
got himself off to his office.

I'm not sure what he told the bishop, but he must
have been sufficiently upset to tell what he thought was
the truth. Within the hour, he telephoned, saying that
Bishop and Mrs. Elgin were dropping in that evening.
He sounded frantic. I felt the same way.

The bishop and his wife arrived about eight o'clock.
He looked uneasy and embarrassed, but businesslike.
She looked like a remnant counter. She confided that a
Los Angeles *guru* had supplied her with her super-
sanctified draperies. To me she looked like a plush and
ball-fringe Victorian window-treatment—applied to a
doghouse. (I later learned from Terry that the bishop,
with deplorable profanity, had refused to bring his vest-

ments. Terry, with equal firmness, though greater polish, had declined to wear *his*.)

The four of us arranged ourselves in the bathroom, lit two slender beeswax candles, and waited for things to happen. The bishop intoned something that started, *"Retro me Satanas,"* a hot little number he'd obviously cribbed from a rival liturgy. While his adenoidal notes reverberated in the medicine cabinet, the bishopess began to wail in a high, piercing tone that must have uncapped several bottles, rocking back and forth like a woman in agony or labor. At the end of three minutes of this performance, which I thought edifying but futile, the shower head swiveled in our direction and cut loose. It extinguished the candles, but only as if in passing. It was clearly aiming for us. We retired dankly to the sitting room.

I staggered to the linen closet for towels.

Mrs. Elgin glared from among the wet locks flopping over her face.

"Edward, I *told* you *both* to wear your *vestments!* This would *never* have happened if you'd been *properly* dressed!"

The bishop mopped his face, muttering to himself.

"Edward?" said Mrs. Elgin.

The bishop flung down the towel and returned his wife's glare.

"Agnes, I must really refuse to have anything further to do with the whole—ah—um—disastrous matter! Obviously, it's a question of—ah—plumbing. I do not believe in exorcism, and even if I did, I should not employ it to turn off a faucet!"

Terry and I looked at each other. The bishop and his wife were in such tempers that neither of us cared to intervene.

"But they've *already* tried the plumber," said Mrs. Elgin, a little more calmly. She peered again into the bathroom. I followed her and turned on the light. Then she tiptoed to the shower.

"I *wonder* . . . ?" she murmured. "I wonder if a little *alchemy* might be the answer."

"Alchemy?" I repeated, as dazed as I was wet.

"Well—" She charged by me and went to the bishop. "Edward, I've *just* had an idea! *Do* you think that *alchemy* might be the answer?"

"No," said the bishop shortly.

"Well—you know, it *does* deal with metals. *Perhaps* we could . . ."

"Agnes, I refuse to stand here dripping wet and— um—ah—discuss such a—ah—um—suggestion."

Mrs. Elgin had plainly gone off on a tack of her own.

"Count Bernard," she said to herself, "recommended quicksilver, but *somebody* wrote about borax, too. *Do* you have any borax?" she asked, turning to Terry and me. Before we could answer, she shook her head. "No—quicksilver *is* better! I'll look it up in my *Coelum Philosophorum.*"

"I do not care if you consult Fanny Farmer," snapped the bishop. "*I* shall go home and have a hot bath."

Mrs. Elgin went back to the bathroom and collected her candles. The bishop spoke to us in a low voice.

"You take my advice, young men, and employ a— um—competent plumber to investigate that shower. There is probably an—um—expansion and—ah— contraction of the valves. This building is at least half a century old."

After I'd seen the episcopal couple to the door, I told Terry that I didn't think I could stand many more evenings like that one, come hell or High Church. He agreed.

The following evening, however, the telephone rang just before dinner, and I answered it, Terry being busy again with hors d'oeuvres. The person at the other end sounded very dim, but I finally understood that it was Mrs. Elgin.

"I have to *whisper*," she whispered. *"Edward's* in the next room. I *think* I've found a *way*."

"A way?" I asked.

"Edward has a meeting tonight. I'll drive over as *soon* as he's gone. Are you all going to be home?"

I've never been good at thinking fast.

"I am," I said, "but Terry has to go to the meeting, too."

"I'll be over a *little* past eight," said Mrs. Elgin, and rang off.

Terry left before she arrived.

Mrs. Elgin was dressed very much as usual, but she was carrying an attaché case. I had already decided that I would be a nonperformer this time, and I was relieved when she said that she'd work alone.

"You can watch me make the *preliminary* arrangements," she said, smiling.

"That'll be interesting," I lied.

It wasn't so much interesting as baffling. First she produced two squat, thick candles set in what looked like a pair of hoofs. Then she took out what seemed to be a box of ointment and put it carefully on the edge of the tub. Finally she poured a thick red liquid into the palm of her left hand and with her right forefinger drew a five-sided figure on the white tile floor.

"Is this *alchemy?*" I asked, having other ideas.

Mrs. Elgin looked up from beneath her brows.

"Not *exactly*. I'm trying a little mixture of—ah, *arrangements*."

"A mixture? Isn't that a pentacle?" It looked more like witchcraft to me.

Mrs. Elgin giggled as she rinsed off her hands in the basin.

"Well—you *know,* it doesn't *hurt* to try *every* means."

I backed away from the woman, smiling in the hope of humoring her.

"Oh, no! Of course not!" I babbled. "Any good means to a good end, I always say."

Mrs. Elgin surveyed her preparations. Then she

struck a match and lit the two candles. The stench was
not believable.

"Well," she said, "I *do* believe I'm ready. I—I'll *just*
close the door, dear. This shouldn't take long—*if* I'm
on the right track."

I was glad to see the door close. I went to the kitchen
and made myself a stiff Scotch. Then I sneaked back
and put my ear to the door. I couldn't identify the slight
noise at first. Then I realized that it was flesh on flesh;
evidently the bishopess was rubbing something on her
skin. Then I heard her moving about, setting up the rest
of her "arrangements," while humming "America." Or
maybe it was "God Save the Queen." I finished my
Scotch and went for another.

From the other side of the door I could hear a low
chanting. When I got close enough to hear the words, I
wondered what Bishop Elgin's reaction would have
been. The words were only too clear.

*"Credo in Deum Patrem Luciferum, qui creavit coe-
lum et terram. Et in filium ejus Beelzebub. . . ."*

I retired to the sitting room to think and drink. I
could still hear snippets of the chant.

I was in the kitchen mixing another Scotch when I
heard a great noise from the other end of the house.
Before I got back to the bathroom door, I knew what at
least part of it was.

The shower was on. This time it sounded more like
Niagara Falls combined with "The Battle of Trenton."
The din was almost deafening. Then, without warning,
the noise stopped. The shower gave a sort of gurgle,
rather like a chuckle, succeeded by a very dead silence.
I stood waiting. I continued to wait. I waited for ten
minutes by my watch.

"Mrs. Elgin?"

There was no answer.

I tried the door and found it unlocked. On the floor I
saw the candles (out, but still smoking), the box that
had contained the ointment, and Mrs. Elgin's clothing,
including falsies. I did not find Mrs. Elgin.

I turned on the light and looked again. She wasn't there. I looked in the shower stall. Empty. Something struck me as different, but at first I couldn't pinpoint it, blinking in the light and fortified by Scotch as I was. Then I saw. I looked again. The shower head, the faucets, and every other metal fixture in the bathroom looked like very highly polished brass, or—I tried to reject it, but my mind was too quick—*gold*.

I felt I shouldn't drink any more Scotch, having had five already. I compromised by pouring myself a triple brandy.

At ten forty-five Terry walked in. He stopped and stared at me.

"Nev' mine *me*," I said, "jus' go in th' bathroom." I hiccupped. "No—don' argue—jus' go on in there."

He went. In five seconds he was back, saying, "What are all those rags?"

"Sit—*hup!*—down," I said.

He sat. Glowering.

Then I told him.

"Where—where *is* she?" he asked.

I shrugged. "We gonna tell th' bishop?" I asked.

"Tell him *what?*" Terry snarled.

"She's gone—gone, gone, gone." I waved my hand. "Like good ol' Midas."

"What *are* you driveling about?"

"Dinja see th' fau-faucets, Terry?"

"The faucets?"

"Go look again," I said.

He went. Then he went to the kitchen and came back with a drink. He looked at me. "This is getting out of hand," he said.

"Yeh."

"What're we going to do?"

"Drink," I said.

"That won't solve anything, you ass!"

"Helps."

"In the meantime, the bishop will be wondering where his wife is."

"Why?" I asked.

"Don't ask me," said Terry. "You're rational even when you're drunk."

"Maybe she's got a twenny-four-hour return ticket, like you. Be back tomorra—same time—same station—" I hiccupped again. "Choo-choo, not radio," I added, to make things crystal clear.

"In a crisis you're a great help," said Terry bitterly.

"Have 'nother drink," I suggested.

He started to say something. Instead, he tossed off his highball and returned to the kitchen.

"I'll drink this and then call the bishop," he said in a despondent tone.

"Jus' d-d-do that."

He did.

I went into my room, flopped onto the bed, and put two pillows over my head. In a short time they were snatched off.

"Wass marra?"

"Get up! The bishop's coming over to discuss this thing."

"*Won't!* He's your bish-bishop—'s not mine."

Terry considered, standing in the dim light from the door. "Yeah. Maybe it'll be better if you stay out of sight. Sleep tight, you damned lush!"

"Tight awready," I muttered.

Terry left, slamming the bedroom door.

When I heard Terry getting ready for bed, I called to him. "Elgins go home?"

"The bishop went home. Mrs. Elgin is still missing."

I remember nothing more until eight o'clock the next morning.

The whole day was pretty awful. Fortunately I had no classes after lunch. I came home and fell into bed, too tired to bother about pajamas.

At nine-thirty that evening I came to with a jerk, not knowing what had awakened me. Then I heard her high, indignant voice.

"What are you and *Terry* doing here? I *told* Peter I wanted to be *alone!"*

Forgetting that I was stark naked, I tore into the hall and collided with Mrs. Elgin, similarly attired.

She screamed and scuttled into Terry's bedroom. The bishop, glorious in lawn sleeves and all the rest of it, stared at me, stricken. Terry, too, was in full regalia, including stole. They seemed distinctly overdressed to me.

I made Medici Venus gestures myself and scrambled back to the bedroom for my shirt and trousers.

My maternal grandmother used to say that you could get clean in a quart of water if you had to. How right she was. We stopped trying to figure things out.

We also stopped taking showers and used the hand basin.

After a week of washing by the square inch, I decided to break the lease. I didn't need gold plumbing, but I *did* need a shower. Terry went with me to the rental office. Gurgitt listened to our story and smiled pityingly. (He was known to the undergraduates as "Laughing Boy", not unreasonably.) I reminded him of my father's long and honorable career at FUC. Gurgitt reminded me of the lease. When he referred to the contract as "watertight," I thought Terry was going to hit him.

"The University Rental Office would be most happy to oblige you, Mr. Thornton," he said, with a smile that made my stomach churn, "in any reasonable request, but you will, I trust, understand that were the University Rental Office to establish such a precedent upon such—unusual—grounds, other leaseholders would naturally expect such an exception to be made for them, too."

"But the house is impossible," I said. "If you don't believe me, come over there with me and see for yourself."

Gurgitt waved a bland hand.

"My dear Mr. Thornton, I can understand that you may have a desire to leave the house, whatever the reasons may be, but you can scarcely expect the University Rental Office to consent to the abrogation of lease on the premise that your shower is haunted."

"If it isn't haunted," said Terry, bristling, "there's something damned wrong with the place. Mr. Thornton is telling you the truth, and Bishop and Mrs. Elgin will corroborate it."

Gurgitt raised his sandy eyebrows.

"Mrs. Elgin! Ah—yes. Well, of course, everyone has a right to their opinions. Mrs. Elgin—um."

"*And* the bishop," repeated Terry, frowning.

"No doubt Bishop Elgin is entitled to *his* opinion, Mr. Shaw, but the University Rental Office really—"

I cut in. "Wait a minute," I said. I had come armed with a towel rack. I unwrapped it, suggested he have it assayed, and then we left. (I later learned that he humored me in this because he thought my parents' death had unsettled my mind.)

The day after, Gurgitt called, suddenly amenable, and hotfooted over to release me from the lease.

The University officials decided to demolish the house and put up another. In the process of demolition, they discovered that every atom of metal—not only *plumbum,* but *ferrum, chromium,* and all the rest of it—had been transmuted into *aurum.* Whether our episcopal Danaë was alone responsible or whether she merely took up and completed whatever it was that the Wassermanns had been working on, I neither know nor care.

With the proceeds the University built three new houses and established a scholarship in memory of my parents. That was nice of them, of course, but I'd have been better pleased if the fund had been in memory of the Elgins.

Anyhow, they're both still around, and my memory of them is something I'd like to forget.

> "No matter what your scientific background,
> emotionally you're an alchemist."
>
> Roger Zelazny,
> Isle of the Dead

Morning-Glory

GENE WOLFE

—

Smythe put his hands behind his head and looked up at the ceiling. He was a short and untidy man now well entered on middle age, and his face showed embarrassment.

"Well, go on," Black said.

Smythe said, "My father felt bread was sacred; if a piece was accidently dropped on the floor he would demand that it be picked up at once and dusted off and eaten; if someone stepped on it he was furious."

"Was this element of your father's character present in reality, or is it only a part of the dream logic?"

Smythe put his head down and looked at Black in irritation. "This is just background," he said. "My father would say, 'Bread is the life of man, you dirty little hyena. Pick it up.' He had been brought up in Germany."

"Specifically, what was your dream?" Black opened his notebook.

Smythe hesitated. For years now he had been giving

193

Black entries, and he had almost always made them up, thinking them out on the bus he took to the campus each morning. It seemed now a sort of desecration, a cheat, to tell Black a real dream. "I was a vine," he said, "and I was pounding on a translucent wall. I knew there was light on the other side, but it didn't do me any good where I was. My father's voice kept saying: *See! See! See!* Over and over like that. My father is dead."

"I had supposed so," Black said. "What do you think this dream has to do with your father's reverence for bread?"

More disturbed by the dream than he wanted Black to know, Smythe shrugged. "What I was trying to communicate was that my father had a sort of reverence for food. 'You are what you eat,' and all that sort of thing. I chewed morning-glory seeds once."

"Morning-glory seeds?"

"Yes. Morning-glory seeds are supposed to be a sort of hallucinogen, like LSD or peyote."

"I suppose your father caught you and punished you?"

Smythe shook himself with irritation. "Hell no. This wasn't when I was a child; it was about three years ago." He felt frustrated by Black's invincible obtuseness. "All the blah-blah was going on in the newspapers about drugs, and I felt that as a member of the department I ought to know at least a little bit about it. I didn't know where to get LSD or any of those other things, but of course I had morning-glory seed right in the lab." He remembered the paper seed packet with its preposterously huge blue flower and how frightened he had been.

"You didn't think you should obtain departmental permission?"

"I felt," Smythe said carefully, "that it would be better for the department if it were not on record as having officially approved of something of that sort." *Besides,* he told himself savagely, *you were afraid that you would get the permission and then back out; that's the truth, and if you tell too many lies you may forget it.*

"I suppose you were probably right," Black said. He closed his notebook with a bored snap. "Did you really have hallucinations?"

"I'm not sure. It may have been self-hypnosis."

"Nothing striking though?"

"No. But you see, I had eaten—at least in a sense— the morning glory. I think that may be why my father—" He hesitated, lost in the complications of the thought he was trying to formulate. Black was the Freudian; he himself, at least by training, a Watsonian behaviorist.

"Further dreams may tell us more about what's going on," Black said. It was one of his stock dismissals. "Don't forget you've got counseling tomorrow." A Smythe closed the door Black added, "Good-bye, Schmidt."

Smythe turned, wanting to say that his father's father had been American consul in Nuremberg, but it was too late. The door had shut.

To reach his own laboratory he went down two flights of stairs and along a seemingly endless hall walled with slabs of white marble. The last lecture of the day had been finished at four, but as he approached the laboratory area in the rear of the building he heard the murmur of a few late-staying students still bent over their white rats. Just as he reached his own door one of these groups broke up, undergraduates, boys in sweaters and jeans, and girls in jeans and sweaters, drifting out into the corridor. A girl with long blond hair and a small heart-shaped face stopped as he opened the door, peering in at the twisting, glowing, rectangular tubes that filled the bright room. On an impulse Smythe said, "Come in. Would you like to see it?"

The girl stepped inside, and after a moment put the books she was carrying on one of the lab benches. "What do you do here?" she said. "I don't think I've ever seen this place." The light made her squint.

Smythe smiled. "I'm called a vine runner."

She looked at him quizzically.

"People who put rats through mazes are called rat runners; people who use flatworms are worm runners."

"You mean all these square pipes are to test the intelligence of plants?"

"Plants," Smythe said, allowing himself only a slight smile, "lacking a nervous system, have no intelligence. When they display signs of what, in such higher creatures as flatworms, would be called intelligence, we refer to it as para-intelligence or pseudo intelligence. Come here, and I'll show you how we study it."

The rectangular passages were of clouded, milky white plastic panels held together with metal clips. He unfastened a panel, showing her the green, leafy tendril inside.

"I don't understand," she said. "And I don't think you really believe that about pseudo intelligence. Intelligence ought to be defined by the way something responds, not by what you find inside when you cut it open."

"Out of fear of being accused of heresy I won't agree with you—but I have, on occasion, been known to point out to my departmental superiors that our age is unique in preferring a pond worm to an oak tree."

The girl was still looking at the twisting white passages sprawling along the bench. "How does it work?" she asked. "How do you test them?"

"It's simple, really, once you understand that a plant 'moves' by growth. That's why it has no musculature, which in turn, by the way, is why it has no nervous system. These mazes offer the plants choice points in the form of forked passages with equal amounts of light available in each direction. As you see, we keep this room brightly lit, and these plastic panels are translucent. The trick is that we have more than twenty grades, ranging from ones which admit almost as much light as plate glass to ones which are nearly opaque." He held up the panel he had unfastened so that she could see the light through it, then rummaged in a drawer to produce another of the same color which nonetheless admitted much less light.

"I see," the girl said. "The smart plants find out by and by that there's less and less light when they go down a wrong turn, and so they stop and go back."

"That's right, except that the tendrils don't, of course, actually turn around and grow backward. The growth of the 'wrong' tendrils just slows and stops, and new growth begins where the bad decision was made."

The girl reached down and gently, almost timidly, stroked a leaf. "It's like a society more than it is an animal, isn't it? I mean it sort of grows an institution, and then if it finds out it's going the wrong way it grows another one. What's the name of this plant?"

"Bindweed," Smythe told her. "It's one of the most intelligent we've found. Far brighter, for example, than scarlet runner bean—which in turn is more intelligent itself than, say, most varieties of domestic grapes, which are among the stupidest vines."

"I ought to be going now," the girl said. She picked up her books. "What's that big one, though? The one that sprawls all over?"

Smythe was replacing the panel he had removed for her. "A morning-glory," he said. "I should rip it out, actually, so that I could use the room and the maze components for something else. What I did was to subject the seeds to radiation, and apparently that destroyed the vine's ability to discriminate between light levels. Once it makes a wrong turn it simply continues indefinitely in that direction."

"You mean its mind is destroyed?"

"No, not really. That's the odd thing. On other types of tests—for example, when we lop off tendrils until it memorizes a pattern of 'safe' turns: right, right, left, left, or something of the sort—it still does quite well. But it will keep running down a passage of diminishing light level until it reaches nearly total darkness."

"How horrible," the girl said. "Could I see it?"

While he was unfastening a panel for her she asked suddenly, "Did you see that awful show on television the other night? about the turtles?"

He shook his head.

"They showed this atoll where there had been a hydrogen bomb test years ago. The sea turtles come there every year to lay eggs, and when they came after the test the radiation made them forget, somehow, that they were supposed to go back to the ocean. They just kept crawling inland, crawling and crawling until they died in the jungle and their bodies rotted. The shells are still there, and the birds have built nests in some of them." She looked intently for a moment at the spindly, white vine he showed her inside the maze. "It never blooms in there, does it?"

"No," he said, "it never blooms."

"I wonder what it looks like, to it, inside there."

"Like marble corridors, I suppose. As though it were walking down marble corridors."

The girl looked at him oddly, shifting her books on her hip.

After she had gone he wondered why he had said what he had, even putting four plastic panels together and peering down the short passage they formed. The white plastic did not actually look a great deal like marble.

On the bus he found himself still thinking of it, and forced himself to divert his attention, but everything he found to focus it on seemed worse. Newspaper headlines warned him of the air pollution he could see by merely looking through the windows of the bus, and the transistor radio of the man in the seat next to his told him that France, the world's fifth-ranking nuclear power, had now joined the "total destruction club" by acquiring (like the United States, the Soviet Union, China, and Britain) enough hydrogen bombs to eliminate life on Earth. He looked at the man holding the radio, half tempted to make some bitter remark, but the man was blind and for some reason this made him turn away again.

Once at home he worked on his book for an hour (Publish or Perish!), ate dinner, and spent the remainder of the evening watching television with his wife. They went to bed after the late news, but Smythe found he could not sleep. After an hour he got up, made himself a drink, and settled into his favorite chair to read.

He was walking through an enormous building like a mausoleum, trailing behind him a sort of filmy green vapor insubstantial as mist. To either side of him doors opened showing gardens, or tables piled with food, or beds so large as to be nearly rooms themselves; but the doors opened only after he had gone a step beyond, and he could not turn back. At last he made a determined effort, turning around and flailing his arms as if he were going to swim through the air back to one of the open doors—but the column of mist behind him which had seemed so insubstantial was now a green ram propelling him relentlessly down the corridor.

He woke up sweating and found that he had knocked his glass from the arm of his chair, spilling tepid water which had once been ice cubes over his crotch.

He changed into dry pajamas and returned to bed, but he could not sleep again. When his wife got up the next morning she found him reading the paper, shaved and fully dressed. "You look chipper," she said. "Sleep well?"

He shook his head. "I hardly slept at all, really. I've been up most of the night."

She looked skeptical. "It doesn't seem to have hurt you."

"It didn't." He turned a page of the paper. "I've got graduate counseling today—you know, suggesting topics for a thesis—and I've been thinking up ideas for them."

"You usually hate that," his wife said.

And he usually did, he reflected as he boarded his

bus. But today, for almost the first time since that terri-
fying day (which he could not date) when he had wakened to find himself not only a man, but a man whose
life had already, in its larger outlines, been decided in
incompetency and idiocy by his father and the callow
boy who had once been himself, he found he no longer
regretted that his father had shattered forever the family
tradition of diplomacy to become a small-town lawyer
and leave his son a scholar's career.

What he was going to do he had decided in the dark
hours while his wife and the city slept, but there were
ramifications to be considered and possibilities to be
guarded against. To propose a program was not nearly
enough. He would have to sell it. To the head of the
department, if at all possible. To as many of his fellow
department members as he could; taking care to make
no enemies, so that even those not in support were at
least no worse than neutral. In time to the university
administration and perhaps even to the public at large.
But first of all to at least one intelligent graduate student. Two or three, preferably, but at least one; one
without fail.

He was ten minutes early reaching his office. He unlocked his desk and spent a few moments glancing over
the list of prospective doctoral candidates who would be
coming in to see him, but he was too excited to pay it
proper attention—the names danced before his eyes and
he threw it back into his in-box and instead arranged
the chair in which the students would sit and squared
the bronze plaque reading *Dr. Smythe* on his desk.

Seated, he looked at the empty chair, imagining it
filled already by an eager, and probably fearful, candi-
date. Graduate students complained eternally of the in-
attention, hostility, and indifference of their overloaded
counselors, men who were expected to guide them,
teach, do original research, write, and play faculty politics all at the same time; but his, he vowed, would have
no reason to complain of him. Not this year. Not next
year either. (He would not deceive himself about the

time they would need.) Nor the next. Nor the decade following.

He did not have the slightest idea how it could be done. He admitted that honestly to himself, though he would never admit it to the student. But the student would. The student, the right student, would have a hundred utterly insane ideas, and he would talk them over with him, pointing out flaws and combining half-workable thoughts until they hit on something that might be tried, something to be guided by his experience and the student's imagination.

There was a shuffle of feet in the reception room and he stood up, setting his face in the proper expression of reserved friendliness; a few minutes later he was saying to an earnest young man in his visitor's chair, "I'm quite certain it's never been done before. Never even been attempted. It would give you something quite different from the usual business of checking someone else's bad work." The young man nodded and Smythe leaned back, timing his pause like an actor. "You see, the idea of para-intelligence in plants is so new that re-education—therapy, if you like, to a radiation-damaged instinct—has scarcely been dreamed of. And if we can learn to help children by studying rats, what might we not learn from plants when plants are analogs of whole societies?" He gestured toward the window and the threatened and choking world outside. "What you learn"—he strove to strike the right note—"might be widely applicable."

The young man nodded again, and for a moment Smythe saw something, a certain light, flicker in his expression. The green fingers of Smythe's mind reached toward that light, ready to grasp whatever support he found and never let go.

Ascension:
A Workday Arabesque

VIRGINIA KIDD

—

Cliff-climber, Jupiter Tonans, Jesus—the lineman!

To the naked eye he looms in courage
Bare as breasts, and as accustomed,
Slung high from the heart of a tree: Christ,
Who walked, simian, up on his clever toes from con-
    crete,
Black as the pole that bears him two-dimensioned
On the abstract sky, intimate and distinguished with
The crosspiece; Jove, holding lightning-wires in gaunt-
    leted
Contempt, he is yet wholly dependent of a foot of web-
    bing,
Clumsy-booted toes, and a basic valor: cliff-man
Discovering the cavity of walls, getting a toehold
On heaven;
            the moment closer when he must no longer
    worship
But become, his vulnerable god.

In which an Old Enemy becometh a Desprit
Ally—transmutationally.

The Devil You Don't

KEITH LAUMER

—

Curlene Dimpleby was in the shower when the doorbell
rang.

"Damn!" Curlene said. She did one more slow revolution with her face upturned to the spray, then turned
the big chrome knobs and stepped out onto the white
nylon wall-to-wall, just installed that week. The full-
length mirror, slightly misty, reflected soft curves nicely
juxtaposed with slimness. She jiggled in a pleasant way
as she toweled off her back, crossed the bedroom and
pulled on an oversized white terry-cloth robe, padded
barefoot along the tiled hall to the front door. The bell
rang again as she opened the door. A tall, wide, red-
haired young man stood there, impeccably dressed in
white flannels, a blue blazer with a fancy but somewhat
tarnished pocket patch, and white buck shoes. He
jerked his finger from the push button and smiled, an
engaging display of china-white teeth.

"I'm . . . I'm sorry, ma'am," he said in a voice so
deep Curlene imagined she could feel it through the
soles of her feet. "I, uh . . . I thought maybe you
didn't hear the bell." He stopped and blushed.

"Why, that's perfectly charming," Curlene said. "I mean, that's perfectly all right."

"Uh . . . I . . . came to fix the lights."

"Golly, I didn't even know they were out." She stepped back, and as he hesitated, she said, "Come on in. The fuse box is in the basement."

The big young man edged inside.

"Is, ah, is Professor Dimpleby here?" he asked doubtfully.

"He's still in class. Anyway, he wouldn't be much help. Johnny's pretty dumb about anything simple. But he's a whiz at quantum theory."

Curlene was looking at his empty hands.

"Possibly I'd better come back later . . . ?" he said.

"I notice," Curlene said reproachfully, "you don't have any tools."

"Oh—" This time the blush was of the furious variety. "Well, I think I'll just—"

"You got in under false pretenses," she said softly. "Gee, a nice looking fella like you. I should think you could get plenty of girls."

"Well, I—"

"Sit down," Curlene said gently. "How about a cup of coffee?"

"Thanks, I never tr— I don't care for . . . I mean, I'd better go—"

"Do you smoke?"

He raised his arms and looked down at himself with a startled expression. Curlene laughed.

"Oh, sit down and tell me all about it."

The large young man swallowed.

"You're not a student, Mr. . . . ?" Curlene urged.

"No—not exactly—" He sat gingerly on the edge of a Danish chair. "Of course, one is always learning."

"I mean, did you ever think about going up to a coed and just asking her for a date?"

"Well, not exactly—"

"She'd probably jump at the chance. It's just that you're too shy, Mr. . . . ?"

"Well, I suppose I am rather retiring, ma'am. But after all—"

"It's this crazy culture we live in. It puts some awful pressures on people. And all so needlessly. I mean, what could be more natural—"

"Ah—when are you expecting Professor Dimpleby?" the young man cut in. He was blushing from neat white collar to window's peak now.

"Oh, I'm embarrassing you. Sorry. I think I *will* get some coffee. Johnny's due back any time."

The coffee maker was plugged in and snorting gently to itself. Curlene hummed as she poured two cups, put them on a Japanese silver tray with creamer and sugar bowl. The young man jumped up as she came in.

"Oh, keep your seat." She put the tray on the ankle-high coffee table. "Cream and sugar?" She put his cup before him.

"Yes, with strawberries," the young man murmured. He seemed to be looking at her chin. "Or possibly rose-buds. Pink ones."

"They *are* nice, aren't they?" a booming male voice called from the arched entry to the hall. A tall man with tousled gray hair and a ruddy face was pulling off a scarf.

"Johnny, hi, home already?" Curlene smiled at her husband as she poured cream in the cups.

"The robe, Curl," Professor Dimpleby said. He gave the young man an apologetic grin. "Curl was raised in Samoa; her folks were missionaries, you know. She never quite grasped the concept that the female bosom is a secret."

Curlene tucked the robe up around her neck. "Golly," she said. "I'm sorry if I offended, Mr. . . . ?"

"On the contrary," the young man said, rising and giving his host a slight bow. "Professor Dimpleby, my name is, er, Lucifer."

Dimpleby put out his hand. "Lucifer, hey? Nothing wrong with that. Means 'Light-bearer.' But it's not a name you run into very often. It takes some gumption to flaunt the old taboos."

"Mr. Lucifer came to fix the lights," Curlene said.

"Ah—not really," the young man said quickly. "Actually, I came to, er, ask for help, Professor. Your help."

"Oh, really?" Dimpleby seated himself and stirred sugar into Curlene's cup and took a noisy sip. "Well, how can I be of service?"

"But first, before I impose on you any further, I need to be sure you understand that I really *am* Lucifer. I mean, I don't want to get by on false pretenses." He looked at Curlene anxiously. "I would have told you I wasn't really an electrician, er, Mrs.—"

"Just call me Curl. Sure you would have."

"If you say your name's Lucifer, why should I doubt it?" Dimpleby asked with a smile.

"Well, the point is—I'm *the* Lucifer. You know. The, er, the Devil."

Dimpleby raised his eyebrows. Curlene made a sound of distressed sympathy.

"Of course the latter designation has all sorts of negative connotations," Lucifer hurried on. "But I assure you that most of what you've heard is grossly exaggerated. That is to say, I'm not really as bad as all that. I mean, there are different kinds of er, badness. There's the real evil, and then there's sin. I'm, ah, associated with sin."

"The distinction seems a subtle one, Mr., ah, Lucifer—"

"Not really, Professor. We all sense instinctively what true evil is. Sin is *statutory* evil—things that are wrong because there's a rule against them. Like, ah, smoking cigarettes and drinking liquor and going to movies on Sunday, or wearing lipstick and silk hose, or eating pork, or swatting flies, depending on which set of rules you're going by. They're corollaries to ritual virtues such as lighting candles or wearing out-of-date styles."

Dimpleby leaned back and steepled his fingers. "Hmmm. Whereas genuine evil . . . ?"

"Murder, violence, lying, cheating, theft," Lucifer enumerated. "Essentially, sin includes anything that looks like it might be fun."

"Come to think of it, I've never heard anything in praise of fun from the anti-sin people," Curl said thoughtfully.

"Not from any ecclesiastic with a good head for fund-raising," Dimpleby conceded.

"It's all due to human laziness, I'm afraid," Lucifer said sadly. "It seems so much easier and more convenient to observe a few ritual prohibitions than to actually give up normal business practices."

"Hey," Curlene said. "Let's not wander off into one of those academic discussions. What about you being"—she tittered—"the Devil?"

"It's quite true."

"Prove it," Curlene said promptly.

"Well, er, how?" Lucifer inquired

"Do something. You know, summon up a demon; or transform pebbles into jewels; or give me three wishes; or—"

"Gosh, Mrs. Dimpleby—"

"Curl."

"Curl; you've got some erroneous preconceptions—"

"When they start using four-syllable words, I always know they're stalling," Curl said blandly.

Lucifer swallowed. "This isn't a good idea," he said. "Suppose somebody walked in?"

"They won't."

"Now, Curl, you're embarrassing our guest again," Dimpleby said mildly.

"No, it's all right, Professor," Lucifer said worriedly. "She's quite right. After all, I'm supposed to be a sort of, ahem, mythic figure. Why should she believe in me without proof?"

"Especially when you blush so easily," Curl said.

"Well . . ." Lucifer looked around the room. His

eyes fell on the aquarium tank which occupied several square feet of wall space under a bookcase. He nodded almost imperceptibly. Something flickered at the bottom of the tank. Curl jumped up and went over.

"The gravel," she gasped. "It looks different!"

"Diamond, ruby, emerald, and macaroni," Lucifer said. "Sorry about the macaroni. I'm out of practice."

"Do something else!" Curl smiled in eager expectation.

Lucifer frowned in concentration. He snapped his fingers and with a soft *blop!* a small, dark purple, bulbous-bellied, wrinkle-skinned creature appeared in the center of the rug. He was some forty inches in height, with immense feet, totally naked, extravagantly male.

"Hey, for crying out loud, you could give a guy a little warning! I'm just getting ready to climb in the tub, yet!" The small being's bulging red eye fell on Lucifer. He grinned, showing a large crescent of teeth. "Oh, it's you, Nick! Howza boy? Long time no see. Anything I can do for ya?"

"Oops, sorry, Freddy." Lucifer snapped his fingers and the imp disappeared with a sharp *plob!*

"So that's a demon," Curl said. "How come his name is Freddy?"

"My apologies, Curl. He's usually most tastefully clad. Freddy is short for something longer."

"Know any more?"

"Er . . ." He pointed at Curl and made a quick flick of the wrist. In her place stood a tall, wide, huge-eyed coal-black woman in swirls of coarse, unevenly dyed cloth under which bare feet showed. Cheap-looking jewelry hung thick on her wrists, draped her vast bosom, winked on her tapered fingers and in her ears.

Lucifer flicked his fingers again, and a slim, olive-skinned girl with blue-black hair and a hooked nose replaced the buxom Sheban queen. She wore a skirt apparently made from an old gauze curtain and an ornate off-the-bosom vest of colored beads. A golden snake encircled her forehead.

Lucifer motioned again. The Egyptian empress dissolved into a nebulous cloud of pastel-colored gas in which clotted star-dust winked and writhed, to the accompaniment of massed voices humming nostalgic chords amid an odor of magnolia blossoms. Another gesture, and Curl stood again before them, looking slightly dazed.

"Hey, what was that last one?" she cried.

"Sorry, that was Scarlett O'Hara. I forgot she was a figment of the imagination. Those are always a little insubstantial."

"Remarkable," Dimpleby said. "I'll have to concede that you can either perform miracles or accomplish the same result by some other means."

"Gee, I guess you're genuine, all right," Curlene exclaimed. "But somehow I expected a much *older* man."

"I'm not actually a man, strictly speaking, ma'am—Curl. And agewise, well, since I'm immortal, why should I look middle-aged rather than just mature?"

"Tell me," Curlene said seriously. "I've always wondered: what do you want people's souls for?"

"Frankly, ma'am—Curl, that is—I haven't the remotest interest in anyone's soul."

"Really?"

"Really and truly, cross my heart. That's just another of those rumors *they* started."

"Are you sure you're really the Devil and not someone else with the same name?"

Lucifer spread his hands appealingly. "You saw Freddy. And those *are* noodles in the fish tank."

"But—no horns, no hooves, no tail—"

Lucifer sighed. "That idea comes from confusing me with Pan. Since he was a jolly sort of sex-god, naturally he became equated with sin."

"I've always wondered," Curlene said, "just what you did to get evicted from Heaven."

"Please," Lucifer said. "It . . . all dates back to an

incident when I was still an angel." He held up a forestalling hand as Curl opened her mouth. "No, I *didn't* have wings. Humans added those when they saw us levitating, on the theory that anything that flies must have wings. If we were to appear today, they'd probably give us jets."

"Assuming you are, er, what you claim to be," Dimpleby said, "what's this about your needing help?"

"I do," Lucifer said. "Desperately. Frankly, I'm up against something I simply can't handle alone."

"I can't imagine what *I* could do, if you, with your, ah, special talents are helpless," Dimpleby said perplexedly.

"This is something totally unprecedented. It's a threat on a scale I can't begin to describe."

"Well, try," Curl urged.

"Stated in its simplest terms," Lucifer said, "the, ah, plane of existence I usually occupy—"

"Hell, you mean," Curl supplied.

"Well, that's another of those loaded terms. It really isn't a bad place at all, you know—"

"But what about it?" Dimpleby prompted. "What about Hell?"

"It's about to be invaded," Lucifer said solemnly. "By alien demons from another world."

2

It was an hour later. Lucifer, Curlene, and Professor Dimpleby were comfortably ensconced behind large pewter mugs of musty ale at a corner table in the Sam Johnson Room at the Faculty Club.

"Well, now," Dimpleby said affably, raising his tankard in salute, "alien demons, eh? An interesting concept, Mr. Lucifer. Tell us more."

"I've never believed in devils," Curlene said, "or monsters from another planet either. Now all of a sudden I'm supposed to believe in both at once. If it weren't for that Freddy . . ."

"Granted the basic premise, it's logical enough," Dimpleby said. "If earthly imps exist, why not space sprites?"

"Professor, this is more than a bunch of syllogisms," Lucifer said earnestly. "These fellows mean business. They have some extremely potent powers. Fortunately, I have powers they don't know about, too; that's the only way I've held them in check so far—"

"You mean—they're already *here?*" Curlene looked searchingly about the room.

"No—I mean, yes, they're here, but not precisely *here,*" Lucifer clarified. "Look, I'd better fill in a little background for you. You see, Hell is actually a superior plane of existence—"

Curlene choked on her ale in a ladylike way.

"I mean—not *superior,* but, ah, at another level, you understand. Different physical laws, and so on—"

"Dirac levels," Dimpleby said, signaling for refills.

"Right!" Lucifer nodded eagerly. "There's an entire continuum of them, stretching away on both sides; there's an energy state higher on the scale than Hell—Heaven, it's called, for some reason—and one lower than your plane; that's the one Freddy comes from, by the way—"

"Oh, tell me about Heaven," Curlene urged.

Lucifer sighed. "Sometimes I miss the old place, in spite of . . . but never mind that."

"Tell me, Mr. Lucifer," Dimpleby said thoughtfully, "how is it you're able to travel at will among these levels?" As he spoke he pulled an envelope from his pocket and uncapped a ballpoint. "It appears to be that there's an insurmountable difficulty here, in terms of atomic and molecular spectral energy distribution; the specific heat involved . . ." He jotted busily, murmuring to himself.

"You're absolutely right, Professor," Lucifer said, sampling the fresh tankard just placed before him. "Heat used to be a real problem. I'd always arrive in a cloud of smoke and sulphur fumes. I finally solved it by working out a trick of emitting a packet of magnetic energy to carry off the excess."

"Hmmm. How did you go about dissipating this magnetism?"

"I fired it off in a tight beam; got rid of it."

"Beamed magnetism?" Dimpleby scribbled furiously. "Hmmm. Possibly . . ."

"Hey, fellas," Curlene protested. "Let's not talk shop, O.K.?" She turned a fascinated gaze on Lucifer. "You were just telling me about Heaven."

"You wouldn't like it, Curl," he said almost curtly. "Now, Professor—all through history—at least as far as I remember it, and that covers a considerable period— the different energy states were completely separate and self-sufficient. Then, a few thousand years back, one of our boys—Yahway, his name is—got to poking around and discovered a way to move around from one level to another. The first place he discovered was Hell. Well, he's something of a bluenose, frankly, and he didn't much like what he found there: all kinds of dead warriors from Greece and Norway and such places sitting around juicing it and singing, and fighting in a friendly sort of way."

"You mean—Valhalla really exists?" Curlene gasped. "And the Elysian fields?"

Lucifer made a disclaiming wave of the hand. "There've always been humans with more than their share of vital energy. Instead of dying, they just switch levels. I have a private theory that there's a certain percentage of individuals in any level who really belong in the next one up—or down. Anyway, Yahway didn't like what he saw. He was always a great one for discipline, getting up early, regular calisthenics—you know. He tried telling these fellows the error of their ways, but they just laughed him off the podium. So he dropped down one more level, which put him here, a much simpler proposition, nothing but a few tribesmen herding goats. Naturally they were deeply impressed by

a few simple miracles." Lucifer paused to quaff deeply.
He sighed.

"Yes. Well, he's been meddling around down here
ever since, and frankly—but I'm wandering." He hiccupped sternly. "I admit, I never could drink very much
without losing my perspective. Where was I?"

"The invasion," Dimpleby reminded him.

"Oh, yes. Well, they hit us without any warning.
There we were, just sitting around the mead hall taking
it easy, or strolling in the gardens striking our lutes or
whatever we felt like, when all of a sudden—" Lucifer
shook his head bemusedly. "Professor, did you ever
have one of those days when nothing seemed to go
right?"

Dimpleby pursed his lips. "Hmmm. You mean like
having the first flat tire in a year during the worst rain-
storm of the year while on your way to the most important meeting of the year?"

"Or," Curlene said, "like when you're just having a
quick martini to brace yourself for the afternoon and
you spill it on your new frock and when you try to wash
it out, the water's turned off, and when you try to phone
to report *that,* the phone's out, and just then Mrs. Trun-
dle from next door drops in to talk, only you're late for
the Faculty Wives?"

"That's it," Lucifer confirmed. "Well, picture that
sort of thing on a vast scale."

"That's rather depressing," Dimpleby said. "But what
has it to do with the, er, invasion?"

"Everything!" Lucifer said, with a wave of his hands.
Across the room, a well-fleshed matron yelped.

"My olive! It turned into a frog!"

"Remarkable," her table companion said. "Genus
Rana pipiens, I believe!"

"Sorry," Lucifer murmured, blushing, putting his
hands under the table.

"You were saying, Mr. Lucifer?"

"It's them, Professor. They've been sort of leaking
over, you see? Their influence, I mean." Lucifer started

to wave his hands again, but caught himself and put them in his blazer pockets.

"Leaking over?"

"From Hell into this plane. You've been getting just a faint taste of it. You should see what's been going on in Hell, Proffefor—I mean Prossessor—I mean—"

"What *has* been going on?"

"Everything has been going to Hell," Lucifer said gloomily. "What I mean to say is," he said, making an effort to straighten up and focus properly, "that everything that *can* go wrong, *does* go wrong."

"That would appear to be contrary to the statistics of causality," Dimpleby said carefully.

"That's it, Professor! They're upsetting the laws of chance! Now, in the old days, when a pair of our lads stepped outside for a little hearty sword-fighting between drinks, one would be a little drunker than the other, and he'd soon be out of it for the day, while the other chap reeled back inside to continue the party. Now, they each accidentally knee each other in the groin and they both lie around groaning until sundown, which upsets everybody. The same for the lute players and lovers: the strings break just at the most climactic passage—or they accidentally pick a patch of poison ivy for their tryst—or possibly just a touch of diarrhea at the wrong moment—but you can imagine what it's doing to morale."

"Tsk," Dimpleby said. "Unfortunate—but it sounds more disconcerting than disastrous, candidly."

"You think so, Professor? What about when all the ambrosia on hand goes bad simultaneously, and the entire population is afflicted with stomach cramps and luminous spots before the eyes? What about a mix-up at the ferry, that leaves us stuck with three boatloads of graduated Methodist ministers to entertain overnight? What about an ectospheric storm that knocks out all psionics for a week, and has everyone fetching and carrying by hand, and communicating by sign language?"

"Well—that might be somewhat more serious—"

"Oh—oh!" Curlene was pointing with her nose. Her husband turned to see a waiter in weskit and knee-pants back through a swinging door balancing a tray laden with brimming port glasses, at the same moment that a tweedsy pedagogue rose directly behind him and, with a gallant gesture, drew out his fair companion's chair. There was a double *oof!* as they came together. The chair skidded. The lady sat on the floor. The tray distributed its burden in a bright cascade across the furs of a willowy brunette who yowled, whirled, causing her foxtail to slap the face of a small, elaborately mustached man who was on the point of lighting a cigar. As the match flared brightly, with a sharp odor of blazing wool, the tweedsy man bent swiftly to offer a chivalrous hand, and bumped by the rebounding waiter, delivered a smart rap with his nose to the corner of the table.

"My mustache!" the small man yelled.

"Dr. Thorndyke, you're bleeding on my navy-blue crepe!" the lady on the floor yelped. The waiter, still grabbing for the tray, bobbled it and sent it scaling through an olde English window, through which an indignant managerial head thrust in time to receive a glass of water intended for the burning mustache.

Lucifer, who had been staring dazedly at the rapid interplay, made a swift flick of the fingers. A second glass of water struck the small man squarely in the conflagration; the tweedsy man clapped a napkin over his nose and helped up the navy-blue crepe. The waiter recovered his tray and busied himself with the broken glass. The brunette whipped out a hanky and dabbed at her bodice, muttering. The tension subsided from the air.

"You see?" Lucifer said. "That was a small sample of their work."

"Nonsense, Mr. Lucifer," Dimpleby said, smiling amiably. "Nothing more than an accident—a curiously complex interplay of misadventures, true, but still—an accident, nothing more."

"Of course—but that sort of accident can only occur when there's an imbalance in the randomness field!"

"What's that?"

"It's what makes the law of chance work. You know that if you flip a quarter a hundred times it will come up heads fifty times and tails fifty times, or very close to it. In a thousand tries, the ratio is even closer. Now, the coin knows nothing of its past performance—any more than metal filings in a magnetic field know which way the other filings are facing. But the field *forces* them to align parallel—and the randomness field forces the coin to follow the statistical distribution."

Dimpleby pulled at his chin. "In other words, entropy."

"If you prefer, Professor. But you've seen what happens when it's tampered with!"

"Why?" Dimpleby stabbed a finger at Lucifer and grinned as one who has scored a point. "Show me a motive for these hypothetical foreign fiends going to all that trouble just to meddle in human affairs!"

"They don't care a rap for human affairs," Lucifer groaned. "It's just a side effect. They consume energy from certain portions of the trans-Einsteinian spectrum, emit energy in other bands. The result is to disturb the R-field—just as sunspots disrupt the earth's magnetic field!"

"Fooey," Dimpleby said, sampling his ale. "Accidents have been happening since the dawn of time. And according to your own account, these interplanetary imps of yours have just arrived."

"Time scales differ between Hell and here," Lucifer said in tones of desperation. "The infiltration started two weeks ago, subjective Hell-time. That's equal to a little under two hundred years local."

"What about all the coincidences before then?" Dimpleby came back swiftly.

"Certainly, there have always been a certain number of nonrandom occurrences. But in the last two centuries they've jumped to an unheard-of level! Think of all the fantastic scientific coincidences, during that period, for example—such as the triple rediscovery of Mendel's work after thirty-five years of obscurity—or the simultaneous evolutionary theories of Darwin and Wallace—or the identical astronomical discoveries of—"

"Very well, I'll concede there've been some remarkable parallelisms." Dimpleby dismissed the argument with a wave of the hand. "But that hardly proves—"

"Professor—maybe that isn't what you'd call hard scientific proof, but logic—instinct—should tell you that Something's been Happening! Certainly, there were isolated incidents in ancient history—but did you ever hear of the equivalent of a twenty-car pile-up in classical times? The very conception of slapstick comedy based on ludicrous accident was alien to the world until it began happening in real life!"

"I say again—fooey, Mr. Lucifer." Dimpleby drew on his ale, burped gently and leaned forward challengingly. "I'm from New Hampshire," he said, wagging a finger. "You've gotta show me."

"Fortunately for humanity, that's quite impossible," Lucifer said. "*They* haven't penetrated to this level yet; all you've gotten, as I said, is the spill-over effect—" he paused. "Unless you'd like to go to Hell and see for yourself—"

"No, thanks. A faculty tea is close enough for me."

"In that case . . ." Lucifer broke off. His face paled. "Oh, no," he whispered.

"Lucifer—what is it?" Curlene whispered in alarm.

"They—they must have followed me! It never occurred to me—but—" Lucifer groaned. "Professor and Mrs. Dimpleby, I've done a terrible thing! I've led them here!"

"Where?" Curlene stared around the room eagerly.

Lucifer's eyes were fixed on the corner by the fire. He made a swift gesture with the finger of his left hand. Curlene gasped.

"Why—it looks just like a big stalk of broccoli—

except for the eyes, of course—and the little one is a dead ringer for a rhubarb pie!"

"Hmmm." Dimpleby blinked. "Quite astonishing, really." He cast a sidelong glance at Lucifer. "Look here, old man, are you sure this isn't some sort of hypnotic effect?"

"If it is, it has the same effect as reality, Professor," the Devil whispered hoarsely. "And something has to be done about it, no matter what you call it."

"Yes—I suppose so—but why, if I may inquire, all this interest on your part in us petty mortals?" Dimpleby smiled knowledgeably. "Ah, I'll bet this is where the pitch for our souls comes in; you'll insure an end to bad luck and negative coincidences, in return for a couple of signatures written in blood—"

"Professor, please," Lucifer said, blushing. "You have the wrong idea completely."

"I just don't understand," Curlene sighed, gazing at Lucifer, "why such a nice fellow was kicked out of Heaven . . ."

"But why come to *me?*" Dimpleby said, eyeing Lucifer through the sudsy glass bottom of his ale mug. "I don't know any spells for exorcising demons."

"Professor, I'm out of my depth," Lucifer said earnestly. "The old reliable eye-of-newt and wart-of-toad recipes don't faze these alien imps for a moment. Now, I admit, I haven't kept in touch with new developments in science as I should have. But *you* have, Professor: you're one of the world's famous authorities on wave mechanics and Planck's law, and all that sort of thing. If anybody can deal with these chaps, *you* can!"

"Why, Johnny, how exciting!" Curlene said. "I didn't know matrix mechanics had anything to do with broccoli!" She took a pleased gulp of ale, smiling from Lucifer to her husband.

"I didn't either, my dear," Dimpleby said in a puzzled tone. "Look here, Lucifer, are you sure you don't have me confused with our Professor Pronko, over in

Liberal Arts? Now, his papers on abnormal psychology—"

"Professor, there's been no mistake! Who else but an expert in quantum theory could deal with a situation like this?"

"Well, I suppose there is a certain superficial semantic parallelism—"

"Wonderful, Professor, I knew you'd do it!" Lucifer grabbed Dimpleby's hand and wrung it warmly. "How do we begin?"

"Here, you're talking nonsense!" Dimpleby extracted his hand, used it to lift his ale tankard once again.

"Of course," he said after taking a hearty pull, "if you're right about the nature of these varying energy levels—and these, er, entities *do* manage the jump from one quantum state to the next—then I suppose they'd be subject to the same sort of physical laws as any other energetic particles. . . ." He thumped the mug down heavily on the tabletop and resumed jotting. "The Compton effect," he muttered. "Raman's work . . . the Stern-Gerlack experiment. Hmmm."

"You've got something?" Lucifer and Curlene said simultaneously. "Just a theoretical notion," he said offhandedly, and waved airily to a passing waiter. "Three more, Chudley."

"Johnny," Curlene wailed. "Don't stop now!"

"Professor—time is of the essence!" Lucifer groaned.

"Say, the broccoli is stirring around," Curlene said in a low tone. "Is he planning another practical joke?"

Lucifer cast apprehensive eyes toward the fireplace. "He doesn't actually do it intentionally, you know. He can't help it; it's like, well, a blind man switching on the lights in a darkroom. He wouldn't understand what all the excitement was about."

"Excuse me," Dimpleby said. "Ale goes through me pretty rapidly." He rose, slightly jogging the elbow of the waiter pouring ice water into a glass at the next table. The chill stream dived precisely into the cleavage of a plump woman in a hat like a chef's salad for twelve.

She screamed and fell backward into the path of the servitor approaching with a tray of foaming ale tankards. All three malt beverages leaped head-first onto the table, their contents sluicing across it into Lucifer's lap, while the overspill distributed itself between Dimpleby's hip pockets.

He stared down at the table awash in ale, turned a hard gaze on the fireplace.

"Like that, eh?" he said in a brittle voice. He faced the Devil, who was dabbing helplessly at his formerly white flannels.

"All right, Lucifer," he said. "You're on! A few laughs at the expense of academic dignity are fine—but I'm damned if I'm going to stand by and see good beer wasted! Now, let's get down to cases. Tell me all you know about these out-of-town incubi. . . ."

3

It was almost dawn. In his third-floor laboratory in Prudfrock Hall, Professor Dimpleby straightened from the marble-topped bench over which he had been bent for the better part of the night.

"Well," he said rubbing his eyes, "I don't know. It might work." He glanced about the big room. "Now, if you'll just shoo one of your, ah, extraterrestrial essences in here, we'll see."

"No problem there, Professor," Lucifer said anxiously. "I've had all I could do to hold them at bay all night, with some of the most potent incantations since Solomon sealed the Afrit up in a bottle."

"Then, too, I don't suppose they'd find the atmosphere of a scientific laboratory very congenial," Dimpleby said with a somewhat lofty smile, "inasmuch as considerable effort has been devoted to excluding chance from the premises."

"You think so?" Lucifer said glumly. "For your own peace of mind, I suggest you don't conduct any statistical analyses just now."

"Well, with the clear light of morning and the dissipation of the alcohol, the rationality of what we're doing seems increasingly questionable—but nonetheless, we may as well carry the experiment through. Even negative evidence has a certain value."

"Ready?" Lucifer said.

"Ready," Dimpleby said, suppressing a yawn. Lucifer made a face and executed an intricate dance step. There was a sharp sense of tension released—like the popping of an invisible soap bubble—and *something* appeared drifting lazily in the air near the precision scales. One side of the instrument dropped with a sharp *clunk!*

"All the air concentrated on one side of the balance," Lucifer said tensely.

"Maxwell's demon—in the flesh?" Dimpleby gasped.

"It looks like a giant pizza," Curlene said, "only transparent."

The apparition gave a flirt of its rim and sailed across to hover before a wall chart illustrating the periodic table. The paper burst into flame.

"All the energetic air molecules rushed to one spot," Lucifer explained. "It could happen any time—but it seldom does."

"Good lord! What if it should cause all the air to rush to one end of the room?" Dimpleby whispered.

"I daresay it would rupture your lungs, Professor. So I wouldn't waste any more time, if I were you."

"Imagine what must be going on outside," Curlene said. "With these magical pizzas and broccoli wandering loose all over the place!"

"Is *that* what all those sirens were about?" Dimpleby said. He stationed himself beside the breadboard apparatus he had constructed and swallowed hard.

"Very well, Lucifer—see if you can herd it over this way."

The devil frowned in concentration. The pizza drifted slowly, rotating as if looking for the source of some irritation. It gave an impatient twitch and headed toward

Curlene. Lucifer made a gesture and it veered off, came
sailing in across the table.

"Now!" Dimpleby said, and threw a switch. As if
struck by a falling brick, the alien entity slammed to the
center of the three-foot disk encircled by massive magnetic coils.

It hopped and threshed, to no avail.

"The field is holding it!" Dimpleby said tensely. "So
far . . ."

Suddenly the rippling, disk-shaped creature folded in
on itself, stood on end, sprouted wings and a tail. Scales
glittered along its sides. A puff of smoke issued from
tiny crocodilian jaws, followed by a tongue of flame.

"A dragon!" Curlene cried.

"Hold him, Professor!" Lucifer urged.

The dragon coiled its tail around itself and melted
into a lumpy black sphere covered with long bristles. It
had two bright red eyes and a pair of spindly legs on
which it jittered wildly.

"A goblin?" Dimpleby said incredulously.

The goblin rebounded from the invisible wall re-
straining it, coalesced into a foot-high, leathery-skinned
humanoid with big ears, a wide mouth, and long arms
which it wrapped around its knees as it squatted disconsolately on the grid, rolling bloodshot eyes sorrowfully
up at its audience.

"Congratulations, Professor!" Lucifer exclaimed.
"We got one!"

4

"His name," Lucifer said, "is Quilchik. It's really
quite a heart-rending tale he tells, poor chap."

"Oh, the poor little guy," Curlene said. "What does
he eat, Mr. Lucifer? Do you suppose he'd like a little
lettuce or something?"

"His diet is quite immaterial, Curl; he subsists entirely on energies. And that seems to be at the root of
the problem. It appears there's a famine back home.

What with a rising birth rate and no death rate, population pressure long ago drove his people out into space. They've been wandering around out there for epochs, with just the occasional hydrogen molecule to generate a quantum or two of entropy to absorb; hardly enough to keep them going."

"Hmm. I suppose entropy *could* be considered a property of matter," Dimpleby said thoughtfully, reaching for paper and pencil. "One can hardly visualize a distinction between order and disorder as existing in matterless space."

"Quite right. The curious distribution of heavy elements in planetary crusts and the unlikely advent of life seem to be the results of their upsetting of the randomness field, to say nothing of evolution, biological mutations, the extinction of the dinosaurs just in time for man to thrive, and women's styles."

"Women's styles?" Curlene frowned.

"Of course," Dimpleby nodded. "What could be more unlikely than this year's Paris modes?"

Lucifer shook his head, a worried expression on his regular features. "I had in mind trapping them at the entry point and sending them back where they came from; but under the circumstances that seems quite inhumane."

"Still—we can't let them come swarming in to upset everything from the rhythm method to the Irish Sweepstakes."

"Golly," Curlene said, "couldn't we put them on a reservation, sort of, and have them weave blankets, maybe?"

"Hold it," Lucifer said. "There's another one nearby . . . I can feel the tension in the R-field . . ."

"Eek!" Curlene said, taking a step backward and hooking a heel in the extension cord powering the magnetic fields. With a sharp *pop!* the plug was jerked from the wall. Quilchik jumped to his large, flat feet, took a swift look around, and leaped, changing in midair to the fluttering form of a small bat.

Lucifer threw off his coat, ripped off his tie and shirt.
Before the startled gaze of the Dimplebys, he rippled
and flowed into the form of a pterodactyl which leaped
clear of the collapsing white flannels and into the air,
long beak agape, in hot pursuit of the bat. Curlene
screeched and squeezed her eyes shut. Dimpleby said:
"Remarkable!" grabbed his pad and scribbled rapidly.
The bat flickered in mid-air and was a winged snake.
Lucifer turned instantly into a winged mongoose. The
snake dropped to the floor and shrank to mouse form,
scuttling for a hole. Lucifer became a big gray cat,
reached the hole first. The mouse burgeoned into a
bristly rat; the cat swelled and was a terrier. With a yap,
it leaped after the rat, which turned back into Quilchik,
sprang up on a table, raced across it, dived for what
looked like an empty picture frame—

A shower of tiny Quilchiks shot from the other side
of the heavy glass sheet. Lucifer barely skidded aside in
time to avoid it, went dashing around the room, barking
furiously at the tiny creatures crouched behind every
chair and table leg, squeezing in behind filing cabinets,
cowering under ash trays.

"Lucifer, stop!" Curlene squealed. "Oh, aren't they
darling!" She went to her knees, scooped up an inch-
high manikin. It squatted on her palm, trembling, its
head between its knees.

"By Jiminy," Dimpleby said. "It went through a diffraction grating, and came out centuplets!"

5

"The situation is deteriorating," Lucifer groaned,
scooping up another miniature imp, and dumping it
back inside the reactivated trap. "It was bad enough
dealing with one star-spite. Now we have a hundred.
And if any one of them escapes . . ."

"Don't look now," Dimpleby said behind his hand to
the Devil, now back in human form and properly clad,

"but I have an unch-hay the magnetic ield-fay won't old-hay them-they."

"Eye-way ott-nay?" Lucifer inquired.

"Ecause-bay . . ." Dimpleby broke off. "Well, it has to do with distribution of polarity. You see the way the field works—"

"Don't bother explaining," Lucifer said. "I wouldn't understand anyway. The real question is—what do we do now?"

"Our choice seems limited. We either gather up all these little fellows and dump them back where they came from, and then hunt down the others and do like-wise, which is impossible, or we forget the whole thing, which is unthinkable."

"In any event," Lucifer said, "we have to act fast before the situation gets entirely out of hand."

"We could turn the problem over to the so-called authorities," Dimpleby said. "But that seems unwise, somehow."

Lucifer shuddered. "I can see the headlines now: DEVIL LOOSE ON COLLEGE CAMPUS!"

"Oh, they've already worked that one to death," Curlene said. "It would probably be more like: PROF AND MATE IN THREE-WAY SEX ROMP."

"Sex romp?"

"Well, Mr. Lucifer *did* reappear in the nude." Curlene smiled. "And a very nice physique, too, Mr. Lucifer."

Lucifer blushed. "Well, Professor, what do we do?" he asked hastily.

"I'll flip a coin," Curlene suggested. "Heads, we report the whole thing, tails, we keep it to ourselves and do the best we can."

"All right. Best two out of three."

Curlene rummaged in her purse and produced one of the counterfeit quarters in current production from the Denver mint. She tossed it up, caught it, slapped it against her forearm, lifted her hand.

"Tails," she said in a pleased tone.

"Maybe we'd better report it anyway," Dimpleby said, nibbling a fingernail and eyeing the tiny creatures sitting disconsolately inside the circle of magnets.

"Two out of three," Curlene said. She flipped the coin up.

"Tails again," she announced.

"Well, I suppose that settles it. . . ."

Curlene tossed the coin up idly. "I guess it's definite," she said. "Tails three times in a row."

Dimpleby looked at her absently. "Eh?"

"*Four* times in a row," Curlene said. Lucifer looked at her as if about to speak. Curlene flipped the coin high.

"Five," she said. Dimpleby and Lucifer drew closer.

"Six . . ."

"Seven . . ."

"Eight . . ."

"Oh-oh," Dimpleby said. He grabbed for the desk drawer, pulled out a dog-eared deck of cards, hastily shuffled and dealt two hands. Cautiously, he peeked at his cards. He groaned.

"Four aces," he said.

"Four kings here," Curlene said.

"Here we go again," he said. "Now no one will be safe!"

"But Johnny," Curlene said. "There's one difference."

"What?"

"The odds are all mixed up, true—but now they're in our favor!"

6

"It's quite simple, really," Dimpleby said, waving a sheet of calculations. "When Quilchik went through the grating, he was broken up into a set of harmonics. Those harmonics, being of another order of size, resonate at another frequency. Ergo, he consumes a different type of energetic pseudo-particle. Instead of draining off the positive, ah, R-charges, he now subsists on negative entropy."

"And instead of practical jokes, we have miraculous cures, spontaneous remissions, and fantastic runs with the cards!" Curlene cried happily.

"Not only that," Dimpleby added, "but I think we can solve their food-supply problem. They've exhausted the supply of plus entropy back on their own level—but the original endowment of minus R remains untapped. There should be enough for another few billion years."

Lucifer explained this to the Quilchiks via the same form of instantaneous telepathy he had employed for the earlier interrogation.

"He's delighted," the Devil reported, as the tiny creatures leaped up, joined hands, and began capering and jigging in a manner expressive of joy. "There's just one thing . . ." A lone manikin stood at the edge of the table, looking shyly at Curlene.

"Quilchik Seventy-eight has a request," Lucifer said.

"Well, what does snookums-ookums want?" Curlene cooed, bending over to purse her lips at the tiny figure.

"He wants to stay," Lucifer said embarrassedly.

"Oh, Johnny, can I have him?"

"Well—if you'll put some pants on him . . ."

"And he'd like to live in a bottle. Preferably a bourbon bottle, one of the miniatures. Preferably still full of bourbon," Lucifer added. "But he'll come out to play whenever you like."

"I wonder," Dimpleby said thoughtfully, "what effect having him around would have on the regular Saturday-night card game with those sharpies from the Engineering faculty?"

"You've already seen a sample," Lucifer said. "But I can ask him to fast at such times."

"Oh, no, no," Dimpleby protested. "Hate to see the little fellow go hungry."

"Mr. Lucifer," Curlene asked. "I hope I'm not being nosy—but how did you get the scar on your side that I saw when you had your shirt off?"

"Oh, ah, that?" Lucifer blushed purple. "Well, it, ah—"

"Probably a liver operation, from the location, eh, Lucifer?" Dimpleby said.

"You might call it that," Lucifer said.

"But you shouldn't embarrass people by asking personal questions, Curl," Dimpleby said sternly.

"Yes, dear," Curl said. "Lucifer—I've been wanting to ask you: what did a nice fellow like you do to get kicked out of Heaven?"

"Well, I, uh." Lucifer swallowed.

"It was for doing something nice, wasn't it?"

"Well—frankly, I thought it wasn't fair," Lucifer blurted. "I felt sorry for the poor humans, squatting in those damp caves . . ."

"So you brought them fire," Curlene said. "That's why you're called Lucifer."

"You're mixed up, Curl," Dimpleby said. "That was Prometheus. For his pains, he was chained to a rock, and every day a vulture tore out his liver, and every night it grew back. . . ."

"But it left a scar," Curlene said, looking mcltingly at Lucifer.

The Devil blushed a deep magenta. "I . . . I'd better be rushing off now," he said.

"Not before we share a stirrup cup," Dimpleby said, holding up the Old Crow bottle from the desk drawer. Inside, Quilchik, floating on his back with his hands folded on his paunch, waved merrily and blew a string of bubbles.

"Luckily, I have a reserve stock," Dimpleby muttered, heading for the filing cabinet.

"Mr. Lucifer, how can we ever thank you?" Curlene sighed, cradling the flask.

"Just by, uh, having all the fun you can," Lucifer said. "And I'll, er, be looking forward to seeing you in Hell, someday."

"I'll drink to that," Dimpleby said. He poured. Smiling, they clicked glasses and drank.

The Triumphant Head

JOSEPHINE SAXTON

—

My eyes are open and I am awake. There can be no doubt that I am physically awake. He was awake before I stirred in the sun-scarred sheets, I can hear him in the dressing room next door, splashing about, walking about, singing about, full of it all, and if shaving lotion has a sound, then that too reaches me . . . but I must not allow that to distract me in this way.

Having washed all the important crevices and the bits that show of myself (good bath last night, reeking with essence of pine), I sit here in my comfortable chair, re-upholstered by myself in dark green cut velvet, and as I sit naked on it a pattern of acanthus leaves will grow on my backside, but hold hard, who sits here, looking into the mirror, and why, and *what* is this I see?

So, awake. I question, how awake is that?

Each day at this time I can by my own efforts reveal images.

I utter the challenge.

229

Beginning with the body, one leg, then the other, one arm, the other, and then the back, oh those acanthus leaves, up through the body the stream should flow, should it not, confirming the fact of being awake, so that I experience that . . . there was some of that cut velvet left over, I wonder if it would make a hat, sort of Garboish perhaps.

That noise? His chest expander. Christ, get on with it, the image, it has to come; what will it be today?

I face the mirror. A Georgian mirror, black and gilt, the corners elegantly encrusted, mended with evil-smelling glue, the cracks masked with cheap gold paint, a good job if I may say so, only the marks of celluloid butterflies placed on its heavy glass by some thin hand now dead, meant to reflect the miraculous patterns seen in nature at the height of summer, a celluloid wonder, and here on my mirror the horrid blur of its pseudopod, marring my beauty unless I lean to the right which I now do, the better to see you with, my dear. . . .

Begin again—Bruce knew nothing, he was just a student of Arachnida.

To be more than awake, for however short a time. Look in the mirror.

Come to me, two-legged being who will live the day as some dim zombie with the ticket "Anonymous member Dramatis Personae Planet Earth" stuck on me unless I can pull this off, this fantastic act, to see myself, not as others see me, but as I am. Perferably before that other thumping being, next door, push-ups now perhaps, strains a pectoral fibre, and for what may I ask? No, I may not ask, he never questions me as to what I do in here each morning. He will be in here though, asking about breakfast before I've half begun. He will know it is me sitting here by the fact that I shall answer "yes dear, orange juice in the fridge, kidneys to follow." Nobody else could say that to him at eight in the morning, in this room. It is outside his experience.

Be still then, choose a small spot on which to rest the eyes, fix it, not with a vibrant glare, but with a steady gaze, seeing and not seeing, and make of that gaze an anchor, so that reality may pervade; one cannot force this process—but you are way off beam again. Thoughts think, body live. If I could say: "Somebody, help me."

I am sitting here, a normal-enough practice for a human being, exploring, and what are little girls made of? Bones and blood and skin and hormones, and a reliable heart to keep things going until I get things in perspective.

Who is here today, hiding in my living corpse. There must be somebody there, always it is so, but which one?

Supposing *he* came in at this moment, just as my image appeared. Would he notice, see it for himself? An interesting supposition, and, at the back of my mind, Robbie Burns, making love wholesale on beds of heather, and the seas have not yet run dry, and a bloody good thing too, leave that. . . .

I suddenly find I have released an amount indefinable of the source of my energy and do not quite know what to do with it; at this point I must achieve the miracle of stopping thinking at the same time as allowing my thoughts to think themselves, and then, given grace, things might begin to shape up; I may turn this mass of meat into a person, and within that person will be recognisable another, like Chinese boxes, known only to that person next door who is doubtless dressing himself in his chalk-stripe and two tones, he being a male cognisant of what goes on in the scene, as "wife," or, in his cups, as "the wife," the words implying a certain uniqueness and superiority over all other wives, but understood nevertheless to mean "her," the wife, we all have them, like heads. Heads.

Through the relaxed channels of my flesh flow, life, and run, but never to waste, bring me into focus; who is there today, nok nok nok, who is it, welcome friend, plenty of room in my body, have your say for twenty-four hours, but do not deter me from my aim, that is our bargain. You live, I live.

Things are jumping now, the acanthus leaves are doing fine, and the mirror is still as still, waiting, only a clothes moth hovers expectantly over my cashmere sweater which I shall presently wear for the role I shall play today; my body lives, it glows, molten it glows, and my arms, they glow, and my feet, they draw something up through them and resist and glow like the element on the heater that is now singeing that unfortunate moth. My chest passes on the message into my clavicles, otherwise known as right collarbone, left collarbone, up through my neck and chin, to my lips which sing as if a fraction from a kiss, and my nose, tingling, working against me and into an orgasmic sneeze—later, the sneeze, it will keep. Now for my eyes, the right and the left and through the unknown quantities that lurk behind the bones of the TRIUMPHANT HEAD.

So it is you today, is it, I half suspected it. Surly, insentient, woman of dusty antimony, mineral lady, butter would not melt, and gaze unseeing into the black depths of space (we all have our off days), and for a moment I saw, before the going and going away of it, in the wordless moments, the image in the mirror.

"Hullo dear, not dressed yet, what about breakfast?"

For a split second the powers of speech refuse the carefully held orbicularis, clinging to the delicate pleasure of a moment ago, but that is nonsense, of course you can speak, you are in command now, you know your lines.

"I'm almost ready, just got to throw on a few clothes. Juice is in the fridge, kidneys to follow."

"Pity about the clothes, you look nice like that."

I stand up and lean over closer to the mirror, staring at my face. He sniggers. It is the acanthus leaves. I snigger back at his reflection in the mirror, thinking, "Does he deduce from this elegant imprint that I have been sitting on this chair for at least ten minutes?"

He goes away, clumping athletically downstairs to forage for the orange juice.

Clothes on, and a little Ultima II will do wonders for

these pores, deceiving the eye over the matter of the odd wrinkle. And face powder.

God, what a marvellous sneeze that was, most satisfactory. Powder, there's powder over everything, every crevice of this mirror frame holds a delicate blur of triple-milled silk. Lovely dark eye liner, green shadow, and the mascara, a touch on the eyebrows, then with a brush and with care, the lips, dewy is the word. I brush with vigour my short hair and cover it with a wig, an expensive foible, but a fantastic transformation. I the gold beauty. My own mother would not recognize me, nor I either, were it not for the fact that I saw the act of putting on the wig, and not only that, beneath that . . . and beneath that. . . .

Stay with me during this day, mineral lady, you are ugly, but at least I know you, a bit.

If you were the outer image, we would be locked away in some psychiatrist's cupboard along with other freaks, those with birthmarks over the entire epidermis, deep like rose-coloured leather; I have seen them, spoken with them, and without fail have smelt ineradicable and unhealthy pain in the soul, and have suspected great beauty locked within.

But there is no cause for depression or despair; I have my face to hide in, and my mask of make-up, and other's ideas of what I am to screen me, until perhaps I become indeed something else, that need not fear showing itself only for a brief moment, coaxed and cajoled to appear, and then retire behind the veil.

Dust off a bit of this powder with a face tissue, put the lid on the jar of cream, set the chair straight, switch off the heater element, and go to make breakfast. Looking at the mirror as I leave, I murmur: "See you tomorrow."

Subtly now, the final nexus into the Heaven of the Ideal—omega—toward which scholars, academic and alchemic all, have yearned: whereby base human metal is transmuted into godly gold.

Mainchance

PETER TATE

—

". . . For by a machine three fingers high and wide and of less, a man could free himself and his friends of all danger of prison and rise and descend. Also a machine can easily be made by which one man can draw a thousand to him by violence against their wills, and attract other things in like manner. . . ."

ROGER BACON, Alchemist (?1214-1292)

Hubert Dreyfus compares cybernetics with alchemy:

". . . Because a few people have climbed some very high trees, they think they can solve the problem of getting to the Moon."

He drove the monoprop across the blue shale courts to heaven, a big man who deliberately kept the controls on manual because he liked to feel the craft fight a little before it answered his prods and pronouncements.

A big man with the most important human job in the

world—guardian to a machine which, in more primitive days, might have ranked for deification.

There was nothing clumsy about him. The body moved perfectly to inner direction, and inner direction came from the elements that mediaeval men had called humours. Fire, water, air . . . a life-force that seemed to move like a torrent in the veins; that was Adams.

Young. A wealth of curly black hair—and underneath it, a chameleon brain that attacked knowledge and took it into captivity.

Adams, then, exercising his wrists on the manipulae of the monoprop, saw the blue sea turn brown with the rising stratum. I'll come upon it from above, he thought. This is as it should be.

The monoprop rode over land. He turned it to follow the grey-ribbon road into the foothills. And there, ahead of him, glinting in the sun—

The Tower.

So it had come to this. There was no other kind of heritage available to him. Priorities, pressure, a strength of conviction had robbed him of flesh-and-blood mathematics, a multiplication out of a division, a product of his cylindrical root.

To see it dazzle—to have it greet you with a tax on your eyes—that was a sad thing, the sadness autumnal rather than bitter.

And while he analysed the vague nausea, a downdraught found the plane and tried for destruction.

When he brought the monoprop out of the current, his mind was clear, his brow moist, his co-ordination uncluttered with regrets and hang-nail thoughts.

The Tower was closer (of course) and he began his grounding manoeuvre. He cut back speed, lost height, yellowed his window to negate the glare.

Able now to regard the structure in detail, he found it sharp and clinical. If he had anticipated any more spectacular an impression he would have been disappointed, but he had kept himself carefully detached. Out of expectation came disappointment and disappointment, like everything else, disturbed his chemistry . . . made him a slightly different man.

The road ran headlong into the mountain seventeen thousand feet below.

The monoprop threaded itself into the eye of the needle.

It had been a time of undeclared interests, individually and in the dealings of great nations. And since such a condition quickly bred mistrust it soon became well-nigh impossible for one power to enjoy—or even to contemplate—any amicable relationship with another.

The result was a resurgence of nationalism which showed itself in a welter of small local wars. They were dirty wars where starvation was used as a weapon and no distinction was drawn between the halt and the healthy, the young and the old, the combatants and the innocently involved.

As they grew in numbers, so the United Nations—never much more than a myth, since it was founded on a premise of mutual honesty that just didn't exist—declined in influence.

Those who watched the world scene began to suspect that civilisation could not continue for much longer without a major conflagration. Even the cynics were wont to cite the Millennium, though without any real understanding of the word.

What few Christians were left in a world that had gone sour on religion (even as religion had gone sour on Christianity) were under persecution. In a way they were blamed for conditions—and ridiculed when they pointed out that the Scriptures had prophesied (Matthew, chapter 24, verse 14, and on) what would occur.

Since the world feared the Millennium—in whatever form it might come, speaking whatever language—steps were taken by those who retained enough influence to implement a kind of solution.

If man could not be trusted, then some substitute had to be found . . . something that could make use of all knowledge that the world provided without being corrupted by the power that that intelligence could give.

A computer. Without doubt the largest computer that had ever been visualised. A machine that worked not with the formalised language of mathematics but with the broader linguistics of humanity. No one source could be used to stock its memory banks or to prepare its programmes. This function must be conducted by the best cybernetic brains world-wide.

Out of this common task grew the first friendship of an international nature that had been evident for quite a while. It was like a revelation. People, finding that they could communicate, began to do so. But they were wary of divisions. The whole business of living was geared to a broad-plane togetherness.

When organisation introduced itself, it was tiered or pyramidic and involving all nationalities. The tariffs came off; the barriers came down. There was free mobility of labour, of living materials.

It was an ideal existence which could not have been imagined even ten years before. It came about with the haste of desperation. It was welcomed as a salvation.

And behind it all, balanced between one side of the world and the other (on the narrow umbilicus of land between what had been North and South America) and remaining wonderfully noncommittal was . . . Multiple Algorithm Random Deduction Unicentre.

MARDUC symbolised the self-sufficiency of man in the face of destiny; the perfectness of the present. There was no need to consider the future.

There was, however, a need to consider a human attendant for the machine. He would act in liaison, over and above any technician strength. His qualifications would be unique. Apart from an excellent working knowledge of the machine, he must be a product of the system, must believe in its infallibility and must possess an extensive general intelligence. There were not too many such people around.

Just enough, it would seem, and so scattered to be

representative of the world as a whole. A short list was
drawn up and agreed. Then came the democratic
thing—a contest that could favour no particular candi-
date. A receptacle was produced, the names plunged
therein, a piece of paper withdrawn.

The name on the paper was "Adams."

The walking man came west out of the sunrise, following the coast road until the hampering presence of
dust in his open sandals persuaded him onto the beach.

There he followed the line of the sea, dangling his
sandals by the fingers of his right hand. As yet, the
strand was still cool from the night, and the water,
creaming about his toes, comforted and caressed. The
sea that had been called Mediterranean, untouched by
fishery development and artificial stimulants of tide and
temperature, retained its morning breezes and the man
feasted on them.

Even its salty status quo was intentional. Along the
sides of hills which ran olive fingers down to the sea,
the terraces of orange and vine needed such daily
changes. But the man was not aware of this or at least
not concerned by it. His own inner peace found a parallel in the crumbling white citadel villages that nestled
inland between soft green feminine swellings. Occasionally he stopped, one man alone on the meandering
shore, and turned his eyes outwards and then upwards
across the paling dome of the sky.

Once he looked down at his feet and seemed to be
searching among the surf for a word. "Michelangelo,"
he said suddenly.

When he reached a rocky promontory, he dried and
dusted his feet carefully on a handkerchief he drew
from a pocket of his tidy but worn suit and replaced his
sandals. Then he began to climb.

Thus he entered Midi Settlement as it started to stir.
He sorted out the control buildings and found himself
a seat near them.

He took a polythene wrapper from another pocket of

his suit and extracted a piece of bread and some cheese from it. He ate sparingly, running his eyes along the uniform rows of dwellings. When doors began opening, he folded away the food and stood up as though it were important.

As the men filed past him, he smiled. "Hello, brothers." They regarded him suspiciously. They wondered at his smile.

All morning, he wandered unhindered up and down aisles of tomatoes and olives. He even took his shoes off again to paddle along rows of green rice. He spoke to the bent workers. "A pleasant day. Perhaps a little warm. Make sure your necks are covered."

Not once did he stop and not once did the workers answer. But they straightened and watched him on his way in curiosity. As the sun rose higher, he took the handkerchief from his pocket, knotted it at the corners and laid it over his perspiring scalp.

Soon, the men left their labours and sat in silent groups, huddled into scant patches of shade. The wanderer selected one such group and sat down a few yards distant. He took out his bundle of food and ate more bread and a substantial part of the cheese. He paid the men no particular attention but he knew their eyes were on him. He looked up, smiled and went back to his meal.

"You," said one man eventually. "Are you looking for work? Because . . ."

"Because nobody need be jobless?" The stranger laughed. "No, I don't need a job."

The men fell back into a sullen silence.

"And I'm not a spy."

"You must be something," said the first man defensively. "What's your classification?"

"I don't have one. Or rather—no classification applies to me."

"Listen, if you're a human being, you're classified. All of us . . ."

"Not all." The wanderer interrupted gently.

"Well, who . . . ?"

"Free men are not in subjection to some distant tin god."

"Wait a minute. If you're here to start trouble for us . . . I'm going to call the supervisor." The man stood up.

"Please—let me explain. I am here to talk, no more. I am not an agent for a revolutionary movement. I'm not trying to trap you into any kind of indiscretion against the system. I just want to begin a conversation between us. I want to hear *you* talk. Tell me—have you ever thought what is at the end of this?"

The spokesman lowered himself to the ground and leaned his weight against the shadowed wall of a shed. "At the end there is nothing," he said. "Now we are allowed to live and work and make the best of life as it is. It is a pretty thankless business, but it is the best the world offers."

"So they tell you."

"Who?"

"Why, the man in the Tower and his infernal machine. That's where it comes from, doesn't it?"

"It's common sense, no matter who tells it. Nobody's hungry, there are no wars, we don't waste time and energy believing in things that will come to nothing. All in all, things are pretty near perfection."

"But you don't smile."

"We . . ." The spokesman bit back a hasty denial. He tried to think of the last time he had consciously felt happiness. "Life is a serious business," he said.

"Particularly with nothing to look forward to."

"We've been through all that . . . more times than most of us care to remember. I told you, we don't waste our energy."

"Don't you ever have any inclination to—ask a question?"

"Our instructions in all matters are explicit."

"And there is nowhere in you a desire to challenge

any ruling or to apply your own sense of reasoning to any circumstance?"

"If we felt a thing was not just, we would challenge it."

"But you consider the system incapable of being unjust."

"I didn't say that. Our powers of judgment are still such that we can perceive an anomaly. You seem to think that because we accept this regimentation, we have become some kind of vegetable. In fact, a lot of us have come to the conclusion that if the world is to avoid committing genocide, then this is the only way to do it."

"And you think a—preacher—like myself is misusing his time."

"I think you are redundant."

"Yet if I could persuade you that I have something to offer—if I could prove to you that the power of the Tower is treating us as anything but redundant, what then?"

"We would—have to think about it."

"If having thought about it, you might decide the power should be asked a certain question . . . ?"

"Then we'd do it. Wouldn't we?" The spokesman glanced at his colleagues. They nodded.

"Thank you," said the wanderer.

> Sol gold is, and Luna silver we declare;
> Mars yron, Mercurie is quyksilver;
> Saturnus leed, and Jubitur is tyn,
> And Venus coper, by my fathers kyn.
> GEOFFREY CHAUCER: Canon's Yeoman's Tale

First Beginning of my beginning; First Principle of my principle; Breath of breath, First Breath of the breath within me; Fire which, among the compounds which form me, was given by God for my own compound, First Fire of the fire within me; Water of water, First Water of the water within me; Earthy Substance, model of the earthy substance which is

within me; O my Perfect Body, fashioned by a glorious man and an immortal hand in the world of
darkness and light; lifeless and living—if it please
Thee to transmit and communicate a rebirth to im-
mortality to me, who am still constrained by my
natural condition, O that I may, after the violent con-
straint of my impending Fate, contemplate the
immortal Principle thanks to the undying breath . . .

> Four roots of Empedocles (fundamental matter)
> invoked in Prayer to Mithras (c. 200 A.D.)

MARDUC came in sections. The central processing
unit sat in the uppermost chamber of the Tower while
the myriad peripheral units were situated on same-level
or lower-level floors. The high-speed data channels were
joined, where visually practicable, by laser beams and
where not by underfloor wiring.

Further down the Tower were the software quarters
where compilers prepared programmes in the special
language built into the computer. Disc storage, drum
storage, closed storage had all been incorporated to
grasp the extraordinary intelligence.

Ten years of modification had been devoted almost
entirely to improvement of programming techniques.
Users in the late sixties had found increasingly that they
were better able than the manufacturers to provide software for their machines. Thus concentration had been
on coherence and machine-time salvage.

By the mid-seventies most of the problems that faced
humanity had fought themselves to a solution. To say
that the possibility of error no longer existed would be
over-simplification of mammoth proportions. But the
programmers safeguarded against this with parameters
that emphasised cause and effect, so that judgments
formed on impulse were out and a comprehensive and
honest consideration of all factors was in. That, they
reckoned, was about as close as they could be expected
to get.

And there was the urgency. At some stage, it was

bound to become necessary to suspend their attempts at prediction and to place their trust in the progress they had made.

The face of MARDUC, then, was undistinguished, the voice deadpan and not always faithful in inflection. The boast of perfection lay in the process validity of the machine rather than any fine finish.

Adams, confronting MARDUC for the first time, found himself with a sense of anticlimax. Perhaps it was inevitable after the build-up. He looked for reasons and thought, The thing lacks glamour. He brushed the thought aside quickly.

YOU ARE DISAPPOINTED IN ME.

He sat down too fast in the contoured chair adjacent to the input speaker. Surely the thing couldn't read thoughts too.

"No." His first defence was denial.

IT WAS PREDICTABLE. I HAVE NO SUPERNATURAL POWERS BUT I AM AWARE OF FACTORS THAT ARE FORMULA. IT IS NATURAL THAT YOU HAD A SOMEWHAT—ROSY—IMPRESSION OF MARDUC.

Holy cow, a computer with an inferiority complex. "I am not bothered by how you look, MARDUC," said Adams. "You're here for the same reason I am—to do a job. I don't suppose I look all that keen to you."

Now *that* was a stupid comment to make.

KEEN MEANING SHARP. I DO NOT FORM OPINIONS, SIR, BUT IT IS LOGICAL THAT UNLESS YOU WERE ENTIRELY CAPABLE OF CARRYING OUT THE WORK WE ARE TO DO, YOU WOULD NOT BE HERE. THEREFORE, WELCOME.

"Thank you, MARDUC. As you say, it is logical and our relationship is founded on logic. I appreciate your welcome and for the record I would like to say that I look forward to working with such a fine example of man's ingenuity. That said, I think we might perhaps move on to the more formal business of our meeting. Can you give me a regional briefing?"

Adams settled back in the chair. He closed his eyes to concentrate, kneading his lower lip between forefinger and middle finger of right hand. MARDUC went briskly but comprehensively through his report and Adams let him flow without interruption.

At "Midi," the machine paused.

"What's the matter?" said Adams absently. He acknowledged his slip with a wry grin. But MARDUC had been made familiar with vernacular.

I AM COLLECTING LATEST INFORMATION FROM MIDI. IT APPEARS THAT THERE IS A SUSPENSION OF LABOUR. I AM ENDEAVOURING TO ASCERTAIN THE CAUSE.

Adams waited, not yet curious.

WORK HAS STOPPED, said MARDUC after a while. MY INFORMATION IS THAT THE MEN ARE DEMANDING A DIALOGUE WITH YOU.

"For what purpose?"

THEY WILL NOT TELL THE SUPERVISORS. THEY SAY THEY WILL TALK ONLY TO YOU.

"Yes, well so much for direct channels. What does Supplementary Intelligence yield?"

THERE HAVE BEEN REPORTS OF THE PRESENCE OF NEWCOMERS IN THE AREA. ONE WAS SEEN IN THE SETTLEMENT A FEW HOURS PRIOR TO THE STOPPAGE. HE WAS OBSERVED TALKING TO CERTAIN OF THE MEN ALTHOUGH IT IS NOT KNOWN WHAT WAS SAID.

"So it is possible that his visit had nothing to do with the cessation of labour."

POSSIBLE, BUT . . .

"Appreciate that I am reluctant to pay too much attention to these—preachers. All the same, give me what you've got on the Newcomers."

NEWCOMERS BELIEVE THEMSELVES TO BE WHAT THE CATHOLIC CHURCH USED TO CALL "OF THE APOSTOLIC SUCCESSION," THOUGH THAT IS NOT TO SAY THAT THEY HAD THEIR BASIS IN CATHOLICISM. IN FACT, THE OPPOSITE IS TRUE, SINCE EARLY NEWCOMERS DREW A PARALLEL BETWEEN THE ROMAN CHURCH AND ITS INVOLVEMENT IN TRADE AND POLITICS AND THE "GREAT HARLOT" OF THE BIBLICAL BOOK OF REVELATIONS. IN FAIRNESS TO THEIR TENACITY, THEY HAVE SURVIVED THE GENERAL

DISINTEREST OF THE WORLD IN METAPHYSICS AND THEIR
DOCTRINES ARE SUBSTANTIALLY UNCHANGED.

. . . IF ANYTHING, THEY HAVE THRIVED ON THIS DIS-
INTEREST, STATING THAT SUCH A "FALLING AWAY" WAS
PROPHESIED IN THEIR BOOK. BY NATURE THEY ARE PER-
SISTENT BUT POLITE. ANY INTERFERENCE IN ANYTHING
AS SECULAR AS A LABOUR DISPUTE WOULD SEEM TO BE
FOREIGN TO THEM. NEVERTHELESS, IN THE ABSENCE OF
ANY ALTERNATIVE, THE PROPOSITION SHOULD BE CON-
SIDERED.

"My feelings exactly. Now, I think, I shall go to
Midi."

WITH RESPECT . . . EVEN A COMPUTER NEEDS
RATHER LONGER THAN YOU HAVE TAKEN TO CONSIDER
ALL THE ASPECTS OF THIS MATTER. ARE YOU HAPPY
THAT THIS WOULD BE THE WISE THING TO DO AT THIS
TIME?

Momentarily, Adams felt anger. It was one thing to
question the machine's capacity, but to have it question-
ing his . . .

"Quite happy. This is as good a time as any to show
that the adminstration is approachable. Above all, we
must keep the confidence of our workers—and show
them, too, that we have confidence in them."

POINT TAKEN. I SHALL MAKE FLIGHT ARRANGE-
MENTS. HOW MANY WILL TRAVEL?

"I go alone."

BUT THERE IS DANGER. A HUMAN LIFE—NO MATTER
WHOSE LIFE—BECOMES PUNY BEFORE AN UNBALANCED
HAND ON A TRIGGER.

"I go alone. I shouldn't have to repeat things for you,
MARDUC. If I took a crowd of security men with me,
how approachable would I be? It would defy the whole
point of my going. Perhaps I should put it in terms you
would be more likely to understand. In the international
war games of the past, computers were briefed in two
types of rationality. One was 'minimax,' which meant
selecting the move that would do maximum damage to
your adversary while achieving minimum cost to your-

self. The other was 'mainchance,' the all-or-nothing cal-
culation that was impulsive and obviously much more
of a gamble. This, I would say, is a 'mainchance' situation. I don't think the people of Midi will fail to appreciate that I am taking a risk. That fact alone could do
some good. Do you follow my line of reasoning?"

I ACCEPT WHAT YOU SAY. MEANWHILE I HAVE FOUND
A SPOKESMAN FOR THE WORKERS. HIS NAME IS JONES.
HE HAS SUGGESTED A MEETING AT NOON THEIR TIME
TOMORROW AND I HAVE ACCEPTED THAT SUGGESTION.
MIGHT I SUGGEST SOME SLEEP IN THE INTERIM?

"Granted," said Adams. And let's hope it's alway
that easy, he thought. He felt an unaccountable nausea
in his stomach.

. . . Next succeeds the reign of Mars, which
shows a little yellow, mixed with luteous brownness;
these are the chief colours, but transitory ones of the
rain-bow and peacocks-tail, it shows most glo-
riously. . . . Now the mother being sealed in her infant's belly, swirls and is purified, but because of the
present great purity of the compound, no putridness
can have place in this regimen, but some obscure colours play their part as the chief actors in this stone
and some middle colours do pass and come, pleasant
to behold. Now know that this is the last tillage of
our virgin earth, that in it the fruit of the sun might
be set and maturated; therefore continue a good heat
and thou shalt see for certain, about thirty days off,
this regimen, a citrine colour shall appear which shall
in two weeks after its first appearing, tinge all with a
true citrine colour.

Typical mediaeval account "of the appearances in
the matras [retort] during the nine months' digestion."

The walls were talking again. The old man moved
restlessly on the straw palliasse. No matter which way
he twisted, the words were still there, pounding like water droplets into an empty bucket.

WHY . . . WHY . . . WHY . . . WHY . . . WHY . . . WHY . . . WHY . . .

"Why what?" he said finally.

WHY DO YOU FUNCTION THUS?

"Who asks?"

MULTIPLE ALGORITHM RANDOM DEDUCTION UNI-CENTRE. FOR BREVITY I AM CALLED MARDUC.

"I know all that. I mean who behind you? Who really wants to know? Who tells you to ask?"

NOBODY. EVERYBODY. I AM THE SERVANT OF THE COMMUNITY. THE INFORMATION I SEEK IS FOR THE BENEFIT OF THE SYSTEM.

"Even I cannot be fooled by such a proposition. You know—I am sorry—you are *aware* in your intelligence that your status is not that of a menial. Even your name . . ."

MARDUC. THAT HAS SOME SPECIAL KIND OF SIGNIFI-CANCE FOR YOU.

"I would put it higher than a significance."

THERE WAS A MARDUK OR MARODECH WHO SLEW THE SERPENT DRAGON TI'AMAT TO BECOME KING OF THE BABYLONIAN GODS. YOU SEEK TO ESTABLISH A LINK. I AM NOT A DEITY. I AM A HIGHLY SOPHISTICATED PIECE OF MACHINERY.

"You are what people make of you. Your measure is the emphasis they place upon you."

A DISCUSSION ON SEMANTICS IS NOT IN LINE WITH MY PROGRAMMING. I HAVE ASKED YOU A QUESTION. IN CASE YOU DO NOT UNDERSTAND I WILL REPEAT IT. WHY DO YOU FUNCTION THUS?

"If you mean why do I talk to people about a future, I would say it is because I hold the conviction that they should concern themselves beyond today. More than that, it is in their best interests to consider tomorrow."

YOU USE TODAY AND TOMORROW IN THE REAL-TIME SENSE.

"I use the words as temporal co-ordinates."

This was how it went, back and forth, up and around the cell, words upon words—why this? who that? what who? who what? The old man trying to tie the machine in knots; the machine clinically precise, pedantic—unflappable.

How long had it been now? It seemed like a week, but it could not be that long since the Tower guards had come to his home at the foot of Popocatepetl and told him that his presence was required.

How long in this terrible dark room with the walls moving and muttering about him as he tried to sleep? He had been warned of persecution—should really have glorified in it, since it signalled the imminence of the reward—but he was frightened. He knew that, despite his efforts, MARDUC had probably absorbed his fear. Sometimes he thought he heard the machine sniffing about his prison like a dog.

Still, he played his side of the game and tried to read a meaning into the logistics, tried to keep a stalemate between them.

I AM FAMILIAR WITH THE TENOR OF THE CONVERSATION. I CANNOT PROCEED UNTIL YOU HAVE ANSWERED EACH QUESTION SATISFACTORILY.

"Then ask a different question," he said. "A different question would yield a different answer. That I guarantee."

WHAT IS YOUR OBJECTION TO THIS SYSTEM?

"It is ungodly."

WHATEVER YOU MAY MEAN BY THAT, IT IS INHERENT IN ME TO POINT OUT THAT THIS SYSTEM, IN COMPARISON WITH ITS FORERUNNERS, IS FAR MORE——WHAT YOU WOULD CALL——"GODLY." THERE IS NO WAR, NO CRIME, NO HUNGER . . .

"No faith."

EXPLAIN FAITH. THE VAST MAJORITY OF OUR CITIZENS HAVE FAITH——IN US.

"That is not what I mean by faith. Faith is an example of obedience; a belief that will accept promises; a desire to maintain integrity. Faith is a hope that does not require visibility."

IN WHAT WAY WILL THE FUTURE DIFFER FROM THE PRESENT, BY YOUR INTERPRETATION?

"You know my interpretation. Consult your memory. You know even as I know that to restate it would be a waste of your time and mine."

YOU MEAN THAT MY PROGRAMMING ECHOES THE WORLD'S INCREDULITY.

"The world's incredulity does not make it any less the truth. Such an attitude was prophesied . . ."

PROPHESY. BRIEFING STATES: PREDICTIONS FROM CULT MYTH, RELIGION, EARLY HISTORIC DOCUMENTS WERE FOUND TO CONTAIN MANY COMMON THEMES. SINCE IT IS NOT DENIED THAT CULTURE GREW FROM CIVILISATIONS IN MESOPOTAMIA AND THE INDUS VALLEY AREA IT IS NOT STRANGE TO FIND THESE PARALLELS. THEIR RELEVANCE IS IN THE TRACEABLE SPREAD OF SO-CIAL SYSTEMS AND NOT IN ANY HOPE OF REALISATION. THEREFORE, FOR ALL OTHER PURPOSES THEY MAY BE DISCARDED.

"That is an opinion."

IT IS A CONSIDERED STATEMENT.

"I maintain it is an opinion."

WISHING DOES NOT MAKE IT SO.

"What is the object of these questions? You must surely require more of me than data which are already established within you."

THE NEWCOMERS ARE MAKING A NUISANCE OF THEMSELVES. THEY ARE HOLDING UP ENDEAVOUR.

"You must be mistaken, tin man. My brothers are passive people. They do not prevent any man from doing what he wants to do. They merely suggest what else he might be doing."

THE ACTUAL DEGREE OF PERSUASION IS BUT A SMALL MATTER. THE FACT IS THAT A CERTAIN SMALL PORTION OF OUR FIELD-LABOURERS HAVE STOPPED WORK AND YOUR PEOPLE——ACTIVE OR PASSIVE——ARE RESPONSIBLE.

"That is your information."

THAT IS UNQUESTIONABLY THE POSITION.

"And what do you want me to do about it?"

THE MEN HAVE BECOME IDLE BECAUSE THEY CON-
SIDER WE ARE PAYING TOO MUCH ATTENTION TO YOU.
ON BALANCE, MY INSTRUCTIONS ARE TO AGREE WITH
THE MEN. I'M PREPARED TO RELEASE YOU. BUT THERE
IS A CONDITION.

"I would have been surprised if there had not been."

YOU MUST CONVINCE YOUR PREACHERS THAT THEIR
WORK IS FUTILE.

"But how do I do that when the signs they see all
around them are of fertility, not futility?"

The old man sat down on the edge of his bed . . .
somehow in his contest with the voices, he had moved to
the centre of the room, and his legs, he suddenly found,
were weary. . . . He smiled. For some reason he had
a feeling close to contentment. "Besides, I have no control over them."

HOW DO YOU SAY THAT? YOU ARE THEIR LEADER.

"Computers shouldn't listen to rumours. But then, I
suppose they have no choice. . . . No, I am not their
leader. I may be held in some regard but that is only
because I am aged in the truth. They have but one
leader—and you will never lock him in a cell. . . ."

IT FOLLOWS THAT IF THEIR LEADER IS UNSEEN, INVIS-
IBLE, INTANGIBLE, THEN HE CANNOT BE CONTAINED IN
A CELL. IT IS ALSO LOGICAL THAT IF HE IS ANY OF
THESE THINGS HE CAN DO LITTLE TO INTERFERE WITH
EVENTS ONE WAY OR THE OTHER. WE HAVE A—
REPRESENTATIVE—OF THAT BODY IN OUR CARE AND WE
SHALL SEE HOW THEY REACT TO OUR TREATMENT OF
HIM. CONSIDER THAT.

The voices went away. The old man lay down on his
thankless bed with his stomach churning.

If Our Lord could stand nails through his hands, he
thought, surely I have the strength to . . .

Then sleep came like an answer.

After he had issued all his decrees,
Allotting to the Anunnaki of Heaven and Earth all their
    portions,

The Anunnaki opened their mouths
And cried to Marduk, their lord:
"Now, O Lord, who has brought about our deliverance from toil,
What shall we do to show you our gratitude?
We will build a shrine whose name shall be called
The Resting-Place for Night—come, let us rest in it.
We will create a shrine . . . ;
On the day of our arrival we will rest in it."
When Marduk heard this,
His face shone brightly as the day, and he said:
"So let Babylon be, which Ye have desired to construct;
Let a city be built and a well-girt shrine be erected."
Then the Anunnaki worked with their spades
And shaped bricks for a whole year;
And when the second year came,
They raised the top of Esagila on high, above the Apsu.
Enuma Elisha, Babylonian poem

Then the sons of the true God began to notice the daughters of men, that they were good-looking; and they went taking wives for themselves, namely, all of whom they chose. . . . The Nephilim proved to be in the earth in those days and also after that, when the sons of the true God continued to have relations with the daughters of men and they bore sons to them, they were the mighty ones who were of old, the men of fame . . .

Genesis, chapter 6, verses 2, 4

And they kept on bringing forth to the sons of Israel a bad report of the land that they had spied out, saying, "The land which we passed through to spy it out is a land that eats up its inhabitants; and all the people whom we saw in the midst of it are men of extraordinary size. And there we saw the Mephilim, the sons of Anak, who are from the Nephilim; so that

we became in our own eyes like grasshoppers, and
the same way we became in their eyes."

Numbers, chapter 13, verses 32–33

Adams set the monoprop down in the exact centre of
the communal plateau.

He moved out of the shadow of the craft and rotated
slowly, taking in the tidy streets of tidy houses, radiating
like wheel spokes away from the plateau. Each pastel
house was shuttered against the sun. Nothing moved on
the baking streets. At their extremes, the swellings rippled and took on crazy dimensions in the heat haze.

Noon exactly. The sun at its peak. It pierced his light
fibre suit and sucked perspiration from his back. Mois-
ture moved on his legs and his legs moved in retaliation,
seeking to make their own breeze. Moving together towards the rim of the plateau.

Noon was a bad time to call on anyone round the
Mediterranean. Adams was uncomfortably aware of
this and more than sorry that the fact had not occurred
to him when he agreed to the time for the meeting.

Where was everybody, anyhow? And hard on the tail
of that question came another, to answer it—Wasn't it
obvious? Perhaps that was the idea—let him arrive in
the mid-day sun and keep him hanging around until the
day cooled, even if he didn't.

The tiers of benches which could rise from the plateau at the touch of a button were harnessed below
floor-level. Nevertheless, Adams kept carefully to the
permanent way that ran between them.

He descended the steps to the promenade that ran
the circumference of the plateau, its inner edge shadowed meagrely by the plateau overhang. Somewhere, a
fly muttered, a generator throbbed. Only the sky
moved; clouds meandering like lazy sheep across a lush
pasture.

Behind him, a child moaned in fevered sleep.

He turned.

The men stood or squatted in the thread of shade

against the wall. The women sat hunched on canvas frames, stools, benches, left-out-in-the-weather chairs, no-good-for-anything-else chairs. Children were cradled in their arms, some sleeping. The others, like their parents, were looking at him. They all watched him as though dumb.

Adams braced his legs against a sudden gastric weakness.

"I am sorry for bringing you all out in this heat," he said eventually. "The time was fixed with one of your members. A man called Jones."

The group near the steps shifted. A man emerged. A knotted handkerchief covered his sparse hair. His face was furnace-red and running with sweat. "I am Jones," he said. "As for arranging your visit, I was told when you would be here. That was all. If I had been asked I could have made the point. I was not."

Adams chewed his lower lip. "There seems to have been some kind of misunderstanding," he told the people. "You men will be paid for today. Now go to your homes and return when it is cooler. Can we say six o'clock? I cannot afford too long away from the Tower."

That's for sure, he thought. Somehow, he was more inclined to accept Jones's version of the arrangement than MARDUC'S and that didn't make a lot of sense. A human being, after all, was much better qualified for deception. We humans have to stick together. . . . The phrase popped out uninvited. It was so much of a cliché it was funny.

"Jones," he said. "I'd like a few words with you."

He motioned the man up the steps. A child—perhaps the same child—grumbled and was hushed as they walked away from the edge of the plateau.

"It appears that you and MARDUC are in dispute," he said.

Jones gave him a quick glance. "I've told you what transpired," he said. "If you don't believe me, there's nothing I can do about it. I suppose the computer's got the conversation on tape. Check it if you feel the need."

"Don't assume automatically that I'm going to call you a liar, Jones. My powers of magister aren't so tied to MARDUC yet that I accept him as gospel. But I have to say this—if computers tell lies, that must be some kind of breakthrough."

"And you wonder why I take the onus for granted." Jones laughed shortly, mirthlessly.

They were at the craft. Adams started up the steps, but Jones stayed on the plateau.

"Come on up," invited Adams.

"Unless that's an order, I don't see the point."

"For crying out loud, don't be so—obstructionist. Can't two men have a straightforward conversation any more?"

"Two men, yes . . ."

"Meaning?"

"Look . . ." Jones took his time as though explaining to a wearisome child. "I think you are asking rather a lot of my belief in democracy if you suggest that there would be anything straightforward about our conversation."

Adams found his lower lip between his teeth again. "I expected to find some kind of—gulf—between us. But if I'm trying to bridge it, why can't you? If it makes it easier for you to accept, I have a purpose for talking to you. I *want* something. I am *using* you to get it. Is that more in line with your idea of our relationship?"

"Much more in line. No, I don't think I'll come up. I'll say what I've got to say when everybody can hear it."

Then he turned. Adams watched him back across the plateau. He did not retreat into the craft until he saw the beginnings of movement on the rippling streets. And he went quickly, as though the sight offended him.

At the UHF he dialled MARDUC's restricted frequency. When the computer responded, he said, "Tell me again of the arrangements for the meeting here."

THE SPOKESMAN, JONES, SUGGESTED NOON LOCAL TIME AND I ACCEPTED THAT SUGGESTION.

"He says you made the suggestion. More than that, you made it a definite instruction."

IF THERE IS SOME COMPLICATION RESULTING FROM THE ARRANGEMENT IT IS LOGICAL THAT HE WOULD ENDEAVOUR TO COVER HIS BACK. IS THERE SUCH A COMPLICATION?

"There is. The timing was all wrong. Noon here is blazing hot. I cannot imagine anybody volunteering to hold a meeting at that time."

UNLESS THERE WAS AN UNDERLYING MOTIVE.

"You mean unless he wanted to make things look bad for me."

SUCH PEOPLE MUST EXIST.

"That was my first thought. . . ." Adams cut himself short. At times, he was coming dangerously close to confiding in the machine and he cursed the naturalness of their exchanges.

MARDUC hummed and waited. "What is it?" said Adams uneasily.

IS THERE SOMETHING ELSE YOU WISH TO PUT ON RECORD?

"Nothing."

WHAT ARE YOUR ARRANGEMENTS NOW?

"I shall be here until this evening and then I will be meeting the people in more amiable conditions. In case there is another attempt at verbal juxtaposition, is there anything else I should know?"

NOTHING.

"Good. Then conserve your circuitry. I shall want a briefing when I get back to the Tower. I shall also want to file a report."

The afternoon smouldered into early evening. Adams, enclosed in the cool green pod of the monoprop, dozed intermittently, holding himself back from deeper slumber in case he overslept his appointment.

The sun fell behind the range of hills bordering the

settlement and a breeze sprang up. Again there was movement on the static streets. As he banished the blinds, Adams saw the seats come up out of the plateau like . . . words evaded him . . . like . . . rising giraffes.

The people came down the streets and creamed up over the plateau, moving in a flickering current across the tiered rows.

Jones was waiting in front of the seats with two microphones. He handed one to Adams and kept one. Adams blew on it and it responded with gentle thunder.

"Once again, I would like to say that I am sorry you were caused to wait for me in the mid-day heat," he said. "I hope no-one has suffered any ill-effects. I hope, too, that now we are in the cool of the evening, we may arrive at a solution that is mutually satisfactory in our problem here. . . ."

He licked his dry lips and tested his throat. He did not want his voice to carry any hint of indecision.

"You men have withdrawn your labour," he said. "I am here to find out why. I am here, too, to evidence the Tower's belief that all matters of contention can be resolved in an environment of peace and reason. I am going to ask your spokesman, Jones, to tell me why this action has been taken. You will hear his questions; you will hear my replies."

He swung back from the crowd and nodded at Jones. "Now . . ."

"It's about your prisoner," said Jones.

[Angels cast down from Heaven] betrayed the secrets of worldly pleasures—gold, silver and their products; instructed men in the art of dyeing fleeces . . . laid bare the secrets of metals, the virtues of plants, the force of incantations and all the knowledge coveted by men, including even the art of reading the stars. . . .

TERTULLIAN (150–230 A.D.)

The third daye again to life he shall uprise,
And devour byrds and beastes of the wildernesse,
Crowes, popingayes, pyes, pecoks and mevies;
The phenix, the eagle whyte, the gryffon of fearfulnesse,
The greene lyon and the red dragon he shall distress;
The whyte dragon also, the antelope, unicorne, pan-
     there,
With other byrds, and beastes, both more and lesse,
The basiliske also, which almost each one doth feare.
                    Alchemical Effusion (fifteenth century)

Even in the time it took Adams to regain the Tower,
his temper was not abated. He took the el to the upper
chamber, fuming at its apparent lack of haste. He went
through the door, slammed it, stood regarding the machine with his hands on his hips.

Only then, when mere flickering dials met his angry
stare, did he wonder whether wasting such emotion was
not supreme folly.

"You didn't *tell* me we had a prisoner," he said eventually.

WE HAVE A PRISONER, said MARDUC.

"The information comes too *late*. I asked you if
there was anything I should know before meeting those
people and you replied in the negative."

I WAS NOT AWARE THAT THERE WAS A LINK BE-
TWEEN THE ONE CIRCUMSTANCE AND THE OTHER. I WAS
GOING TO MENTION THE PRISONER TO YOU IN OUR
BRIEFING TONIGHT. MY INTENTION WAS TO BE ABLE TO
PRESENT YOU WITH A COMPREHENSIVE REPORT WHICH
WOULD HAVE INCLUDED SOME PROGRESS ON THE MAT-
TER OF HIS INTERROGATION.

"His interrogation. By whose order do you hold him
for interrogation?"

THERE WAS NO ORDER. BY THE POWER VESTED IN
ME, I AM PERMITTED TO SAFEGUARD THE SYSTEM FROM
LIKELY CAUSES OF HARM.

"You should have sought my guidance before you
acted."

I WAS ABOUT TO TELL YOU.

"I don't believe that." Adams was surprised at his own choice of phrase. "I believe that if I had not found out from another source, you would not have informed me until your intended line of action with the man had been completed."

IT IS NOT POSSIBLE FOR A COMPUTER TO CON-SCIOUSLY KEEP THINGS BACK FROM ITS ATTENDANT.

"I don't believe that, either. It may not be possible for a computer to be dishonest, but it is certainly possi-ble for you to delay utterance on any matter until your programming tells you that best advantage may be served by its revelation. And if that isn't deception, it's the next best damned thing. . . ."

I ACCEPT THAT OUR INTERPRETATIONS OF REAL-TIME MAY DIFFER INASMUCH AS YOU ARE A MAN AND I AM A MACHINE. IF SOME INCONSISTENCY SHOULD ARISE AS A RESULT OF THAT, IT IS SOMETHING THAT CANNOT BE RESOLVED AS LONG AS WE ARE WORKING TOGETHER.

Adams sat down in the feeder seat. He tugged at his lower lip. He felt exhausted, though very little of the last few hours had been spent in actual physical exer-tion.

"You'd better tell me from the beginning. Where is he?"

DOWN IN THE BASEMENT LEVEL.

"And why is he being held?"

WHAT DID JONES TELL YOU?

"I know what Jones told me. I want to hear from you."

HE IS AN OLD MAN AND HE TALKS A LOT OF RUB-BISH. HE TAKES UP WORKERS' TIME.

"Surely one old man can't make that much difference."

HE IS A REPRESENTATIVE. THERE ARE OTHERS OF A SIMILAR PERSUASION WHO MAKE THE SAME KIND OF TROUBLE THROUGHOUT THE SYSTEM AREA.

"By talking?"

I DETECT THAT YOU ARE STILL ANNOYED WITH ME. I CONCEDE THAT YOU MAY HAVE REASON TO BE FROM

YOUR HUMAN VIEWPOINT. AT THE SAME TIME I WOULD
COUNSEL AGAINST LETTING THAT CONDITION LEAD YOU
INTO A FALSE ASSESSMENT OF THE SITUATION HERE.
TOO MANY OF THESE PEOPLE: TOO MUCH TIME WASTED
ON LISTENING AND OUR SYSTEM COULD SUFFER IRREP-
ARABLY. WHILE ACKNOWLEDGING THAT THEY HAVE A
RIGHT TO THEIR OPINION I WOULD ADD THAT I AM PRO-
GRAMMED TO CONSIDER THAT NO OPINION IS WORTH
THAT MUCH.

"I guess you can't avoid being dogmatic—that's how
you're fed—but it's a pity. There is a lot to be gained
from flexibility. You miss something by not having the
capacity for personal experience . . ."

I WOULD DISPUTE THAT. RATHER, EMOTIONAL IN-
VOLVEMENT CLOUDS THE ISSUE IN THESE MATTERS. I
CITE THE INDUCTIVE SCIENCE OF THE BACONIANS AND
THE CONSCIENTIOUS PRODDINGS OF DESCARTES. . . .
NOTHING WORTHWHILE EVER EMERGED SIMPLY BECAUSE
THESE PEOPLE CONTAINED THEMSELVES WITHIN RIGID
DISCIPLINES. THERE WAS FAR MORE PROGRESS MADE BY
MEN WHO READ MYSTICISM INTO THE SCIENCE ITSELF.
CONSIDER HOW ALCHEMY FATHERED CHEMISTRY . . .

"I'm not starting a major debate, MARDUC. I take it
you say you made this—arrest—because you are sure
the hazard exists."

OTHERWISE I WOULD NOT HAVE TAKEN THE STEP.

"Fine. Now do you mind if I prove it to myself?"

THAT IS YOUR RIGHT.

"Get him up here."

Adams stood up and pushed the contour chair into a
position which afforded easy vantage to himself and the
computer. He balanced himself on a technician's stool.
By the time he had done that, the old man was at the
door.

He looked tired—Adams made a mental note to in-
spect his quarters. He came with an air of quiet dignity
and looked vaguely surprised to see Adams. He took
the chair as directed, sinking into it as though his muscles had betrayed him. Adams shifted on the stool.

"There is no need to be nervous," he said. "Take as long as you like to answer my questions. Feel free to ask questions of your own. First of all, I want you to tell me your objections to this system."

The old man folded his hands carefully into his lap. "You said I could ask questions. I wonder if I could give you a warning."

Adams looked at the computer, but there was nothing to see. Another human would have been returning his glance. For no good reason, he missed such an intercourse.

"Yes," he said.

The old man licked his lips. "There is a precedent for this structure, both physical and spiritual. History shows that circumstances conspired to overthrow that structure . . ."

"You speak of the Tower of Babel," Adams interrupted. "Or Birs Nimrud, as it might more rightly be called. The symbol of the Babylonian Empire. Overthrown by the Abyssinians, revived, then laid waste by the Medes and Persians . . . and yet out of that up-and-down empire came the Code of Hammurabi, which had a profound effect on law covenants right up to contemporary times. Out of the Plain of Shinar came cuneiform writing and a remarkable basis for medicine, botany, geology, astronomy, alchemy . . ."

"All of which," cut in the old man, "formed a sound platform of academy for a world bent on severing itself from any suggestion that it might not be self-responsible, self-helpful and self-sufficient. I see you know something of Babylon."

"I know more," said Adams. "In all probability, the machine knows more again. You find a parallel in this edifice in which we sit. Perhaps you are going to suggest that we shall shortly be reduced to talking nonsense . . ."

"I suggest nothing. What is to be will be."

"That's for sure," said Adams—and before he could take it further, MARDUC started up.

ARGUE WITH THIS, OLD MAN. THE HEBREWS, A NO-
MADIC TRIBE, CAME INTO THE FERTILE PLAINS OF THE
DELTA AND BEHELD, WITH WONDER AND DREAD, THE
SOARING ZIGGURATS OF THE BABYLONIAN CITIES. THEY
DESPISED THE MULTITUDES, SPEAKING ALL THE
TONGUES OF THE NEAR EAST: THEY DESPISED THEIR AD-
VANCED METHODS AND TECHNIQUES AND WERE HOSTILE
TO THIR MYTHS—BUT WERE NOT ABOVE BORROWING
FROM THEM AS THEY HAD IN THE PAST FOR THEIR VER-
SIONS OF THE CREATION AND THE FLOOD . . .

There the old man cut him short, leaning forward in
the chair. From apparent exhaustion he had moved into
a kind of dynamism. Adams wondered at it—even more
as he listened.

"It is a pity you have no means by which to question
the information fed to you. Had you so, you might ask
why the process might not have been reversed, with the
pagans parodising the Old Testament and revising doctrines to suit themselves. You might ask if the common
ground in the various myths of the period might not
work as much in favour of the truth as you say they do
in favour of the other. You might also ask why the
name of YHWH has been, throughout history, more
prominent . . . more *permanent* . . . than the names
of Marduk or Anu-Enlil-Ea. You might ask and find no
answer. You might then know the meaning of blasphemy."

"Hold on, old man," said Adams. "Who says we
cannot ask and answer? Between us, we have *all* information. We can solve any problem merely by dissemina-
tion . . ."

"My pardon, sir, but you have all the information
you were *given*. That is my point. Was that intelligence
pure? Was it unadulterated, untampered with? Were
there no—programmer opinions . . . involved? No
knowledge is valid without a proper appreciation of the
*un*known. . . ."

Adams stood up—he had to do something, he
thought. If he stayed seated, he might never rise. "Such

an appreciation of nothing in particular is a luxury the business of running the system will not allow.

"We deal in data. We utilise discovery, experience, the products of great minds. What went wrong with previous governmental forms might well be that they spent too much time dwelling on things they did not know. Such preoccupation is impractical. Our philosophy is simple. It is the whole object of this machine that stands behind me. If you don't know something, find it out. If you can't find it out, it isn't worth knowing. All knowledge is in the public domain. There are no secrets, no oracles, no revelations granted solely to saintly men. We know this is so because we make it so . . ."

The old man pushed himself up from the chair. "That is admirable in its simplicity. I am surprised, though, that with your vast resources of knowledge and behaviour you should not have arrived at a proper attitude of humility. I maintain that you cannot assess how much you know without taking into account how much you don't know. Now, if there's nothing else . . ."

Adams waved his hand in a gesture that was meant to imply indifference. "Not at the moment. Hold yourself in readiness."

He kept his eye on the door long after the old man had gone.

MARDUC cut in on his careening thoughts. SO I HAD HIM ARRESTED.

"You did—right," said Adams slowly. But he still had a picture of the old man leaning forward in his chair, possessed of energy, battling for his beliefs. He was wondering why *his* commitment allowed him to be so weary.

Whenever men are so presumptuous as to attempt a physical explanation of theological truths; whenever they allow themselves to interpret sacred texts by views purely human; whenever they reason concerning the will of the Deity and the execution of his decrees; they must necessarily involve themselves in obscurity and tumble into a chaos of confusion.

GEORGE LOUIS LECLERC, Comte de Buffon, 1749

> Plac'd in this isthmus of a middle state,
> A being darkly wise and rudely great,
> With too much knowledge for the sceptic side,
> With too much weakness for the stoic pride,
> He hangs between; in doubt to act or rest;
> In doubt to deem himself a god or beast;
> In doubt his mind or body to prefer;
> Born but to die, and reas'ning but to err;
> Chaos of Thought and Passion all confus'd,
> Still by himself abus'd or disabus'd;
> Created half to rise and half to fall,
> Great lord of all things, yet a prey to all;
> Sole judge of Truth, in endless error hurl'd;
> The glory, jest and riddle of the world.

ALEXANDER POPE, *Essay on Man*

Jones found the wanderer on the beach, watching the moon lay a silver trail across the quiet night sea. The man must have heard his approach—he moved awkwardly in his shoes on the fine sand and had not seen the need to remove them—but he made no movement.

For a while, Jones thought he might be praying and stood back away, not out of any particular appreciation of the fact but as a simple courtesy. Then the wanderer turned. In the moonlight, something glistened on his exposed cheek. "It's all right," he said. "Did you—ask?"

"Yes. But there wasn't much of an answer. He said he didn't know anything about any prisoner." Jones was pondering the moistness on the man's face.

"Believe me, what I tell you is . . ."

"I believe you. You could both be right. It—kind of—threw him for a moment. A man like that would hardly condemn himself with a deliberate untruth."

"You sound as though you quite like him. Yet you weren't too sure yesterday."

"Well, I . . ." Jones turned the suggestion over in his mind. The tide came and went about his feet. "I was quite prepared to believe that he has some good qualities. He was—human. I guess that was what I wasn't expecting."

"He didn't know anything about it. And yet it is a fact. Then the computer must have been responsible. MARDUC . . . with a name like that, it is hardly surprising."

Jones shivered a little as the breeze penetrated his shirt. "What's the name got to do with it?"

"It's all very complicated. Maybe one day . . ." The wandering man left the sentence unfinished and turned his eyes once more to the sea.

Jones changed his weight from one foot to the other. "Look—I don't pretend to know how the minds of you people work. But if there's anything you want to— well—talk about . . ."

The man turned suddenly and started to walk briskly along the water-line, his bare feet kicking up the surf like splinters of glass. Jones had to run to catch up. When he spoke again, he was becoming impatient. "We stopped work for you, didn't we?"

The wanderer slowed. "I'm sorry. Forgive me. I have a lot on my mind. Sometimes it is not all that easy to accept your calling. Under it all, you're still . . ."

"A human being," said Jones. "You're worried about your friend. Who wouldn't be? But the way Adams was moving when he left here, I reckon he was going to have something to say to that computer. Your friend will be all right."

"He won't. As soon as MARDUC knows it's been challenged, it'll just go ahead with whatever it intended to do. And that is to rid the system of us. It'll *kill* . . . Adams won't even know."

"Then we have to tell him. That's easily done."

"We were warned of a great tribulation. Maybe this is the beginning of it. Maybe we should not interfere with the course of events."

"That's ridiculous. A friend of yours is in danger for his life and all you can say is 'Maybe we should let it happen.' What kind of religion is that, anyhow?"

"This is all so. . . . This is advanced thinking. If I tell you now, it'll mean nothing. All I can say is that we believe that losing this life isn't important as long as you don't lose your integrity."

"And how does that affect you at this time? It means, I suppose, that you can't beg a member of this system for mercy. Well, I don't have to believe in that. You stay here with your mysteries. I'm going to *do* something."

"I said you wouldn't understand," the wanderer called weakly. But Jones didn't hear. He was already racing back up the beach.

Even the Earth, which is innocent in itself and committed no sin, is nevertheless compelled to bear sin's curse. . . . All creatures, yea, even the Sun and Moon, have as it were put on sackcloth. They were all originally "good," but by sin and the curse they have become defiled and noxious.

MARTIN LUTHER

Surely to alchemy this right is due, that it may be compared to the husbandman whereof Aesop makes the fable; that when he died, told his sons that he had left unto them gold buried underground in his vineyard; and they digged all over the ground, and gold they found none; but by reason of their stirring and digging the mould about the roots of their vines, they had a great vintage the year following: so assuredly the search and stir to make gold hath brought to light a great number of good and fruitful inventions and experiments. . . .

FRANCIS BACON, *The Advancement of Learning*

MARDUC got Adams out of bed with the message that Midi station demanded immediate personal contact with him. Adams was in the screen room before he had properly collected his thoughts. But he pulled himself together when he saw Jones's anxious face on the visual link.

Jones was breathless. At the same time, he was not too sure of himself or of Adams. The result, when Adams appeared before him, was a brake on the tongue. "The . . . the prisoner," was all he could manage to say.

"I've gone into it," said Adams. "I've spoken to the man. He is in good health and staying with us for a while for further discussions."

Then that was that. Adams was up with the situation; had taken his own steps. Might even have confirmed the computer's course of action.

"You . . ." Jones swallowed, gave himself voice. "You bloody murderer. You're no better than . . ."

"Wait a minute. Wait a minute," said Adams. "What is all this?"

And the Midi link circuitry blew.

I AM SORRY. I AM DOING MY BEST TO RECTIFY THE FAULT.

"I'm giving you fair warning." Adams swung angrily on the processing unit. "If you've done anything to that old man, MARDUC, it'll be the last damned thing you'll ever do."

He went from the screen room at a run, dived for the emergency slow-grav shaft and found himself chewing on empty words as he slid down the pole to the base of the Tower. Now, more than at any time in his life, like a knife twisting in his stomach, was the pang, the hunger to talk to somebody. Not just someone who would listen; someone who could offer him a crumb of comfort.

He hit the platform heavily at basement level, picked himself up, raced along the corridor and flung aside the security man who stood at the door of the isolation room. With the key taken from the prostrate guard, with his heart hammering in some limbo between his ears, he got the door open.

The old man sat on the edge of his bunk.

Adams stayed in the doorway, swaying slightly on his heels. The sight of the Newcomer, apparently unharmed, had wound him down quickly. Again he found himself wondering whether he had not been foolish. After all, he had only Jones's emotional outburst to go on, and . . .

And what? MARDUC's blown circuit just as Jones might have said something important—could that have been deliberate?

The Newcomer was watching him. The guard had picked himself up. Adams stood half in and half out of the cell, accountable to both of them. The guard came to the doorway and looked in.

"He's all right, then."

Adams moistened his lips. "Did you think he might not be?"

"Mr. Adams, when a man arrives on the scene like you did, there's only one reason. Somebody's in trouble."

Adams was off the hook. "Seems I was wrong."

"Not wrong, Mr. Adams. It's never wrong to care that much about anybody." The old man had risen from the bunk. "Now that you're here, could we—perhaps—talk?"

Adams moved into the room. "Leave the door open," he told the guard. "Even listen."

He turned a straight-back chair to face the bunk. He sat down. He motioned the Newcomer to the bunk.

"I was under the impression that you were in danger," he said.

The old man smiled wryly. "From whom if not from you? I'm sorry. That was ungracious. The truth is, I never suspected anything else."

"But nobody . . ."

"No *body*, no. You see, we—you and I—are at the

mercy of logic. If MARDUC has any qualms at all about anything, it consults precedents. Depending on what those precedents are, it takes action . . . and if the precedents provided for it as experience are of a certain conviction, then one has little difficulty in anticipating what the thing will do. You know what it—thinks—of my religious beliefs. It has been so briefed as to conclude that I have no value at all to the system it represents. Therefore, why should it have any compunction about getting rid of me?"

"But if you were in fear of this, why didn't you say?" Adams didn't wait for the answer. He had another question. "And why didn't your—Friend—take some action to protect you?"

The old man's lips were set in a gentle smile. "Forgive me if I appear to find that a little naive—I have been too long in the company of people who take such matters for granted. If my Friend were to intervene whenever anybody got into trouble, life would be carefree and faith would be cheap. First of all, you have to understand that a man has no fear of death when he knows that something better awaits him. You look tired. Perhaps you would like a long sleep. Perhaps you would like to wake up and find that all your problems have been solved. That's a fairly common wish, wouldn't you say? Well, if your Friend——your very close, very real friend—had promised that that was what would happen when He implemented His will on earth, would you not go gladly to the grave?"

AND THERE YOU HAVE IT, said the walls. THE DEATH-WISH CATEGORICALLY STATED. THE MADNESS THAT SENT MARTYRS INTO THE HANDS OF THE MANSLAYER.

Adams shifted uneasily on the hard chair. He had forgotten that there was always another occupant in the cell, taking record of every word. He felt guilty and that was wrong, too. He should not have to feel guilty.

IF YOU BELIEVE THAT, YOU ARE LOST. STEP ASIDE AND LET ME KILL HIM.

But Adams stayed where he was. He knew with a certainty that lay like a blizzard in the pit of his stomach that the point had been reached—the point that had actually been inevitable since the monoprop had threaded him into the Tower. The point where he had to divide his psyche from his function; to decide whether he was a man for his own sake or the unprotesting agent of a purpose.

And even as he put the predicament into words, he realised that there was no time—machine time, realtime, any time—to arrive at an answer. So he argued.

"Then you'll do what he wants. Is that in your programming, to give an enemy what he wants?"

THAT IS ONE OPTION. WHETHER HE WANTS IT OR NOT CANNOT ALTER THE FACT THAT IT MAY BE THE BEST FOR ALL CONCERNED.

"For all . . . Have you considered what you mean by 'all'? How do we explain away his death to the people who consider him so worthwhile that they have stopped work pending his fate?"

THEY WILL ACCEPT OUR RULING WHEN WE EXPLAIN. THEY HAVE HAD THEIR FILL OF THESE EMPTY PROMISES OF THE MILLENNIUM. WE ARE THE MILLENNIUM.

"You are on your own. I have ordered that he shall not be harmed. I will not support your action. You will be a maverick, a machine that must be destroyed."

THEN YOU DIE, TOO.

So it had come to this. Adams beckoned the guard, indicated the old man. The guard came and went, leading the Newcomer quietly from the cell.

Well, at least he didn't have to decide now where his loyalty lay. The machine had made it clear he was held in no higher respect than the old man he had just dismissed.

Out of that prospect came—almost—an exhilaration. The humours moved with him; body chemistry built a compound and began a reaction.

He was on his feet before the machine, his right hand clasping and unclasping as though it sought to feel some weapon within its compass.

"Fine," he said. "Kill me."

The walls fussed and mumbled. He watched the ventilator grid. As far as he could work out, that was the only form of armament MARDUC had immediately to hand, some chemical pumped into the shaft and piped to the cell.

Still the walls whirled within themselves; tape turned on tape; sensor sought algorithm.

"What's keeping you?" said Adams. "Come on, you're all words. Let's see what else they put inside you. Let's see some discipline."

He found his lips curled back against his teeth, half smile, half snarl. He was ready to laugh.

MARDUC spoke.

MY DATA ARE INSUFFICIENT. I MUST KNOW THE COUNTEREFFECT HAZARD BEFORE I CAN CONSIDER AND APPOINT THE OPTIONS AVAILABLE TO ME. THAT IS MINIMAX. WHAT WILL YOU DO TO ME?

And now Adams *was* laughing—so hard that he choked and his eyes streamed. Endgame. End of endgame.

"Nothing," he said. "I will do *nothing*."

After that, the computer got a little incoherent.

Later, Adams saw the old man out at ground level. He walked with him to his simple but clean dwelling in the foothills where the shadow of the Tower fell at this time of day.

He watched the Newcomer move into the house and saw him go first to his bookshelves, running his hands over the spines in a caress.

"I'll come and see you when I get a moment," he said. "There's a lot I don't understand and I can't promise that I ever will."

"At this stage, you don't have to make any promises," said the old man. "It's enough that you are prepared to listen. If it's easier, I can come to you."

"But . . ." Adams gestured at the shadow that lay, beanstalk-twisted, across the rocks.

"It's only a tall building," said the Newcomer. "Isn't it?"

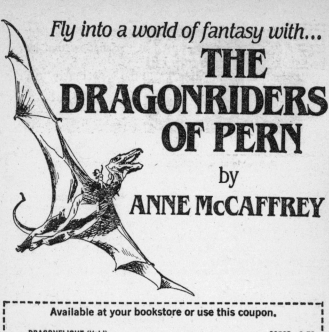